“Well, lass. Th

I’ve ever witnessed.

Laurel jerked upwards at the low angry brogue. *Stupid*? She’d fallen off a horse, for crying out loud. It happens.

She peered into the dense fog trying to get a glimpse of the disembodied Scot. The thick mist swirled, thinned, and parted to reveal a pair of well-worn, brown riding boots with red cuffs at the top. Her eyes climbed higher, following the boots to a pair of large muscular thighs encased in dark-colored breeches. Her eyes continued upward, past the flat stomach, which led to a broad chest and shoulders covered in a mostly unbuttoned white shirt.

She craned her neck and finally saw his face. Roughly chiseled, he had a square jaw with high cheekbones, a slightly off-centered nose, and full lips pursed into a frown. She forced herself to meet his eyes, and her jaw dropped. The light gray eyes were almost opalescent against his dark lashes and black shoulder-length hair—eyes that pierced right thorough her.

“Every bloody year the tourists just get dumber,” he declared.

She clamped her mouth shut on a sharp retort and shook her head. “Gee, thanks for your concern. It’s not like I planned to fall off.” She started to push off the ground, but her right arm collapsed under her. Before she could fall back, the man reached her side and grabbed her good arm, pulling her to her feet.

Honors for CJ Bahr

Winner
2014 Florida's Romance Writers Contest
"The Golden Palm" in paranormal category

~*~

Second Place
2014 Chesapeake Romance Writers Contest
"Finish the Damn Book Contest"
The Rudy Award in paranormal category

~*~

Fourth Place
2014 MORWA's "Gateway Contest"
paranormal category

~*~

Sixth Place
Utah RWA's "Great Beginnings Contest"

Enjoy!
CJ Bahr

Walking Through Fire

by

CJ Bahr

This is a work of fiction. Names, characters, places, and incidents are either the product of the author's imagination or are used fictitiously, and any resemblance to actual persons living or dead, business establishments, events, or locales, is entirely coincidental.

Walking Through Fire

Contact Information: info@thewildrosepress.com

Cover Art by *Debbie Taylor*

The Wild Rose Press, Inc.
PO Box 708
Adams Basin, NY 14410-0708
Visit us at www.thewildrosepress.com

Publishing History
First Faery Rose Edition, 2014
Print ISBN 978-1-62830-615-6
Digital ISBN 978-1-62830-616-3

Published in the United States of America

Dedication

To my parents, Catherine and Allan,
avid readers who gave me a love of books by example.

~*~

Thanks, Mom and Dad,
I hope they have books in heaven.
I miss you both.

Acknowledgements

A novel may start out with a single person and a computer, but a large family joins in its birth. Be they family, friends, mentors, or even you, the reader, this story would just be another document on my computer without the community effort.

First, a huge thank you to my fellow Friday nighters: Marla White, Bekah Wright, and Heidi Carson. Your input, critiques, and "but whys?" along with good wine, friendship and conversation made this book what it is today. I couldn't have done it without you gals.

To my beta-readers, Nahmi, Bill, and Maureen—Thank you for braving the rough versions and your brilliant advice.

To my editor, Amanda Barnett at Wild Rose Press, for her amazing support and help in polishing *Walking Through Fire* and making it the best book it could be. Also, a special thank you to my cover artist, Debbie Taylor, for bringing Simon to life. And of course, to the rest of the gang at Wild Rose Press; it's a pleasure and honor to be a member of the garden.

Last, but in no means last, a huge thank you to my parents. I wish they could have been here to witness the birth of my first book. They were responsible for instilling in me a love of reading. I don't remember a time they were without a book. They led by example. I was brought up believing that if I worked hard, stayed persistent, there wasn't anything I couldn't accomplish.

And thanks to you, my readers, for picking up this book. I love sharing Simon and Laurel's story with you. Enjoy!

Chapter One

Northern Scotland, Near Durness
July 1809

The first tingle of fear raced up Simon MacKay's spine as he found himself alone in the pitch dark—kneeling on rough, wet granite. Waves thundered and crashed around him in the gloom. He must be in one of the sea caves on his estate. A blast of salty, cold air struck him, clearing his muddled, throbbing head to frightening awareness. He staggered clumsily to his feet, pain shooting through his arms and shoulders. He couldn't move his hands.

"Nay!" His shout echoed in the darkness. He was bound to the cave's wall. He struggled, arms stretched tautly behind him, his muscles strained against the ropes tying his wrists. Ignoring the bite of the coarse fibers and the pain of his tortured joints, panic set in. He had to get free. He had to get out. His family was in danger.

A wave slammed in close, spraying water onto his face. Sweat mingled with salt water as he thrashed. The metal mooring ring trapping him clanked against the limestone rock, as his heart raced with equal parts dread and exertion. Clasped hands turned sticky with blood from the rough bindings biting into his flesh. Simon ignored this too.

Ice water drenched him as the next wave crashed against the wall. The chill soaking froze him in place. The tide was coming in, and the cave was rapidly filling. He hung his head and water dripped from his long hair to streak down his face, mimicking the tears he couldn't shed. His body started to shake as shock and disbelief speared his mind. If he didn't free himself, he'd drown and his family would be left unprotected.

"I canna die like this. I won't!"

He lifted his head and peered into the shadows. Another wave hit him waist high before he felt the dragging pull of the ocean's retreat. He could now hear lapping water.

I will die here, his traitorous thoughts declared, *and for what?*

A choked laugh escaped Simon, and he shook his head. "Never!" He strained once more against his bonds, but they held fast. Whoever tied the knots had done it well.

How had he gotten here? His last recollection before waking in the cave was leaving the manor and walking to the stable. He entered, but then it all blurred together. His throbbing head held the missing clue. He'd been struck. There had been no warning, no telltale movement.

The next wave hit him chest high, slamming him against the wall, crushing his arms behind him. This time however, as the wave retreated, frigid water remained clawing at his ankles.

Simon prayed the high water mark wasn't above his head. With no light, he couldn't tell. In his soul though, he knew. He was meant to die, and at the rate the tide continued to rush in, his fate would soon be sealed.

"Damn you to hell, you bloody devil!" His cry was lost in the booming darkness. He should have known better, should have anticipated. There had been threats. He ignored them all. More fool he. Now he would pay the ultimate price.

He shook with rage as the icy water swirled about his waist. Numb to his physical discomfort, his inner turmoil was dagger sharp. Who had done this to him?

The thoughts of his tormentor fled from his mind when an incoming wave crashed above his head, submerging him. He instinctively held his breath until the arctic wash drained away to chest level. He braced and waited in the darkness for the wave set to finish. He knew the sea's rhythm, it was in his family's blood.

Three. Four. Five. The last wave pulled him from the wall, stretching his arms painfully behind him. He floated back and his feet found ground. The sea now reached his neck.

Regrets flooded him. Who would care for his family? He would be leaving behind a little sister and a sick mother. Sadly, the sea had already claimed his father, and now she would have the son. Were the men in his family cursed? Simon would disappear, and the MacKay name would die with him. Would the sick bastard who killed him now go after little Jean or his Ma? Who would stop him?

A sob escaped his throat, and he ruthlessly bit his lip. He would not die a sniveling coward.

The water lapped his chin and reached higher to caress his mouth.

The bastard would pay. Though he knew not who his murderer be, Simon saved his last thoughts to curse his enemy.

The water closed over his head, submerging him into a liquid world. He held his breath, willing the water to retreat, but the sea would not be cheated.

His lungs burned, tears squeezed from his closed eyes, and mingled unseen in his watery prison. He bit his lips, drawing blood in his effort not to breathe, but his body betrayed him.

Purely reflexive, his mouth gasped open sucking in air for his oxygen-starved lungs. All they received was the cold water of the north Atlantic.

On the second inhalation, his body started to convulse when the ocean filled his lungs.

On the third, Simon MacKay drowned.

Chapter Two

Northern Scotland, Near Durness
July, Present Day

Laurel Saville breathed a sigh of relief. Cleitmuir Bed and Breakfast appeared before her in the parting strands of fog. She coasted her rental car to a halt on the circular gravel driveway and shut off the engine. It had been a long trip, almost twenty-four hours worth. It started in Chicago with two plane connections ending in Inverness, followed by the almost three and a half hour drive on mostly single lane roads. Home felt light years away.

Letting out a pent up breath, she closed her eyes. No sound reached her through the fog. Peace at last.

"Lori!"

Laurel's eyes snapped open and she smiled while watching a tiny bundle of blonde energy break into a run. All of five-foot-one (if you measured generously), Beth Leighton, now Murray, reached the car, grinning.

"Lori, Lori, Lori, you made it!"

Laurel opened the door, and stepped out to embrace her best friend.

"I can't believe you're finally here. God, how I missed you." Beth squeezed her tight before releasing her to peer upwards.

"Me, too." Laurel vowed it wouldn't be so long

between visits. It had been so much easier when Beth lived in Chicago, but at least now Laurel had a great excuse to visit a country she always wanted to see. The Scottish Highlands, a beautiful land of craggy mountains, rough coastlines, heather-filled hills, and hardy, hospitable people. A land filled with history. She couldn't believe she was finally here.

"Though I have to admit," she teased. "I wasn't sure I'd make it. I swore I was lost the last few miles. Thank God for GPS, since you picked a pretty isolated spot to live. There isn't a soul around, unless you count the sheep."

"But there will be! Things are really growing in Cleitmuir, and we're in at the ground floor."

"With sheep for guests?" Laurel joked. Looking around, she only caught hints of the grounds and hotel through the tendrils of fog.

Beth slapped her shoulder. "Quit it. You'll love the place. It's a nice change from Chicago, and," she stated with a knowing look in her eyes, "you need a break. Come on." Beth wrapped her arm around Laurel's waist, "you have to meet Grant."

Heading toward the hotel, Laurel's happiness morphed into guilt. Beth was more than just a best friend, she was family, having grown up with her since kindergarten. They'd been so close, inseparable. What one did the other did also. It couldn't last of course. By college they started making their own lives. Laurel became a history nut and started work for a museum, while Beth chose interior design as her life's pursuit. On a trip to Scotland where Beth studied Celtic design, she met and fell in love with Grant. A soul mate, she had claimed, and love at first sight. How was it possible

Laurel had missed one of the biggest events of their lives? How could she not have made time to be at her friend's wedding?

"Beth," she sighed and shook her head. "I'm so sorry I missed your wedding—"

"Not another word," Beth wagged a finger. "I'm the one who got married at the last second and across the pond. You're here now and that's what counts."

"But almost a year?"

"Nope. Nada. Zip it my giant friend."

Laurel looked down. "Are those gray hairs I'm seeing?"

"Bite your tongue!" They both laughed as they reached the hotel.

Laurel felt herself unwind. It was always like this. No matter how long they'd been apart, with Beth, time stood still. She was glad Beth had called when she had and then insisted Laurel come, right now, for a visit. It was exactly what she needed after Derek. How Beth always knew when things weren't right with her, she couldn't guess.

They mounted the wide stone stairs to the double doors, one of which stood open.

"*Ceud mile failte gu,* Cleitmuir," Beth flung wide her arms as they crossed the threshold. "That's a 'hundred thousand welcomes' in Gaelic, don't you know?"

"Ah, Beth, you're sounding a bit Irish, and you married to a Scot..." she shook her head in mock dismay.

"So, what do you think?" Beth asked grinning.

Envy swept through Laurel, while she took in the warm inviting entrance. The large vaulted ceiling stood guard over rich hardwood floors, covered with thick throw carpets of dark greens, rusts, and golds. Padded benches lined either side of the walls, and a wide grand staircase occupied the far end of the hall. There were two rooms on either side, one obviously used as a lobby/office to check in guests and the other an inviting sitting room complete with a huge fireplace, bay windows, and the requisite comfortable chairs and couches. When the fog lifted, sunlight would flood through the large windows and light the entranceway with a warm glow. The hotel oozed an upper crust aristocracy yet somehow remained enchanting, welcoming. Romantic. Laurel cringed inwardly. She'd leave the romance to Beth, who was living her dream.

"It's lovely, Beth. You've outdone yourself. It puts Pemberley Hall to shame. I'm sure Mr. Darcy would be quite put out."

"He's English. We Scots have better taste."

Laurel looked up at the booming voice, and saw a man built like a bulldog, walking down the stairs.

"Grant! Come meet Lori."

"Ah, the infamous Laurel, we meet at last." Grant stopped in front of Laurel and gave her a quick hug and kisses to both cheeks. "I've heard so much about you."

"I'm so happy to finally meet you," Laurel returned. "It's hard to believe I'm actually here. Cleitmuir is amazing, I can't wait to see the rest of the hotel. Beth emailed during the renovations, but the pictures don't do it justice. Between you and Cleitmuir, it's no wonder why Beth makes her life here." She smiled at Grant. She had seen pictures of him, too. Laurel had to admit she was still a bit shocked. He wasn't at all the physical type Beth had dated while in school. Back then she'd gone for the dark, lithe, dancer types. Grant resembled a bruiser—all muscle, broad shoulders, stocky. Though the twinkling brown eyes, and a great smile softened the image. She looked forward to getting to know him. "Thank you so much for inviting me, I hope it wasn't too much of an imposition."

"Och, never mind. Bethy is paying for it with a return of favors," Grant winked.

"Grant!" Beth punched his shoulder. "You've only just met her!"

Grant laughed. "After everything you've told me about you and her, I doubt I even caused a slight blush." He scooped Beth close to him, keeping his arm wrapped about her shoulders. "You're welcome to stay as long as you like. We even gave you the best room in the house, well, besides the master suite," Grant grinned. "By the way, we'll be busy, a full house soon. The Primrose Festival is taking place this month."

"A festival?"

"Aye. Not as grand as September's Northern Lights Festival, but we have our moments," Grant replied.

"Wow, I didn't know it was party time. I really don't need a fancy room, and wouldn't want to take the income away from you. Any room will do. Or I can find another place, a sleeping bag in the stable or something. Beth knows I did field work for my degree. I can pretty much sleep anywhere in comfort."

"Absolutely not," Beth frowned at her. "I won't allow it. You hated fieldwork and besides there's not another place close by. Grant and I wouldn't dream of having you camp out in our stable. No way."

Grant laughed again. "Just give in. My wee spitfire has a habit of getting her way, as I'm sure you know. Moreover, we rarely let the room you'll be staying in during the summer months, so we won't be losing any income."

"I thought you said it was the best room?"

"Well, it may be, but you have to be a fan of the *Ghost Hunters* show, like you and Bethy, to really appreciate it. She mentioned the two of you never missed an episode."

"Grant, I told you not to say anything," Beth admonished.

"*Ghost Hunters*? Ah, Beth, is there something you forgot to tell me?"

"Now you've done it," Beth scooted out from under her husband's arm and shot him a dirty look. "It was supposed to be a surprise. Be gone. I'll deal with you later."

"Is that a promise?"

"Grant!"

He faced her with a sheepish smile. "It's really nothing, Laurel. It was great to meet you. I'll see you again after you've settled in. Drinks before dinner." Grant walked away whistling as he entered the office.

"Beth?" Laurel caught a mischievous glint in her best friend's eyes.

"Later. It's a surprise. Wait until you see the room."

"Oh, my suitcase..."

"Don't worry, Ian will bring your bags up and park your car. Just give me your keys and follow me."

Laurel exhaled and shook her head as she handed over her car keys. What had she gotten herself into? But that was Beth—instigator, troublemaker galore. For someone so petite, Beth had the affinity of leading them into trouble. Mostly harmless escapades, but it was usually Laurel who ended up with the egg on her face. How they had managed to stay friends all their lives, she couldn't guess. Probably because, deep down, Laurel admired Beth's adventuresome spirit, something she sorely lacked.

She followed Beth up the stairs to the second floor, through carpeted hallways and past several doors.

"You're at the end of the hall. You're going to love it. There's only one room at this end of the house, so it'll be nice and quiet."

Beth led her to the final door and in a grand gesture flung it open. Laurel stepped past her and into history. Or at least, what she thought a room in a manor house would look like from the Regency Era. Mister Darcy, indeed. The room was wide and open. The far wall held a bank of large windows, including one with a window seat. Thick carpet in a dark green lined the floors. There was an antique writing desk, lots of comfortable looking chairs, and a couch. It even had a fireplace. The room's vibe was masculine, but inviting.

"Beth, it's fabulous, but, ah, where's the bed?"

"Knucklehead, it's the room off to your right."

Laurel went through the door and walked into the bedroom. It was just as wonderful as the sitting room. Maybe even better. Decorated in warm autumn colors like the other room, the bedroom had only minimal furniture. The reason for this was obvious. Straight in front of her stood the biggest, comfiest bed she'd ever laid eyes on. A large oak, four-poster with a down comforter and pillows galore. Just looking at it made

Laurel want to take a nap and never get up again.

She dragged her gaze away from sleep heaven to study the rest of the room. To her left were more sets of large windows along the wall, but instead of a window seat there were a pair of glass double doors. She walked over and pushed aside the long white filmy drapes and opened a door. A cool breeze entered bringing with it mist as she stepped outside onto a small balcony. The fog was still too thick to see the surrounding area.

"Wait till the fog clears," Beth said as if reading her mind. "The view is spectacular. On a super clear day you can see across the plain to the ocean, which looks like it touches the sky. There's nothing like the bright blue Scottish sky. You're going to love it here."

Laurel was sure she would. Scotland had been a dream of hers—now a reality, and much better than staying in Chicago facing the broken dreams of a shattered love affair.

"And that's not all," Beth interrupted her depressing thoughts, "you've got to see the bathroom. We've just remodeled it. Very twenty-first century."

She allowed herself to be tugged along to the opposite side of the room. Beth was right, the bathroom was gorgeous, and the only thing modern about the suite of rooms. White granite with dark variegations lined the floor and counter tops. The claw-foot bathtub beckoned her to take a deep soak, and a built-in corner shower which contained the clearest glass it almost appeared there wasn't any, would make getting ready quickly a snap. The interior had some sort of stone, with multiple showerheads and even a stone bench. And for a romantic touch, candles of all shapes and sizes were strategically placed in various locations. The whole room looked like a Poseidon paradise.

Her jet lag began to set in, as did her reason for being here. "I need this, thanks so much, Beth."

They hugged.

"I'm glad you came. I've missed you so much. Relax. Take a good long bath, then meet me for tea. We have a lot of catching up to do." Beth gave her another quick hug and a kiss on the cheek, before departing, leaving Laurel standing in the bathroom door a bit dazed and exhausted.

Like a robot, she walked into the bathroom and turned on the faucet to the tub. Keeping her fingers under the water until the temperature heated to almost hurting, she then plugged the tub. She noticed the plush robe on the back of the door and plenty of towels. Her luggage hadn't arrived, but there certainly was no reason not to get naked.

By the time she added some lavender oil to the water, organized towels, robe, and shed her clothes, the water almost reached the tub's rim. Turning off the tap, Laurel tentatively dipped a toe and winched. Hot, but a good pain.

Steeling herself, she stepped into the tub and sank with one swift movement up to her neck. A gasp escaped her throat, as she closed her eyes against the heat. With a few deep breaths, her temperature and the water regulated, and a contented sigh passed her lips. She took another breath, inhaling the lush lavender aroma. Tension from the past month and the long travel day oozed away, sending Laurel into an almost sleep state.

Derek's image floated through her mind. Handsome, milk chocolate brown hair and vivid green eyes stared back at her. When she'd first laid eyes on him in the museum, she couldn't speak. Never had she reacted so physically to a guy. Simply gorgeous. Her heart had actually raced. In no way, not in a million years had she suspected he'd developed any interest in her. Although three years ago, Laurel still vividly remembered when he approached her and asked her out for coffee.

A single tear escaped from behind her closed eyes. Damn it, no. She wasn't going to torture herself. Her eyes snapped open. Enough. It was over, and she was done with crying. Her toes sought the plug under the water. Finding it, she pulled. The water glugged then started to empty. She watched the whirlpool swirl down the drain, almost like a replay of watching her dreams of a loving relationship, a true partnership, disappear forever.

Chapter Three

Laurel knocked on the door one floor directly above her own room. Beth answered and invited her in. The room was decorated more femininely and much larger than hers. A tea service rested on a table in front of the couch.

Beth led the way. "You're looking much better. You were fading there. The soak helped."

"The tub was wonderful. I can't believe I could submerge myself to the neck and stretch out! I'd kill for one at home. Did you have to custom order it?"

Beth laughed. "Nope. Apparently they grow large men in the Highlands, the tub was a stock item. Awesome, huh?"

They reached the couch and sat. Beth picked up the beautiful teapot decorated with pink heather, and poured tea into two similar hand-painted china cups.

"It's Earl Grey with lavender," Beth explained. "Let me know if you like it."

Holding the steaming cup, Laurel sniffed the fragrant steam before tentatively taking a sip. Happily, she discovered it wasn't too hot to drink.

"Mmmm, it's really good."

"I knew it. Now," Beth set her cup down and met Laurel's eyes directly. "How *are* you really doing?"

She sighed. "I'm okay." She saw her friend's skeptical look. "Really. I put Derek out of my life.

Moved on."

Laurel knew she was kidding herself. She had taken Beth's invitation to visit as a chance to escape Derek. She needed time away to heal her broken heart and figure out what to do next. The added benefit of visiting Scotland was hanging with her best friend who knew her so well. Beth even knew when Laurel was currently lying to herself.

"Honey, you were with that skeeving lowlife for three years, with no ring, no commitment, and apparently no monogamous understanding. It's okay to hurt."

"Yeah, I know. Why do you think I took you up on your offer of a vacation getaway?" Laurel took a long sip of her tea then stared into the cup. "The long flight helped put things into perspective. Derek is a loser. He always was. Apparently all looks and no substance. I just romanticized him, and apparently wore blinders."

Romance. What a fickle emotion. She might be in one of the most romantic places on earth, but too bad, no more faux relationships. Derek had fooled her, and broken her heart. She really needed to change the conversation before she started crying.

"My family says 'hi'. They want to know when you're planning on coming back for a visit."

Beth smiled. "Even your brothers?"

"Well, Tom thinks you're insane for marrying a *foreigner*, but forgives you and would love to see you."

"Ah, the one that got away," Beth laughed. "He was never interested in me when I practically lived in your backyard, seriously crushing on him. How are the other two hooligans, Sam and Chance?"

"When they heard about Derek, they, as well as

Tom, wanted to go beat the shit out of him," Laurel grinned, remembering the argument.

"You should have let them, that's what protective brothers are for."

Air escaped from Laurel's lips in a sigh. How in the world did they get the conversation back to Derek again?

Time for a new topic. "All right, spill the beans. Is my room haunted? It has to be if you won't book it during your busiest time. The room's amazing, and being in the middle of nowhere, I figured you'd want to fill it with an actual paying guest."

"Trying to change the subject, are we? You're transparent as a window. I'll let you get away with it for now, but by no means are we finished," Beth challenged. "Yes, your room is probably haunted."

Laurel grinned. Her love for the supernatural, shared equally with Beth, was well known. She couldn't wait to hear more. "So, give me the 411 on your spooky Casper. I assume it's not harmful or anything, unless you have a desire to off me that I don't know about?"

"Nope. Sorry, still want you around. No worries. Our ghost is harmless, and pretty much quiet. It's weird, though," Beth added. "It's like a seasonal haunting or something. Our ghost appears to love the summer, but then again who wouldn't, especially this far north?"

"Summer? Are you only getting activity when it's warm?"

"July, actually. Only the month of July," Beth replied with a slight frown.

"I've never heard of a ghost haunting for only a

month at a time. Bizarre. So what are the claims?" Laurel held her breath for the answer. She'd tried to stay in a couple of haunted hotels before but walked away with no personal experiences.

"Well, it's nothing bad, just some noises, and occasional misplaced objects. Sometimes people complain about it being cold, or a feeling of being watched, but that's it. Honest."

"Ah, where's *TAPS* when you need them." Laurel chuckled, thinking of "The Atlantic Paranormal Society", whose show, *Ghost Hunters* had been her and Beth's perennial favorite television series.

"Are you freaked out? I can move you if you want, but you've told me about the other haunted places you stayed. You never had ghost sightings with them but maybe this room will be the one. Grant's owned the hotel for several years and swears it haunted, but I'm not so sure. I've been here a year now and nothing's ever happened around me."

"Ha, you sound like Jason or was it Grant? I can never remember which one of the *Ghost Hunters*, kept refusing to list a place haunted. I guess we should just keep it listed under paranormal activity?" Laurel paused for a moment, when she realized something. "Hey, wait a sec. You married a Grant! Is there some weird coincidence or fetish going on?"

"You wish. Nope, nothing weird or abnormal, just your everyday coincidence," Beth replied. "And honestly, if you're uncomfortable, we'll put—"

"Absolutely not!" Laurel allowed herself a half smile. "You know me too well, especially after I saw the rooms there would be no way I'd back out. I've never stayed any place so fancy. I adore my room and even more now with a chance for a *spectral* encounter."

Beth smiled. "Yeah, well, you are the history buff, and we're not best friends for nothing. And speaking of that, how are you handling seeing Derek all the time?"

Laurel inwardly winced. How neatly her friend brought them back to their original topic. "Not great, but I'm hoping time away will make things easier. I know it's silly, but seeing the cheating sleaze on a weekly basis, hasn't been great for my work," she admitted. "Your timing was perfect. I was driving myself insane. He's an ass, and I'm determined not to let him interfere with my life."

"I'm glad. You deserve so much better," Beth reached over and gave her a quick hug. "And I have just the solution to help you," a mischievous grin lit her face. "A handsome Highlander to take your mind off your troubles."

"Oh no, Beth, absolutely not." Laurel was so not ready to dive into another relationship. She promised to swear off men, cold turkey it for a while, not get back into the dating pool after only two weeks. Her friend was insane.

"Too late and too bad. It's already done," Beth countered. "He's perfect for you. You're going to love him."

"Really, no. I'm not ready for this."

"Stop freaking yourself out. Look, there's no commitment. If you don't like him, don't date him. If you do, have some holiday sex. I'm not asking you to marry him, though he's certainly a keeper," Beth argued. "I'm hosting a small dinner tomorrow, which he is attending. His name is Alex MacKenzie, a neighbor actually. You've got a lot in common. I really think you'll like him. Please, just give it a try?"

Oh what the hell. Laurel sighed as she nodded. Her life wasn't over. Maybe a Highland fling was just the thing.

Chapter Four

Cleitmuir Manor
February 1809

The wind blasted into his face carrying a sheet of icy rain, as Simon and his horse carefully picked their way onto the plateau. He urged his mount into a trot, then a canter, all the while praying the gelding was sure-footed. It was madness to be out in this storm.

Yet he had been gripped by insanity since the dreaded news had reached him on the Continent. "The Earl of Cleitmuir is dead, you are needed at once."

What had happen?

He immediately sold his military commission in order to return home and take up his duties as the new Earl. The war against Napoleon wasn't his problem any more. His responsibilities to his mother and sister took precedence. He regretted leaving others to do what Simon wanted to accomplish, but he shirked his family long enough. It was finally time to return home. Simon found the first ship headed north, but sailing around Cape Wrath had been a nightmare of violent currents, wild winds, and lashing waves when the ship ran into a winter North Atlantic storm. The Captain and crew deserved a medal for reaching port at Balnakeil Bay intact.

Simon wasted no time in Durness. He grabbed a

meat pie, bought a horse, and then rode south. Only a few minutes into the ride, he had been soaked through and chilled to the bone. His pace was forced to a crawl by the storm, but none of this mattered. He needed to reach his home. He needed to see his family and to find out what happened.

So he rode. Lifting a hand from the reins, he shoved a wet hank of hair from his eyes, and then through the heavy mist and dense rain Cleitmuir Manor appeared in the far distance. Home at last, its warm glow a safe port in the dark storm.

Simon urged his mount faster, eyes fixed on his goal. He knew this land like the back of his hand. He approached the manor from the rear and thundered up to the stable. He leapt off his horse and took hold of the reins to lead the gelding into the stable.

He barely crossed the threshold when the stable master greeted him. Brian showed his age with thinning gray hair instead of the busy thick red of his younger days. He had been stable master since Simon was born, even taught him how to ride. Brian was always there for Simon, comforting him when as a wee lad felt he had nowhere else to go. No judgment, only sternness when needed, and comfort always.

"Simon, ah, I mean my lord, we weren't expecting you so soon. Here, let me take him."

He passed the reins, and ran his free hands through his soggy hair pushing it away from his face. "Thanks, Brian. I couldna stay away." He glanced worriedly over his shoulder back to the stable's entrance in the direction of the manor. "Are they well?"

"As to be expected, sir."

"Right," he sighed. He gave a quick pat to the tired

rain-soaked horse. "Treat him like royalty. He has a stout heart and iron will. We'll have to think of a name..." Simon hesitated. What was he doing? He should be running to the house, not bantering with Brian, who stood staring at him.

The stable master gave him a sad smile. "Go on now, lad. The beast will be well seen to. Your family needs you."

With a brief nod, Simon left the stable. The cold wind hit him as the rain continued to pelt down. He broke into a jog, following the path to the manor. He was running by the time he passed under the trellis and sped through the garden. He reached the kitchen door and yanked it open.

The door had barely closed behind him when he heard a shout.

"Simon!"

He scarcely managed to open his arms and catch his sister, Jean, as she flung herself at him. His arms wrapped around her, both heedless of his soaking clothes.

"Och, Jeanie. I'm here now." It broke his heart to hear Jean's sobs, as he held her shaking in his arms. "Quiet, lass."

"It's horrible. Everything is wrong." His sister's muffled broken voice pierced him.

"Shush," Simon reached up a hand to stroke her hair. "Calm yourself. Jeanie, lass, look at me." He pried her away from him, holding her by the shoulders to look down into her grief stricken face.

She gave a few more choked sobs, before sniffling and meeting his eyes.

"Tell me what's happened."

She took a deep breath. “Da went...he...” She shook her head, then straightened her shoulders under his hands. She’d grown while he had been away, matured. He always thought of her as his baby sister, but the six years separating them from birth seemed to have shrunk. A lady stood before him now.

“He took one of the boats out. The day was clear, but Da didn’t return. The lads set sail to find him, but all they discovered was his abandoned boat.” Jean stifled a sob, and bit her lip. “Two days later...two...they found his body on the bank of the Kyle.” Tears started to streak down her face once more, returning the little girl of his memories. “When they brought...him home, Ma collapsed. Oh, Simon! She’s been in bed ever since, barely ever awake!”

She collapsed against Simon. “You weren’t here! Why weren’t you here?”

Her muffled accusations made him cringe. “Hush now, Jeanie. I’m sorry. I’ll make it right.” He stared past her shoulder and noticed the servants gathering in the kitchen. He and Jean needed to set an example. Be strong for the household. Keep appearances so the servants were reassured their livelihood and safety would remain intact even though the MacKay family was in turmoil. For most of the help who managed the estate, this was their only home, a safe haven from a rough life, and the difference between life and death. His military training took hold and he shoved his emotions and grief aside. He gently pried Jean away from him. Meeting her eyes, he gave a brief smile. “It’ll get better. Why don’t you take me to ma?”

Jean sniffled once, and nodded after noticing the servants as well. “She’s in her rooms.”

Once again, she put on a brave front and the mask of a well-bred lady, and led him through the kitchen, past the servants who parted as they passed. Simon hardly noticed the spoken condolences and greetings as he left the room.

Why had his father sailed out alone? Or for a fact, sailed at all? He had left the sea to younger men and rarely even supervised his shipping and ferrying business, leaving it to his handpicked people. Murdoch MacKay spent his time with the land and his tenants. *What could have sent him out?*

They climbed the stairs to the third landing and made their way to the back of the house, to the rooms almost identical to his, a floor below. Colin, the butler, waited outside her door.

"Welcome home, my lord. You have made good time."

Simon shook his head. "Not nearly as fast as I wished." He looked down at the aging man. How had everyone grown so old the few years he'd been away? Simon met Colin's gaze. "How is she?"

"It has been hard for milady. She is much better today, having one of her good days. I believe the thought of your return has given her some strength. She is awake now if you would enter."

"I would indeed," Simon reached out a hand and squeezed Colin's shoulder. "Thank you for all your care. It gave me great comfort knowing you were here looking after the family."

"No thanks are needed, my lord. I serve the MacKay's gladly." Colin gave a slight smile, than departed down the hallway.

Simon turned to his sister. "Jean, I'll go in alone."

It was best if he saw his mother by himself. He'd run away at the age of six and ten, and it would be the first time she'd see him since he'd left. A tense reunion at best. Would she be happy to see him after all these years? Or angry he hadn't been there for the family? There was no telling how she would react, and Jean didn't need any more stress or grief than she currently experienced. "Wait for me in the library?"

"Yes, of course," she turned to leave, yet hesitated. "If you need me, send for me. And Simon," tears filled her gray eyes once more. "I'm glad you're home." After a quick hug, she left, her footfalls silent on the carpet runner.

Simon braced himself and entered his mother's sitting room. A roaring fire in the hearth crackled merrily in stark contrast to the weather outside and his mood inside. Rain pounded on the windows and a burst of lighting burned across his eyes. He blinked rapidly, blaming the sudden welling of tears to the storm. He had been right to leave all those years ago, but he had sorely missed wee Jean and his mother. He couldn't change the past. He had left for everyone's benefit, for the peace and welfare of his home, but he highly doubted if his ma saw it that way.

He looked at the open door to the bedroom when the clap of thunder struck. Simon shivered wondering if the menacing boom had been an omen. Enough of this superstitious nonsense, he admonished himself. His mother needed him.

He walked across the room, but reaching the doorway, he hesitated.

"Don't stand there lurking, come in Simon," Cora MacKay greeted her only son while propped up in bed.

Simon expelled a sigh, but crossed the room in a few strides to reach his mother's bedside. She held out her hand, which he raised up and gave a brief kiss before clasping both his hands around her own. "Ma, I came as fast as I could."

"I ken that, lad. You look like you've ridden hard. You're dripping wet."

He shrugged and stared down at her. She didn't look well, though she was trying to put a brave face on. The handsome woman, he remembered, had grown old in the eight years Simon had been gone, belying her forty-two years. Always a petite woman, she now seemed shrunken and lost in the blankets of the massive bed. Her thick, shiny red hair hung limp and flat, and her green eyes usually holding teasing mischief, were bloodshot and swollen.

She noticed his scrutiny and pulled her hand from his, and patted at her head, fussing with her hair. "Stop glaring down at me, son. I'm just feeling a little under the weather." Another clap of thunder greeted this statement causing them both to glance out across the balcony. "You should look to yourself. You need to get out of those wet clothes, before you end up in bed like me."

Simon shook his head, "I will. Dae nae worry about me." He ran his hand through his hair, pushing it away from his eyes. "Tell me what happened. Why was he out to sea?"

"He wouldn't tell me." Her already soft voice, lowered to a whisper. "I told him Duncan could handle anything he needed. After all the man has looked after his business for ten years now, but your father wouldn't listen, he was so stubborn. He said he had to go, do it himself."

Simon watched as a single tear trickled down his mother's cheek. His hand clenched into a fist, when she brushed it aside and then pressed her fingers to the bridge of her nose.

"Does your head ache you?"

"Only a wee bit."

He watched her forehead crease, and she inhaled sharply.

"I think it's more than that. Let me get you something—"

"No, no, I'll be all right. I just need some rest..." She reached up to grip his arm, pulling at him. "But I need to tell you..."

He dropped to his knees alongside the bed, bringing his face close to hers. "What is it, Ma?"

Her grip tightened on his arm, her voice barely a whisper. "Simon...your father was murdered. Careful...Find his killer..." her eyes closed and her hand slid from his arm to drop limp beside her.

"Ma? Ma? Are you all right?"

Cora sank deeper into the bedding and fell asleep before his astonished eyes. His mother was obviously ill and now this revelation. *Murdered? Murdoch MacKay had been murdered?* Was this truth or just a fantasy his ailing mother had conceived? He wanted to wake her and demand answers, but kneeling beside her, he knew she needed rest. With a light touch, he traced a finger across the back of her hand and sighed. "Sleep easy."

He stood, not taking his eyes from her diminutive form. He knew his mother. She was sharp and quick, even an illness wouldn't change that. Stunned, he let reality sink in. His father murdered. His intuition had warned him when he first read the message in France. He knew something had been terribly wrong. *But why would someone kill him?* His thoughts were broken by a thunderclap, and he turned to face the storm.

Simon stared blindly out the windows as the storm increased its fury. *What had his father needed to handle personally?* Therein lay the key, but it just didn't make any sense.

He left his mother's bedside, and reached the balcony doors. Placing a hand against the cold, damp glass, he brooded. He didn't want this added burden. He hadn't been ready to be Earl, and now he had to track down a killer.

When Simon left for France, his da had been robust and it seemed he would live forever. He was a stubborn man—too tough to ever die. It was hard to believe he was gone, his death brought about by foul intentions.

Simon would unearth the murderer. He was good at finding the enemy, and had plenty of experience working behind French lines. He'd start by finding Fiona. She was the first person who might be able to shed some light on this mystery. She knew everyone in the county and had her ear to the gossip. Simon only wondered if his jilted betrothed would even deem to speak with him.

He silently walked across the room. As he reached the bedroom door he stopped and gripped the frame's molding. Someone would pay for tearing his family apart. He glanced back at his mother's sleeping figure lost in the large bed. His knuckles turned white as his hand tightened with his fury. He would make it right, or die in the trying.

Chapter Five

Near Cleitmuir
July, Present Day

Laurel turned on her side to face the windows and snuggled deeper into her cozy nest of sheets and blankets, letting the filtered sunlight from the gauzy curtains warm her face. It was the best night's sleep she'd had in a long time. She hadn't realized how poorly she'd been sleeping these past weeks. Derek had gotten to her. But apparently being over-tired from jet lag, and hanging with her best friend until one in the morning was just the medicine she needed for a peaceful night's sleep. Even finding it still light as day out when she'd finally gone to bed hadn't affected her. It was weird, even though Laurel had read about it, but definitely another thing to experience it. This far north during summer, Scotland could get up to twenty hours of daylight.

She smiled and opened her eyes while taking an internal inventory. Laurel felt great. No hangover. What a relief considering the amount of wine and scotch she had consumed last night. She hadn't drunk that much since her freshman year in college. At least this time it had been stretched out over the evening in hours instead of binge at a frat party. Her smile changed to a grin, as she remembered her first college party Beth had dragged her to, claiming they had invitations, but were actually crashing. The things Beth had gotten her to do.

Last night had been relaxing and fun. It was easy to see why Beth had fallen in love with Grant, and drastically changed her life for him. It was a relief to see how much in love Grant was with Beth. Laurel should have been jealous, but she wasn't. If anything, seeing what true love looked like had opened her eyes to the three years she had wasted with Derek.

After dinner, Beth and Grant shared stories on how they had met, and the comedy of errors their wedding had become. They had her laughing so hard, she once again regretted the fact she hadn't made the wedding. Work, as it always seemed to do, had demanded her time. The museum had received a generous donation of Inca artifacts needing verification and the exhibit to arrange. There hadn't been a chance for her to sneak away for a surprise last-second marriage. After that, it was always something rearing its head, keeping her from getting to Scotland.

But she was here now, almost a whole year later. Laurel opened her eyes and stretched before throwing back the blankets and sitting up. Somehow she always let her job take over, leaving little time for a personal life. Maybe if she hadn't, she might have spotted what a fraud Derek really was or possibly been able to hold his interest. *Stop!* That train of thought would drive her insane. Besides she had a country to explore and no time to waste in bed, mulling over the past she couldn't change.

Laughing, she stood and stretched again. The irony of it all, mulling over the past *was* her job, but she was on vacation, a much needed and long overdue one. She wasn't going to waste another minute.

****

A short time later, Laurel entered Cleitmuir's inviting kitchen and stopped short in wonder. Controlled chaos met her eyes. Beth presided over a staff of four and everyone seemed to be heading in a different direction.

"Dear God, is this normal?"

"Oh Lori, you're up early. I expected you to still be in bed." Beth dusted the flour off her hands. "We have a dinner party to get ready for, remember?" She walked over and gave Laurel's beat-up tall riding boots, faded blue breeches, and long sleeved T-shirt a long look. "I think it's time you invested in some new riding duds. Your boots and breeches have seen better days."

Laurel shrugged. "They're comfortable."

"Are you sure you still want to ride out on your own? I know you won't get into any trouble, but maybe you've changed your mind and would like some company? It'll only take me a moment to change and join you. You can grab some breakfast while you wait."

Laurel grimaced and gave a brief shake of her head. "No thanks, you know I'm not the breakfast type, besides, we talked about this last night. You're much too busy, and there's no way I'm waiting for you to free up some time. I've been looking forward to this ever since you wrote and told me you renovated the barn and filled it with everything equine."

"One of these days I'll get you to eat breakfast," Beth gave a shrug, and grinned. "For now, I'll ignore it, 'cause I can't wait for you to see the barn. Grant's amazing. I'm still shocked he let me do it," Beth smiled warmly. "Here, let me walk you out at least."

Beth untied her apron and flung it onto a nearby chair and led the way across the kitchen. Reaching the back door, she grabbed a slicker/windbreaker from a hook on the wall and handed it to Laurel.

"You'll need this. The weather is unpredictable up here, besides, the wind off the Atlantic can be cold."

"Thanks," she slipped into the jacket shocked it fit so well.

Beth caught her look and shrugged. "It's an extra. Some guest left it behind. It's yours if you want it."

They walked outside and into a small herb garden. Crossing through, they passed under an arching trellis covered in blooming roses and onto a gravel path. Laurel took in the view. The ground opened up, and directly ahead stood a large stone building surrounded by mostly flat land, with an occasional rolling hill. It was the view from her balcony. She glanced over her shoulder and saw the hotel and in the far distance a large mountain range reaching up to touch the puffy white clouds floating in a crystal clear blue sky. A sky appearing so low, Laurel felt she could reach up and touch it.

"I still can't believe I own a stable full of horses and get to ride whenever I like," enthusiasm filled Beth's voice. "Remember in high school how we had to beg and bargain for our rides? Let alone scrap together the money to compete? It's great to be an adult!" Beth smiled. "I've picked you out a great mare. Her name is *Rògair Gailleann*."

Laurel gave a half-skip jog to catch up to Beth. "Ah, that's a mouth full."

Beth laughed. "Yeah, well, that's Gaelic for you. Her name translates roughly to rogue storm. We simply call her Gale. You're going to love her. She's an English thoroughbred, ex-steeplechaser. Right up your alley. I can't wait for you to try her."

It was right up both their alleys. As kids they hungered to run and jump cross country. None of the prissy show hunter stuff for them, and dressage was just a phase they endured in order to run like maniacs on uneven terrain, flying over ditches, up and down banks and solid jumps that wouldn't fall down if they hit them. They both loved it so much they made time in college to continue to ride. It was harder for Laurel now with a full time job, but every once in a while she still managed to get in a ride. She was completely jealous of Beth. What would Laurel do in order to own her own stable full of horses?

"A tempest is she?" Laurel laughed. "I'm not sure I should thank you just yet. You do remember I haven't ridden in a while, right?"

"Phsst, you'll be fine. You said it's only been a few months. And here we are," Beth gestured to the large gray stone building.

She followed Beth into the well-lit and ventilated barn. At once the welcoming smells of hay, horse and leather reached out to her.

"The tack room is here to your right, the crossties are across the aisle." Beth walked right past said items with only a slight gesture and continued to the first corner stall.

An elegant, well-shaped gray head popped out of the open split door. Large brown intelligent eyes observed them as they approached. Beth stopped in front of the horse and reached out to affectionately pat her.

"Gale, I'd like you to meet my best friend in the whole world. Laurel, this is Gale."

Laurel stepped near and raised her hand for the mare to sniff. A warm puff of air blew across her open flat palm in greeting. She smiled and reached up to stroke Gale on the neck.

"Hey sweet girl, aren't you the pretty thing?" And she was too, Laurel thought. A good sixteen-three hands, tall for your average horse. Refined, yet muscular, with a gleaming dappled gray coat, she was the pin-up girl of the equine world.

"You're going to love her, Lori. I'll just leave her to you. You do remember how to groom and tack, right?" Beth teased and raised an eyebrow at her.

Laurel returned the eyebrow. "It hasn't been *that* long. I think I can manage." She gave the mare a pat.

"Well then, her saddle and bridle are marked, and there's a grooming kit in the crossties. I really should go," Beth hesitated. "As long as you're sure you'll be all right..."

"Yes, get out of here. We'll be fine." Laurel gave Beth a smile then reached up to remove Gale's halter from a nearby hook.

"Okay then, have fun, and I'll see you for lunch." Beth turned and left the barn.

Laurel opened the mare's stall and slipped the halter over her head. "Let's get to know each other and then go out and raise some hell."

She led the horse out of the stall, smiling to herself. Laurel decided this vacation was off to a fantastic start.

Chapter Six

Near Cleitmuir Manor
July, Present Day

The wind rushed past Laurel's face and she let out a wild whoop of joy as the mare muscled into a gallop up the steep grade of the ravine. She hadn't felt so alive in months. With the lush rolling green hills, the brilliant Scottish sun sparkling off the distant ocean, and a horse who didn't know the meaning of stop, all of Laurel's problems disappeared as she galloped on.

She leaned forward, lightening her seat as she urged the mare forward. They crested the top, reaching a plateau, and ran straight into a bank of fog.

"Holy hell!" Laurel cried out as both she and her mount were enveloped in a thick misty cloud. Visibility shrunk to just herself and the mare, the entire world disappearing. Sinking deep into the saddle, she pulled on the reins. "Easy, girl. We can't see a thing."

The horse slowed to a trot and then to a walk. As they meandered slowly forward, she looked around.

The fog was thick with eerie bright white wisps threaded throughout. They twisted and turned, giving it a sense of motion. Laurel shivered as the damp cold penetrated her borrowed jacket. The fog hadn't been there when they had dropped down into the ravine. The day had been brilliantly clear. How had the plateau been engulfed so quickly? This must be the changing weather Beth warned her about. Dropping one hand from the reins, she reached for the partially closed jacket zipper, pulling it up so the collar closed around her neck.

The mare continued to pick her way carefully along the path. “This is ridiculous. I guess we should head back, Gale.” The horse snorted as if in agreement, while Laurel began to turn them around.

Suddenly, the mare froze. Laurel squeezed her legs, and then jabbed her heels into Gale’s side when the horse didn’t respond. “Come on, git up.” She thumped the mare again.

The horse started to prance and hop around in place, before shooting backwards.

“What the...”

Laurel over-handed the reins, smacking the mare’s neck, causing the horse to lurch forward. She grabbed a fist full of mane as Gale slid to a stop and reared. The horse slammed her front legs back to the ground, only to reload and launch herself upward again, completely vertical.

Laurel felt herself lose her grip, beginning to slide off, she desperately squeezed her thighs trying to clamp on. The mare spun on her hind legs, sending Laurel spiraling off her back. As she fell, the fog closed around her, and she looked for the ground but couldn’t see any.

Oh my, God! An involuntary scream burst from her throat when something grabbed her upper arm, abruptly halting her plunge. Her shoulder wrenched painfully, then again when she was yanked upwards. Her legs scraped against stone as her body was dragged. But then she was released as fast as she was seized, to land sprawled on her side, panting, eyes closed. *Holy hell, what just happened*? She rolled onto her back as she tried to get her breathing under control.

"Well, lass. That was about the stupidest thing I've ever witnessed."

Laurel jerked upwards at the low angry brogue. *Stupid*? She'd fallen off a horse, for crying out loud. It happens.

She peered into the dense fog trying to get a glimpse of the disembodied Scot. The thick mist swirled, thinned, and parted to reveal a pair of well-worn, brown riding boots with red cuffs at the top. Her eyes climbed higher, following the boots to a pair of large muscular thighs encased in dark-colored breeches. Her eyes continued upward, past the flat stomach, which led to a broad chest and shoulders covered in a mostly unbuttoned white shirt.

She craned her neck and finally saw his face. Roughly chiseled, he had a square jaw with high cheekbones, a slightly off-centered nose, and full lips pursed into a frown. She forced herself to meet his eyes, and her jaw dropped. The light gray eyes were almost opalescent against his dark lashes and black shoulder-length hair—eyes that pierced right thorough her.

"Every bloody year the tourists just get dumber," he declared.

She clamped her mouth shut on a sharp retort and shook her head. "Gee, thanks for your concern. It's not like I planned to fall off." She started to push off the ground, but her right arm collapsed under her. Before she could fall back, the man reached her side and grabbed her good arm, pulling her to her feet.

Laurel shivered as cold lanced through her. She

looked up to meet his disconcerting pale eyes. She shivered again and suddenly realized just how much larger he was than her. At five-foot-eleven, she rarely ever felt short, but next to this man, who was easily five to six inches taller, she felt practically petite. She never felt that way. She rubbed her right arm to ease the sting still pounding in her bicep, until Laurel realized it might make her appear vulnerable. She quickly dropped her left hand back to her side.

Squaring her shoulders, she met his icy gaze. “Thanks for your help, I’m fine. You can stop lurking now.” She watched as something flashed through his strange eyes, but she noticed he hadn’t taken a step back. “If you’ll excuse me, I need to find my horse.”

She tried to shoulder past him, but he stepped in front of her, blocking her way. A tinge of unease coursed through her, but she defiantly met his eyes. “Is there something else?”

“Aye, there is. A warning. If you’re not a competent rider, you shouldna be out on the plateau.”

“What the...of all the crass, stupid...” Laurel fumed. *Smug jerk*. “Get out of my way!”

“The horse has more brains than you.”

“How dare you? You don’t even know me. I’ve been riding since I was twelve.”

“Then you should know by now if you can’t see where you’re going, and a horse balks, you lean to caution and figure out why.”

Laurel took a deep breath, she didn’t want to argue with him, all she wanted to do was get the hell away from him. “Look, I thanked you, but you’re stepping way out of bounds. I fell off a horse. It wasn’t like I was going to die.”

"Are you so sure, lass?" He nodded past her shoulder. "I think it would take more than a helmet, which I might add you're not wearing, to save that pretty head of yours."

Laurel turned and gasped. The dissipated fog left a clear view of the Atlantic Ocean. She was a scant few steps from a sheer drop-off. She looked down over the ledge at the thin strip of beach far, far below and barely heard the crashing breakers from the waves as they reached the shore.

"Oh, God!" The whispered exclamation escaped her. She had fallen off a cliff.

Laurel took two steps back and slammed into the solid wall of her rescuer. His hands grabbed either side of her waist to steady her. She started shaking at the sudden release of adrenaline, realizing how close she came to dying.

"You're not going to faint, are you?"

"I... not...I don't faint." She shook her head. "Can we move away from this ledge?"

His laughter, low in his chest, vibrated through her. "Aye, lass. If you promise me you won't faint."

She spun in his arms and glared up at him. "I already told you, I don't faint." She placed both palms flat on his chest and pushed. He didn't budge, not an inch. She felt his hands tighten on her waist.

He chuckled. "A feisty wee thing."

She tried another shove with the same results and earned herself a raised eyebrow. He was a handsome man, however, Derek's life lesson taught her packaging couldn't always be trusted. Laurel frowned. "Cute. Let go of me. Now!"

He released her immediately and stepped to the

side giving her a sweeping courtly bow. Her rescuer straightened and stared at her as she rubbed her right shoulder. He frowned and took a step toward her.

She dropped her hand. “I’m fine.” He stopped and retreated, as if sensing her discomfort. *Great*. She hated showing weakness of any kind, especially in front of strangers. Could this day get any better? She needed to get out of here.

“Where’s Gale?” She scanned the plateau and then spotted the mare, standing a few yards away, cropping grass. “Oh thank, God. Beth would have killed me.”

Laurel completely missed the irony of her words, and ignored the slow smile of the man beside her. She started to walk to the horse but stopped, realizing how rude she was being. Just because she thought he was an ass wasn’t an excuse to lose all manners, after all he did save her life. It was a miracle he had been there and seen her drop over the side, let alone reach down and grabbed her in time. How had he lifted her over the ledge, one handed, as if she had weighed nothing? Laurel turned and faced him.

“I don’t know what to say. Thank you seems really lame.”

He wore an easy smile while his silver eyes stared straight through her. “It’s no worry. You’re welcome.”

He walked alongside her as they approached the horse. Reaching Gale, Laurel took hold of the reins and gave her a pat. It would have been a long walk back if she’d run off, and her shoulder and arm were really beginning to throb.

She turned toward the man to thank him again when she saw his hands cupped for a leg up. Laurel placed her left leg into the cradle and pushed off with her right. His timing was good as he flung her up into the saddle, but he had to quickly grab her thigh to steady her as she almost slipped off the opposite side from the force of his throw.

His hand burned warm on her thigh as she looked down at him. “Ah...thank you, again.”

“My pleasure. Just promise not to throw yourself off any more cliffs.” He removed his hand and swatted the mare on her hip, startling Gale into a walk. The horse turned back to the path and broke into a trot.

In a few seconds, Laurel reached the descent off the plateau and realized she hadn’t gotten his name. Even if he was sort of condescending, she owed him. She should at least know his name.

She halted Gale and turned in the saddle to call out, but the words froze in her throat. The man was gone. Disappeared. There was no one on the plateau.

Laurel stared at the empty expanse then shook her head and faced forward. She nudged the mare into a walk. She’d ask Beth if she recognized him. The whole thing was so surreal, all starting with the fog appearing and disappearing out of nowhere. Just like the man. He had been wearing riding clothes, but where was his horse? How had he gotten off the plateau so quickly? Who was he? The researcher in her stirred, as she sensed a puzzle to be solved.

She urged Gale to a trot as she reached the bottom of the ravine, trying to shake off the odd feeling still with her. Laurel already knew she wouldn’t tell Beth about her close call. There was no need to worry her, after all. She was safe and sound except for a sore shoulder.

She lifted a hand from the reins to rub her shoulder

again. Her hand slid down to her bicep. It felt warm and tight. Like the man's hand still gripped her. She'd probably get one hell of a bruise, but if all she got out of this experience was a sore arm, she'd count herself lucky.

Chapter Seven

Laurel stared back at her reflection in the freestanding mahogany framed mirror and frowned. She couldn't believe she was nervous. This wasn't a date, just an informal dinner party, no matter how much Beth wanted her to think otherwise.

She smoothed her hands down the pleated jewel-toned skirt that swished around her knees and glared at the non-descript black flats she wore. Laurel never wore heels, they caused her to tower over most men, which was never a good thing. She stared back at the too tall and intense woman in the mirror. Feminine, she wasn't, no matter the wrapping. Derek had been right about one thing, she just wasn't built correctly to wear dresses and skirts. Give her a good pair of jeans and a T-shirt and her confidence soared. Girl trappings made her mind spin self-consciously.

Tilting her head, she studied her hair. She'd twisted the long straight strands and fastened it with an alligator clip high on her head. Slippery tendrils had escaped to frame her sharp-featured face, softening it just a bit. At least Laurel hoped it did. She glanced at her plain white blouse and popped an extra button open. What the hell? Maybe her cleavage, her one God given asset, would distract him from her appearance. If judging by the other men who thought her eyes were located chest level, she had a good chance in succeeding.

Laurel turned her back resolutely on the mirror, and with a swish of her gauzy skirt, left the bedroom and didn't look back. She told herself not to worry. Tonight held no pressure. She didn't have to like the guy, and who cared if he liked her? She could do this. "Screw you, Derek." Rebound guy look out!

Striding down the hallway, she rubbed her right shoulder and thought of the mystery man from this afternoon. Beth hadn't recognized him from her description, but mentioned with the festival starting there were many new people in the area. Well, he'd have to settle for just her thanks, unless she crossed paths with him again. And she was completely divided by that idea. He was handsome in a rough and rugged kind of way, but she could definitely do without the attitude.

Reaching the top of the wide stairs, she paused and took a deep breath, putting all thoughts from her head. She *would* have a good time tonight. Who knows? Maybe Alex MacKenzie was just the man she needed. Beth was always good at reading her, and if she thought Laurel would like him, then she probably would.

Laurel descended the stairs and paused outside the sitting room, not quite ready to enter. The rumble of deep Scottish voices reached her, and she smiled. She loved the Scottish brogue. But the smile disappeared from her face when she caught sight of a man leaning casually against the mantel of the lit fireplace. Tall and lithe, he looked athletic even when relaxed, a dancer's physique. Dark trousers hugged his slender hips and covered long legs. His tie-less white dress shirt was open at the throat giving the smallest glimpse of his broad chest and shoulders. With his sleeves casually rolled up to reveal well-defined forearms, it took little imagination to envision sculpted biceps.

But it was his face that garnered most of her attention. Clean-shaven, his face was *GQ* perfect with short tousled blond hair framing a strong jaw, a straight aquiline nose, high cheeks bones, and full lips. Lips presently curled up into a contagious smile. She felt herself drawn to him.

He turned his head, then stared directly at her from across the room. Clear blue eyes, the color of a cloudless Chicago winter sky, captured hers, pinning her in place. His smile widened, and he inclined his head.

"Lori! It's about time."

Beth's voice broke the spell and she dragged her attention away from the man, to watch Beth walk to her side.

"It took you long enough. Come on in," Beth grabbed her hand and dragged her into the room. Most of the conversation stopped as Laurel entered, all eyes drawn to her. It was like that dream everyone has of walking into school as the new kid only to discover you're naked. Talk about awkward.

"Everyone, this is my best friend Laurel from the States." The guests smiled at her, a few called out greetings before they went back to their conversations.

"Beth," she hissed under her breath. "I thought you said a *small* dinner." She gazed around the room in dismay. There were probably a good twenty people whereas Laurel assumed it might be five or so.

"Oh, hush," Beth smiled up at her. "They're all neighbors, community members involved with the Primrose Festival. And it's not like you're not used to crowds with all of the museum's highfalutin shindigs." Beth tugged on her hand to get her walking. "We're using tonight as a last meeting before the show gets rolling. Now relax, there's someone I'm dying to introduce you to."

Beth was right. The Chicago Field Museum held parties on a regular basis. She dealt with crowds at those required functions. That didn't mean she liked it. One of the many perks of becoming a historical researcher allowed her to hole up with her computer and dusty moldy tomes and lose herself. Nary a person in sight. However, Laurel thought as she saw where Beth was taking her, there were drawbacks in being secluded. She didn't get to meet a lot of new people. And after Derek, she didn't think she could trust her own opinion, especially when it came to good looking strangers—like the man Beth was leading her toward. Was he another wolf in sheep's clothing?

Laurel didn't realize she held her breath as Beth stopped them in front of the man at the fireplace. He straightened and his smile grew larger as his blue eyes stayed focused on her face. Relax she mentally admonished herself.

"Alex, I'd like you to meet Laurel."

"Hello, it's a pleasure to finally meet you," his soft burr rolled over her, and she managed a breath.

"Laurel, this is Alex MacKenzie. He leases Sinclair House, a neighboring property a few acres away."

Beth turned to Laurel and grinned. "I'll leave you in his capable hands. Alex," Beth nodded at him and walked away, making Laurel a bit speechless as she watched her go.

His low chuckle drew her attention back to him.

"Not very subtle, is she?"

She could do this. After all, Laurel hadn't picked Alex out all on her own as she had Derek. He came pre-vetted by Beth. Alex was exactly what he looked like—a gorgeous guy any woman would dream of and want. So she forced a smile as she shook her head. "Beth isn't well known for that attribute. Hi." She held out her hand. "I'm happy to meet you."

Expecting a handshake, she was startled when his hand lightly gripped her fingers and raised them up. His lips were warm and soft as he pressed a kiss to her skin. She could have sworn she felt his thumb lightly brush the inside of her palm at the same time. Warmth flushed through her, all the way down to her toes. It was definitely getting warm in here, or maybe she was standing too close to the fire. But which fire, the hearth's or Alex's?

The Scotsman continued to smile and slowly released her hand. "Again, the pleasure's all mine. Welcome to Scotland. I understand this is your first trip?"

Laurel realized she was staring blindly at him and focused. "Yes, yes it is. I've always wanted to visit, but never could make the time."

"Ah, yes, the Chicago Field Museum. It's kept you busy I understand."

"What else has Beth told you?"

He grinned. "That you're a workaholic history detective, single from a freshly broken long-term relationship, you're smart and have a great sense of humor. I was told to distract you and make you forget all your problems."

"Oh, is that all," she swallowed hard. Best friend or

not, Beth's day's were numbered. "I guess she pretty much told you everything."

"Not everything. She didn't tell me, for instance, that you had the softest, shiniest hair," he reached out and fingered a tendril before tucking it behind her ear. "Hair that changes colors by firelight. I bet candlelight would suit you as well."

"Ah...really?" His sharp blue eyes held a mischievous twinkle as he stared into her eyes.

"And she didn't tell me that you have the most intriguing eyes. What color are they? Green? Brown? Gold?"

Wow, did this work on the local girls? He was laying it on a bit thick. Was he teasing her? Laurel wondered and shook her head. "My brothers always said mud colored," she took a step back, giving herself some distance. She wasn't sure if she should feel flattered or creeped out. But she did know she tingled from his single-minded attention.

Alex chuckled. "I don't think I'd use that adjective."

She was spared from more uncomfortable banter by Grant's entrance into the room.

"Dinner is ready."

"Here," Alex extended his arm beside her. "Let me show you the way."

Laurel placed her hand on his arm and walked alongside as he escorted her from the room. He turned his head and smiled at her. "I don't know about you, but I find myself verra hungry."

Her stomach flipped as he deliberately broadened his accent. She had a feeling he wasn't talking about food. The man certainly knew how to flirt. And damn it, it felt good to be the object of a handsome man's attention, even if he was pouring it on a bit thick.

Laurel smiled back at him. A little highland fling indeed.

Chapter Eight

The dinner meeting came to a close as Beth rattled out the final touches. "So, as long as Liam stays out of the scotch," she said which was greeted by a round of laughter at the table. "And, it doesn't rain on the opening picnic, bad omen, we should be all set." Nods and murmured agreements came from all sides of the table. "Oh, Jenny," Beth looked down the table to a red-haired, middle-aged woman. "You've confirmed the orchestra for the ball, right?"

"Aye, got it this morning. I even heard them play. They're fabulous."

Laurel took in all the satisfied faces at the table. Dinner had been interesting with all the strategizing and bantering. The Primrose Festival, a local tradition in July, culminated with Highland Games consisting of tossing the caber, stone putting and hammer throws, along with competitive dancing, at the end of the month. It sounded like fun. And it all began with a brunch picnic followed by a costume ball that night. She sighed. The ball was a sore point. Alex had been at her all through dinner to make sure she would attend, but she had yet to agree. It just wasn't her cup of tea. She didn't dance, and lord knows how goofy she'd look in a period gown. She much preferred jeans. Being tall and gangly, gowns only accentuated her awkwardness.

"So, it's settled, then," Alex got her attention.

"You'll be my guest at the Festival's opening ball," he grinned at her from across the table.

"Wait a second, it certainly is not," she shook her head. "First, it's a costume ball, so where in the world would I find a dress in time? I don't see how this would work."

"Oh, you're not missing the ball," Beth chimed in at her side. "All we need is a road trip. I'll drive you down to Inverness, I've errands to do there. I know the perfect shop, and you can sightsee, too. Maybe you'll spot ol' Nessie?"

"You're both ganging up on me," Laurel accused.

Grant laughed from the head of the table. "You might as well cut your losses."

"Easy for you to say. I don't dance." She stared down at her plate and stabbed a lone piece of asparagus. "Don't think for a moment I won't get even." She glared first at Beth then across the table at Alex, who tried hard not to laugh.

"Speaking of the Loch Ness monster—"

"Changing the topic won't save you, MacKenzie," she challenged. He grinned back at her.

"But all I wanted to know was if you've met the ghost yet?" He asked, now looking perfectly innocent.

"Oh, dear God, really? If that room is haunted, the ghost is extremely shy."

"Well, from what I understand and correct me if I'm wrong," Alex looked to Grant and Beth, "but this is prime haunting time. Apparently the Festival sets him off."

"Him?"

"Simon MacKay."

"You know who the ghost is?" Laurel shook her

head. "Beth, you didn't tell me that. How do you know it's him? Who is he?" That was so cool if they knew who the ghost was. She wondered why Beth had held that tidbit to herself? She wondered what Simon MacKay's story was.

"Now you've done it," Beth replied. "You started this, Alex, so you get to tell the story."

"My pleasure. There's nothing better than a tale filled with intrigue, scorned love, treasure, and murder." Alex pushed his empty plate away and picked up his wine glass. He swirled the red contents and leaned back in his chair. He met Laurel's gaze from across the rim as he took a sip.

Laurel picked up her own glass and settled in for Simon's saga. She wondered if Alex was a good storyteller. It didn't really matter. Anything would sound great with a Scottish burr, and besides, she wasn't bored with the view yet. A hush fell over the lingering guests as Alex took up his tale.

"It all goes back to the Jacobite gold."

"Ha, doesn't it always go back to Bonnie Prince Charlie?" an elderly man inserted.

"It does indeed, James," Alex nodded in agreement. "Laurel, you know about the Jacobites?"

"Of course. They were the men and woman who favored Charles Stuart as the true King of Scotland and England over King George," Laurel smiled, after all, history was her specialty.

"Excellent," Alex replied. "Then I'll just dive right in. Our story begins in 1746. A ship named, *Hazard*, was sailing to Inverness. It carried over £13,000 in gold coins sent by France to aid the bonnie Prince's rebellion. They were spotted by the royal frigate, *HMS*

Sheerness, and chased into the Kyle of Tongue. The *Hazard's* crew escaped and took the gold ashore to carry it overland." He paused and took another sip of wine.

"The MacKay's gave chase and caught up with the rebels the very next morning at Lochan Haken. The Jacobites, realizing they were trapped, threw the gold into the Loch to keep it away from the royal English coffers."

"Hang on, the MacKay's are Highlanders. They weren't Jacobites?" Laurel asked.

"Now, therein lies another tale, but suffice to say, the MacKay's were Royalists, supporting King George."

"Wow. I thought all Highlanders were with Prince Charles."

"Some weren't, and they all had their reasons, no matter how wrong they were. Many of them hedged their bets and figured out a way to fight on both sides. But we're getting sidetracked. This is a ghost story, remember?" Alex teased.

"Oh yeah, excuse me for getting sucked into history. Oww!" Laurel glared at Beth and rubbed her arm from her friend's slap. "So, how does gold sitting at the bottom of a lake make a ghost?"

"Of course the gold didn't remain in the loch. Historical documents prove the government later recovered most of it. But that's the key phrase, 'most of it'."

"Ah, here it comes, the balderdash of hidden treasure," someone muttered from the far end of the long table.

Alex glanced down the table and shrugged, before

fixing his attention back on her. “Rumor has it, the MacKay’s acquired some of the gold, and stashed it away, supposedly here in Cleitmuir. The gold was the family’s legacy handed down from father to son, but the inheritance was broken.

“Around the early 1800’s, the last Earl of Cleitmuir died under mysterious circumstances. It was said his only son, Simon, was responsible.”

“He couldna have,” a man rebutted. “He was in France fighting Napoleon.”

Alex smiled. “Or, he snuck back home, tired of war and the wee pay of a common solider and murdered the Earl,” he replied with a slight shrug to his shoulders, countering the grumbles from around the table. “It was said, Simon wanted the gold for himself. He was tired of the MacKay’s hoarding it and decided he wanted to live the life of the rich he’d witnessed on the Continent, regardless of the consequences to his family. But, here’s where the story gets interesting.”

Laurel took in the rapt faces of everyone at the table, some frowning, some smiling, but all hooked by Alex’s words. It was obvious they all knew where the story was headed, but like any good urban legend, they still wanted to hear it once more.

“Simon MacKay disappeared, without a word to anyone—not to his mother or sister or even to his betrothed.”

“So? He stole the gold and left. How does that make him the ghost?” Laurel asked.

“Because he never got the gold. It’s believed someone in the household found out Simon’s intent, had him killed, and then secreted the gold to a new location to protect the treasure. But something went wrong and the gold disappeared forever."

"He's trying to find the gold," Laurel grinned. "Why does he only search during the festival time?"

"The Primrose Festival is old, dating back before Simon MacKay was even born. It's run pretty much unbroken for hundreds of years except during the Clearances," Grant replied. "As to why he haunts during festival time, it's more like he makes the most impression during that time. He's probably at it all year long.

"And..." Alex paused, letting the word hang into the expectant silence of the crowd. "The anniversary of young Simon's disappearance which was the first day of the festival, is only a few days away."

"Cool." Laurel continued to grin. She loved nothing better than a good ghost story.

"And it's a fitting end to the tale," Grant replied. "The ghost of Simon MacKay is supposed to haunt the halls of Cleitmuir Manor until he finds the gold that was hidden away from him." Her host stood up. "And on that note, enough with these silly old tales, why don't we adjourn back to the sitting room for a wee dram or two."

Laurel stood and placed her empty wine glass on the table. Her head swam a bit, and she was not at all surprised to find herself tipsy. All this drinking was going to kill her, or pickle and preserve her for the future like some poor creature stuck in formaldehyde. She caught up to Beth and walked with her. Alex and Grant were already leading the way to the front of the house.

"So, how does Alex know all about the gold?"

Beth gave her a quick glance. "He didn't tell you

what he does for a living?"

She felt a blush heat her cheeks. It hadn't come up in their conversation while he had been outrageously flirting with her earlier. Laurel was torn between feeling flattered by his attention and leery of his handsome face. Reminders of Derek's betrayal had crossed through her mind all evening, making her cautious of Alex. Burned once… But was she supposed to put her life on hold indefinitely, to suspect any attractive man's attention?

"I'm going to punch that blond lummox!" Beth's exclamation interrupted Laurel's thoughts. "It was the one of the main reasons why I thought you two would hit it off," Beth sighed. "He's a professional treasure hunter."

"You're kidding?"

"No, not at all. He's dived shipwrecks, crawled through tombs, and searched caves, all in the name of treasure. He hears of a tale or rumor, researches the myth behind the legend, and *voilà*, he's a good deal richer. He's a lot like you—well, except for the richer part."

"Wow, I had no idea," she stared, lost in thought at Alex.

Laurel dismissed Beth's grin as she walked toward Alex, quite intrigued now. She stopped beside him and Grant.

"Laurel," Grant greeted. "Would you like some scotch?"

"No, really," she waved him off. "I don't think I should drink anymore, my head's already mushy. I need some fresh air." She looked at Alex. "I'd love some company."

He nodded and joined her as she walked to the front door.

"Have you seen the moors by moonlight?"

Laurel shook her head and laughed. "I guess I still won't. It's daylight outside."

"Ah yes, the Highlands during summer. At least we won't fall into a ditch."

"There is that."

Alex opened the front door, allowing her to exit first. She waited for him at the bottom of the steps as he closed the door and joined her. They strolled in companionable silence, gravel from the circular drive crunching beneath their feet. The sun rested low on the horizon, nearing the gloaming hour since it was close to midnight. Magic time.

"How have you enjoyed your first day in Scotland?"

"It's been...spectacular. I saw a lot of the area today. I borrowed one of Beth's horses."

"You ride?"

She nodded as they drifted off the driveway and took a groomed path leading around the side of the house.

"You'll have to come to Sinclair House. It's not that far, an easy ride, and quite beautiful. I'm letting it for the duration."

"That's right, for the treasure hunt."

"I see word has spread." Amusement colored his reply.

"It's fascinating. Right up my alley as a historical researcher, except for the whole physical retrieving thing. I like my nice safe desk, computer, and books. I'm surprised you didn't mention it during dinner."

He shrugged as they came to a path that took them further around back. At an intersection, Alex chose right, leading them toward the garden. "I try not to make a big deal about it. Besides, the locals believe it's a bunch of nonsense, and it's not like we've had a lot of time together to bring it up."

He was right about that. They had barely met and yet, she felt a connection to him. It was amazing they shared an interest in history, but Derek had as well. Was her past repeating itself? She was over thinking things, and needed to stop comparing everyone to her ex-boyfriend. It was time to move on. She decided she wanted to know more about Alex. A small weight shifted off her shoulders with her decision. "Well, it would have been better time spent, conversationally speaking that is, than trying to convince me to go to a ball."

"We'll just have to disagree on that," Alex replied as the corners of his mouth curled up.

"I'd love to look at your research, if you don't mind of course. I might even be able to help."

"That's a generous offer, one I'll probably take you up on. I must confess when Beth told me about you, it was one of the first things that crossed my mind. Here," Alex gestured to the steps of a faded white gazebo. Hedge roses in full bloom scented the night air with a light delicate fragrance where they surrounded the structure. It created a nice illusion of privacy.

"You don't need to apologize, I'd love to help."

"Yes, but you're on holiday. I didn't want to impose."

"It's not—" Her foot caught the last step, and Laurel stumbled forward. Before she could fall flat on her face, strong arms wrapped around her waist, steadying her. Dear God, when had she become such a klutz? At least she hadn't fallen off a cliff this time. She must be drunker than she thought.

"Uh, thanks."

"My pleasure."

Laurel turned in his grip to face him. She was near his height, just a few inches shy. She realized he hadn't let go of her. In fact, he took a step closer and smiled.

"If I wasn't a gentleman," his soft words raced through her, "I could take advantage of this situation." He glanced down at her lips before trapping her gaze. "Alone, with a beautiful woman in my arms, who's slightly tipsy."

Was he really going to kiss her? She decided she liked the idea. "What would you do?" Her voice came out low and husky, surprising her.

"I might do this." He leaned in, and Laurel closed her eyes.

The first brush of his lips was brief and almost questioning. When she didn't pull away, his lips closed over hers placing soft kisses, caressing back and forth, tender and light. Her breath quickened, when he added just the teasing tip of his tongue to trace around and between her lips.

On a soft sigh, her lips parted. It was all the encouragement he needed. Alex deepened the kiss, his tongue sliding into her mouth, stroking. She kissed him right back, tangling with his tongue. He tasted of zinfandel, scotch, and some exotic spice she couldn't quite place. He tasted wonderful and foreign. She was warm all the way down to her toes and her mind whirled. She moved closer, pressing into his hard lean body. His hands shifted to her hips, tightening their grip and holding her to him, as she reached up to entwine her fingers into his thick soft hair.

Laurel felt his chuckle more than heard it. With one last swirl of his tongue, he broke the kiss. Her hands dropped to his shoulders, steadying herself. She was grateful he still held her close, because she actually felt weak in the knees. Derek certainly had never made her feel this way.

The soft touch under her chin, made her open her eyes. Alex smiled at her.

"But, I am a gentleman, so I'd never take advantage."

"Ha."

"It's getting late, let me walk you back." He escorted her from the gazebo, and in a short while they were on the path to the kitchen garden. He stopped under the rose trellis.

"Do you have plans for tomorrow?"

"Well, at some point, I need to go to Inverness and get a costume."

"I can't wait to see you dressed in historic garb. You'll be perfect." He grinned at her. "It'll take a good portion of the day, but if you make it back by late afternoon and aren't too tired, why don't you come over for a late tea?"

"No promises. With Beth in charge of the schedule, God knows what will happen."

"We'll keep it open, then. You're on holiday after all, and should be enjoying yourself. I wouldn't want to take advantage of you." He leaned in and gave her a brief kiss, before walking away.

Laurel watched him leave. She was tingling from

her head down to her toes. How had this happened? She'd traveled half way around the globe to forget a handsome traitorous man, and now seemed to be getting entangled with another guy. What was wrong with her?

She sighed as she turned and entered the kitchen. Nothing. Nothing was wrong with her. With new determination, she took a deep breath. It was time to step up and live her life.

Chapter Nine

Simon MacKay tried the door. Locked. His eyes narrowed as he glared at the barrier. Was the room actually occupied? Hadn't they learned their lesson? They would now. He had little patience left.

His eyes closed as he concentrated. He hated this, but he'd use whatever tricks granted him—if it meant ending his personal hell, no matter how uncomfortable it might be—he needed in that room. Grimacing, he felt his body contort and then thin. He stepped forward and pushed his way through the solid wood door. Each strand of wood fiber pierced his being like hot knives, but he ignored the pain, shoving it into a corner of his mind that lived in constant torment. This pain was just another acquaintance introduced to an already crowded gallery.

He stepped into the room. On a silent exhaled breath, he solidified expending some of his stored energy and opened his eyes. Home once more. The furniture and decorations may have changed throughout the years, resembling little of his past, yet each time he entered his room, it gave a tiny bit of peace. Something to hold and cherish in his cursed life. Little had changed during the past year. But what was a year? Nothing. Not compared to the partial half-life he lived, one month out of every twelve, for the last two hundred years. The other eleven months a black void of limbo, where his self-awareness was lost in a hazy fog only half remembered.

He was close to being free, to finishing it, so very close. Yet, with every piece of the puzzle he found, Fate deemed it not enough. She was a harsh mistress, demanding and not to be cheated of her game. *But what were the rules? Bloody hell, what was the game?* The one hope he clung to, valued the most, the one keeping him sane over these hellish years, was he might find death. He wanted release from his unending prison. Heaven or Hell, he didn't care, just so long as there was an end.

He had been lost when he had first awakened, oh so long ago. No one had greeted him, given him instructions or a guidebook. He was left alone, not dead, but most definitely not alive. Left a ghost to haunt the land where he had lived with no reason why.

Simon had never thought much about spirits or the afterlife when he'd been alive. He had been superstitious like most Highlanders, but it had been more by rote than belief. His best guess was Fate had decided he still had unfinished business, and he wouldn't find his peace until his task was completed.

But it was almost done now. He would find it this time, the treasure his family had guarded through the years, the one his stupidity, while he'd been alive, was now left unguarded and in danger. He would fulfill his family's oath. Nothing would stop him. With grim determination, he strode through the room to the next. First, he'd scare the bloody hell out of whoever was staying in his rooms. He needed the privacy and couldn't be dodging tourists in the short time he was allowed to roam—a little more than a month, the length of the Primrose Festival. He'd be damned if he'd find himself chained in that hellhole of a cave again to drown.

He stopped at the foot of the bed and glared, preparing to do his worst, but froze. By God, it was her, the feisty lass from the cliffs. He frowned down at the woman in his bed. Moonlight sliced through the curtains to spill across the room and highlight her as she slept unaware of his scrutiny.

She lay curled on her side, facing the bank of windows with the covers tucked under her chin. The moonlight made her face glow, ethereal, like a spirit. His gut twisted. She was no ghost. He had held her warm body in his arms, smelled her scent, and had felt desire.

Damn. He wasn't human anymore. He didn't need to eat. So why did he still have his feelings? Urges? Simon continued to stare at the sleeping woman.

If he hadn't been there she would have died. *Foolish, lass*. He frowned and his hand rose to grip one of the bed's poster columns. He gave it a hard shove, causing the bed to shake. The woman didn't move, not even to blink. He released his hold and bent over, placing both hands on the soft sprung mattress. Never taking an eye off the slumbering girl, he jarred the mattress several times. Still nothing. He sighed and straightened, but then as idea struck him, a devilish grin curled his lips.

He reached and grabbed the blanket and sheet that covered her and yanked. It slid away, down her side, past her hips, across her curled legs, to come to rest at her ankles. The smile fled his face.

Moonlight bathed her naked skin. She was pure

glowing white, yet stood out easily from the cotton sheets. No nightrail covered her. She was as bare as the time of her birth. A sigh passed her lips.

She slowly rolled onto her back, straightening her long, well-toned legs. On a second sigh, she raised her arms above her head and stretched in her sleep. Simon's mouth went dry, and his eyes were riveted on the lass. Her movements flattened her stomach, concaving it and accentuating a pair of well-formed large breasts. The dusky nipples taunted him, peaking in the cool early morning air. As he continued to watch, she bent one knee, drawing his attention downward to the thatch of hair so tantalizingly near.

He swallowed hard, his eyes fixed as her leg drew upwards, brushing the soft inner thigh of the opposite leg. On a third sigh, she rolled onto her other side. Moonlight caressed her smooth hip and highlighted her taut derriere as she trailed one hand down her side, finally to rest on one ivory thigh. Sweat broke out across his brow.

He glowered down at the vision in his bed. *Damn.* He choked off a startled laugh. As if he wasn't in hell already. His fingers pierced through his hair. Not once, in over two hundred years had a woman bothered him. Was she a taunt from God? A punishment? Simon had forsaken his family for selfish reasons, and now in death was doing everything to rectify it, so God chose to test his will at this point?

He shook his head and walked to the side of the bed. Reaching for the comforter, he pulled it up over legs and hips, but drew short when he noticed the dark smudge on her upper arm. A blackened bruise marked her porcelain skin. A mark left when he had grabbed her arm as she'd fallen from the cliff. His mark. Simon's stomach did an odd tumble. He had affected a human. In a way, it proved he still existed. He stilled lived. Simon was drawn to her.

He carefully finished covering her, draping the downy blanket around her shoulders. She smiled in her sleep and snuggled deeper into the folds, oblivious to the torment she had created.

Damn, her. He didn't need any more distractions. The last two hundred years were hell enough. Simon turned his back and strode out of the bedroom into the main room. Without hesitation he crossed to the fireplace. Kneeling, he felt for a loose brick on the inside lower left of the firebox. He found it and pressed. On the left side of the hearth a crease appeared in the seams of the flowered wallpaper, undiscovered through the years. Smiling, he rose. He walked to the wall and placed both hands flat against the paneling and pushed. A door formed and swung inward exposing a hidden chamber.

Simon stepped through and found the candle and matches he'd left on the shelf located immediately right of the opening. He struck the match and lit the candle. The deep passage was illuminated in the feeble glow revealing a jumble of items.

Papers and books lay strewn about the hardwood floor. Clothes, crossing the centuries, rumpled and mixed, were on shelves. He stepped into the room and closed the door, concealing it from outside view. Not even the dim light of the candle leaked through to hint of the hidden chamber.

His eyes adjusted to the muted light and searched the area noting the dust that had accumulated in the past year. Nothing had been disturbed. Nodding in satisfaction, he placed the candle on the shelf.

He walked in the dark gloom to the lone wooden stool at the end of the chamber and sat. His shoulders slumped, and his head bowed. Oh, he was tired. Eternal peace was within his grasp, and he yearned for nothing more. He would *not* die cold and alone again. He was owed his peace.

With slow and deliberate movement, he pulled off his boots and tossed them aside. He stood and pulled his shirt over his head. Without thought, he unbuttoned his breeches and peeled them down and off. Standing nude, unselfconscious, he crossed to the nearest shelf. He grabbed a pair of well-worn faded jeans and pulled them on. Next, he snatched a black T-shirt, all clothes he had picked up from prior occupants of the manor and slipped it over his head.

He padded barefoot to the opening where he paused. He stopped and reached out, lightly tracing a framed miniature portrait depicting his parents, his wee sister, Jean, held in his mother's arms and himself as a small lad. A sad smile of remembrance drifted across his face. Simon wished he could turn back the hands of time and become the man his family had needed. Regret washed through him when he thought of his da. He'd never be able to heal the rift between them. Watching through the years of his limbo-death, he witnessed the passing of his mother, Jean's deportment, and the loss of the Cleitmuir, while being powerless to intervene.

His finger trailed off the worn gilt-edge frame as his gaze drifted to the tattered book next to his family's portrait. It held his journey since death. Every ounce of hard earned knowledge of the MacKay's legacy. He had the location, identified the treasure, and now all he lacked was the key. A key he would find during this cycle of half-life. There was only one last place it could be.

Sinclair House. He picked up another miniature and cupped it in his palm. This portrait was of a red-haired woman with a slight smile curling her lips. Her green eyes stared back at him in the ill-flickering light of the candle. Fiona Sinclair, his betrothed. An arranged marriage from the cradle, friendship had bloomed, and he had admired and respected her. Simon had hoped love would come. But that wasn't to be. Only betrayal.

Chapter Ten

Cleitmuir Manor
June 1809

The smell of leather, ink, and books closed in around Simon as he pressed his fingers to the bridge of his nose and closed his eyes. Another headache loomed, and he hoped by force of will he'd keep it at bay. There was work that must get done, regardless how his life might be spinning out of control. He dropped his hand and stared down at the pile of papers and the open account journal on the study's desk.

A harsh exhaled breath pushed past his frown. He sorely missed his father. Simon had thought there would always be time to heal the rift that had torn them apart. Now his Da was dead and running the manor and surrounding lands were Simon's responsibility. Murdoc MacKay, the late Earl of Cleitmuir, lived for the details of running a large estate. Budgeting the income from Cleitmuir's lands was an easy task for his Da. Money allotted so the manor thrived, crops grew, sheep and cattle fed, tenants cared for, all easily planned and executed by his skilled hand. His son, however, thought paperwork was a whole new level of war, one he wasn't skilled to handle. Give him an enemy line to sneak past, a traitor to dispatch, or just a horse and a wide open plain. He lived for action, not numbers.

Simon would rather be out tracking down his father's killer. His mother was correct, it was murder. It hadn't taken any investigation on Simon's part at all, only a mysterious letter appearing one week after his arrival at Cleitmuir. The note was burned into his memory.

> *Give me what I want, or you will share your father's fate. Know this, if you don't fear for yourself, remember you have family that can suffer as well. The treasure is mine.*

Shock came first. Then anger. How dare this cur threaten his mother and sister? Simon vowed afterwards no mercy would be shown the villain. He'd rip his guts out.

More mysterious notes appeared over the next months, each more menacing and yet vague. After ruling out his obvious inheritance he still had no idea what this treasure was. No matter how he had searched, it still eluded him. As time passed, little things began to happen around the estate. First, a small barn fire, then shattered windowpanes, and the latest was flour bags sliced in the pantry and seeded with weevils. With each attack, his frustration mounted. These occurrences were no plain accidents because the notes followed each one.

His hand slammed down on the desk. The stinging blow did nothing to curb his frustration. He had no name, no way to contact the blackguard, no way to fight. The soldier in him yelled. There had to be a way.

"My lord Earl, you wear such a scowl. Is it safe to enter?"

He conjured a half-hearted smile as he looked to the study's entrance. A beauty with fiery sunset hair, piercing green eyes, and a figure most men would be driven to distraction by, stood in the doorway with her face tilted in query. Fiona Sinclair smiled at him.

"You're always safe with me, lass. There's no need to fear."

"That I know," her smiled broadened. "Do you have a moment?"

"For you, always."

He watched his once again betrothed walk gracefully into the room and stop by his side. Simon stood and reached for her hand, pressing a brief kiss to her fingers. "And to what do I afford this pleasure?"

"The festival of course," his petite bride-to-be replied.

"Ah," Simon pushed his hair from his face. "Well then, have a seat."

She rested her hip against the big desk and gestured to his chair.

He shook his head. "You're country roots are showing, Fi. You're not exactly sitting."

Her light laughter filled the quiet study. "And when have you stood on ceremony, my lord? We both know you're not a proper gentleman, even if you currently hold the title of Earl." Fiona laughed again. "I won't be but a moment."

He sat. It was hard getting used to his new address. Fi was right, he did feel like a fraud. But soon Simon would have his Countess by his side and perhaps he wouldn't feel so awkward. If anyone deserved the titled address of My Lady, it was Fi, her beauty put most upper class to shame. He had known Fiona most of his life. The Sinclair family lived on the property next to Cleitmuir. The pairing between them had been set in the cradle when she was born and him just turned seven.

Both the MacKay's and Sinclair's thought it an ideal match. Then he'd left to join the army,

Upon his return from the Continent, his jilting of Fiona seemed to have been forgiven by all parties, though he had a problem with reconciling his guilt and selfishness. He had been so young and stupid. His mother had gained new health with thoughts of the wedding to come. He would do his duty and honor the contract. Simon liked the lass well enough, but he had hoped for more. It was hard when he thought of how very much in love his parents had been and he wished for something like that for himself. Though he had spent a great deal of time with Fiona, and called her a friend, Simon was actually closer to her older twin brothers. He respected and even admired Fiona, but it wasn't right. He tried to push away the wrong feelings, but Fi felt more like a sister, than a lover to be. He hoped after they were wedded and bedded, more might come, though he held little optimism. The few kisses he had stolen hadn't pointed in that direction. Still marriages had been built on much less than friendship.

"How may I help you?"

"Everything is well in hand, which is good since the garden party is just one short week away," Fiona hesitated, and the smile slipped from her face. "I have only one concern."

"Which is?"

"Well, you, Simon."

He raised a single eyebrow. "I don't understand."

Fiona sighed. "You've been distracted. You've canceled on many of our outings. I know something is wrong, though you deny it. I just..." she pursed her lips then fidgeted. Her hand swung out and connected with the ink well shooting it forward, directly toward his lap.

Simon's reflexes saved him. He pushed his chair back and leapt sideways as Fiona let out a cry of dismay and shot to her feet.

"Oh!" She reached for some papers on the desk to help blot the spreading stain, but realized her mistake just as Simon reached out to stop her.

"Not the papers! No worries, I'll just ring for Colin," he took her arm. "Here, step away. You wouldn't want ink on your dress." He led Fiona to a nearby chair and made her sit.

"Simon, I'm so sorry."

"It will be fine, don't fash yourself." He strode past her, signaling to a maid outside the room. "I've spilt ink."

The lass bobbed a quick curtsey and darted off. He turned back and crossed the room to Fiona.

"Now, what were you concerned about? That is, other than the ink?" He smiled down at her hoping to ease her worries.

"Oh, it seems silly now, but I wanted your word you'd be attending the garden party. I," she looked away before meeting his eyes. "I don't want to attend alone."

Again. That was the unspoken word Fiona didn't say. Simon pushed his fingers through his hair. He had a manor to run, a murderer to track down, his family to protect and when things got too much, it was Fiona who was slighted. He was a poor fiancé.

"You have my word, Fiona. I'll be there, come hell or high water."

She rose smoothly to her feet and took his hand. "I'm sorry to doubt you, but now I am relieved of my silly wee doubts. You have given me your word, which is a bond you'll never break." She leaned forward and placed a soft kiss to his cheek. "I'll leave you now," she shot a quick glance to the desk and dark stain. "You've got work to do. Thank you for understanding."

He reached to take her arm, but she sidestepped him. "I'll see myself out." She gave him another shy smile. "I'm looking forward to seeing you at the party."

Simon watched her leave then shook his head. He had been neglecting her. Somehow he'd have to do better. Yes, his family's safety and catching the murderer were of utmost importance, but so was his word and honor. He owed it to both their families, especially after his disappearing act, to forge the best match, to make something lasting, which he wouldn't accomplish by ignoring his beautiful bride-to-be.

The maid returned, bobbing a curtsey before crossing the room and dropping to her knees by the desk. She started dabbing at the black stain.

He sighed again as he watched. The carpet was surely ruined, but that was the least of his problems.

"My lord, here's an envelope. It's fallen. Luckily it's only next to the spill." The maid turned and held out the vellum.

"My thanks," he took the envelope, looking at it as he crossed the room. Scowling, he stopped in his tracks. He tore it open and pulled the folded sheet out.

Your time has run out. By the start of the festival, give me what I want or the killing starts.

He clenched his hand into a fist, crumpling the paper.

"Is everything all right, my lord?"

He glanced to the maid. "Aye, Heather.

Everything's fine. I'll be in the library."

"Aye, my lord."

Simon strode out of the study and down the hall. Entering the library, he slammed the door behind him. In four long steps he reached the whiskey decanter. He threw the crumpled letter down upon the crystal tray and poured himself a dram. The liquor burned down his throat, bringing some sanity back and transforming his rage to a slow smolder. He poured himself another and walked to the large window.

He must think. He had to calm himself. Acting blindly and in anger would not help. Simon willed his muscles to unclench as he took a slow sip of whiskey. Logic. That was how he had dealt with his Napoleon adversaries and the spies within his own ranks. He was known for getting the job done and never failing. Not once. And he wouldn't do so this time either.

The note hadn't been there earlier this morning. The desk had been neat as a pin until he'd entered and made the mess himself. There had been nothing on the floor. So, how had the note gotten there?

He took another sip as he retraced his steps from his morning actions. This was the closest he'd been to an actual note appearance. Always he would enter a room to find the next missive, but he *knew* the note hadn't been there earlier. Who had entered the room since he started work on the accounts? This morning he'd given orders to be left alone and he had been. The obvious choice was the wee maid. She was the one who discovered the note on the floor. She could have easily planted it herself. Simon shook his head. It wasn't Heather. She was extremely loyal. The MacKay's gave her a position when no one else would. They saved her life. Heather would never betray them.

He stared out the window, the glass in his hand forgotten as he spotted a rider in the far distance headed in the direction of Sinclair house.

Fiona Sinclair. She had just been here, and then the note magically appeared. It couldn't be. It was daft to think she was involved. The Sinclair's and MacKay's had shared decades of history. Loyalty and friendship to a Highlander were sacred, never to be betrayed. Fiona would never collude with a murderer, let alone turn her back on family. It wasn't in her blood.

He continued to stare until the rider disappeared from the horizon. But as he'd learned from the military, nothing was impossible. In fact, the more outrageous or hideous something was, the more likely true. Mankind could be innately evil. But, Fi? He couldn't believe it.

Simon racked his brain, sifting through his memories. He had received several notes from his hidden adversary, and could recount at least three more times Fiona had been nearby. She wasn't a killer, but he could possibly see her as an accomplice. Fiona Sinclair, his fiancée, was she loyal or a betrayer? He would find out.

Chapter Eleven

Inverness, Scotland
July, Present Day

Laurel grimaced as she tugged her jeans back on. How could she justify the dress? But in the gown, she felt feminine and beautiful, something she was utterly shocked to discover. She looked at the soft cream creation, with its empire waist, revealing cleavage and smooth straight lines, taunting her from its hanger. £500. With a quick conversion of British pounds into American dollars in her head, she realized the dress was going to cost her a small fortune, the exchange rate was hideous right now.

No dress was worth that for one night!

Well, especially when it was a costume she'd never be able to wear anywhere else, ever again. Where was her fairy godmother when she needed her to give her a free dress made by birds and squirrels? But, dear God, she did love it. It made her feel as if she was in a fairytale. The ugly duckling turned into a beautiful swan.

Always more comfortable in a battered pair of jeans and comfy sweater, this time she was tempted to toss out her tomboy image for something more romantic. It was hard to believe, but when something actually made her feel beautiful, logic and caution was beginning to take a back seat to fantasy.

"Hey, are you alive in there?"

"Yeah. Just a sec." Laurel fingered the dress before lifting it off the hook and draping the long gown over her arm keeping it off the floor. She opened the dressing room door and found a grinning Beth.

"Oh, don't look like your dog got hit by a car." Beth grabbed her arm and dragged her to the sales counter. "I've got great news for you."

"Beth, there's no way I'm buying this dress. I can't afford it."

"Oh yes you are."

"It's ridiculous. I'll never be able to wear it again."

"Pish! You have to buy it. You look fantastic in it."

"I'm not getting it."

"Yes. You. Are." Beth took the dress from Laurel's arm and placed it on the counter.

"Beth, if you think for one moment you're buying me this dress—"

"No, no, no. Of course not. I wouldn't dream of it." The sales clerk and Beth exchanged glances before Beth turned to Laurel. "The price was incorrectly marked. It's on sale!"

"Yeah, right. Even if it was a hundred dollars less, I still couldn't justify this dress. The exchange rate sucks"

"How about five hundred dollars less?"

"What?" Laurel looked at Beth then the clerk.

"Aye, miss. The dress is half off. It's £250."

Disbelief crossed Laurel's face as she stared at the petite clerk, who, for some reason, looked like she was trying hard not to laugh. Laurel did the math. At £250, the dress would be a little over four hundred dollars. It would hurt, but it was doable. And just like an evil small devil on her shoulder, Beth continued to nudge.

"You've got to get it now. Oh, come on. You can't fool me. I saw your expression when you looked in the mirror. If you won't do it for yourself, do it for Alex. You know you'll get lucky if you show up dressed in that."

Beth wore her down. Damn it, she was on vacation and she was coming off a major break-up. How could she turn down something that made her feel pretty? Laurel needed to get out of the rut she was stuck in, think outside the box. A costume ball and gorgeous gown were so not her, it would probably do the trick. Besides, a little shopping therapy was just what the doctor ordered.

"All right, I'll do it. I must be crazy." She dug in her purse for her credit card.

"Hoo yah! Lori's breaking out of her shell. You're actually being extravagant! I can't believe it."

She frowned at Beth as she passed her card to the clerk. "I do wild things every now and again. College, remember?"

"Yeah, right. I believe I was the cause for most of your college excitement. Left to your own devices, the last time you went nuts was when the Inca civilization was around. Actually, it was probably older."

"Ha, ha. Hysterical." She dismissed Beth as she signed the sales slip and watched the girl behind the counter bag her gown.

"Errand time," Beth declared. "It's off to the caterer's, check on the linens, then to the printer's to okay the festival advertisements. Oh, and the florist, how'd I almost forget that?"

"Um, Beth?" She hated to ask her friend the next question, but she'd didn't know when she'd get to Scotland again, and Inverness was such a historic city. Helping Beth run errands seemed like a kind of sacrilege to her. "Would you hate me forever if I bailed on you?"

"Oh, sheesh, I should have thought of that," Beth replied. "I keep forgetting you've never been here. Of course, please go exploring. How 'bout we meet back here in an hour?"

Laurel's grin was huge as she gave her friend a hug. "You're the best. An hour it is."

"Try not to get lost," was Beth's parting shot as she waved over her shoulder as she walked away.

Leaving her gown with the clerk to pick up later, Laurel exited the shop with a spring in her step. Well then, an hour to see Inverness. It wasn't enough time to see Urquhart Castle or try and track down the Loch Ness monster, but it would be enough time to stroll around downtown and take in the sights. With a slight smile on her face, Laurel turned in the opposite direction of Beth and headed deeper into town.

She meandered down the cobblestone sidewalk, pausing here and there to look in a shop window, entirely aimless, and happy for once not to have a stringent schedule to follow. She lost track of how many different stores were displaying stuffed "Nessie's" in their windows and after passing her second woolen mill, Laurel stepped to the curb wondering if she should cross the street. A flyer on the lamppost caught her eye.

An exhibit of Pictish stones at Inverness House. She had studied the Picts, who were an older race than even the Celts, one of the first inhabitants of Scotland. She knew she was heading into "work zone" mode, but a chance to see some of their history in person was like a drug to her system. It couldn't be that far away. She'd find the house and go…which was far more exciting than window-shopping.

After getting directions from yet another friendly Scot, in a short time, she stood outside Inverness House. The house didn't look like a typical museum, but more of a cozy B&B with stone bricks and a welcoming air. She climbed the stairs and pushed open the door to hear tinkling bells. Entering, she felt muscles relax Laurel hadn't known were tensed, and a sense of peace filled her with the familiar features of a museum. Around the world, no matter the foreignness of the city, museums were like returning home. A clear acrylic donation box stood next to the door filled a quarter way with money. She dug into her pockets and pulled out a few pounds and slipped them into the box. Good karma.

"Ah, thank you, miss."

Laurel turned and was greeted by a docent, a petite brunette with laughing green eyes. "You're welcome. Anything for a fellow museum."

"American? Do you work for a museum?"

"Yes and yes. The Chicago Field Museum."

"Oh, brilliant! I've always wanted to go. I've only made it as far as New York, though."

"Well, if you ever do, please look me up," she held out her hand and the docent shook it. "I'm Laurel Saville. I do historical research and verifications, plus some other odds and ends that always need to be done."

"Isn't that the truth? I'm Samantha. Samantha

MacDonald. Are you here for the Pict stones?"

"I saw your flyer when walking around town."

"They're upstairs to your right. It's probably won't be exciting for you, it's only a wee collection. If you find yourself idle, there's a portrait gallery in the left wing. We've got paintings from Scottish artists on exhibit. We even have a couple of George Jamesone's."

"I'm sure everything will be great," Laurel headed for the stairs.

"Enjoy yourself. I'll be around later if you have any questions."

"Thanks."

She made her way to the second floor and turned right into a large open space. She wandered from display to display fascinated by the intricate carvings inlaid on the stones. Most of the exhibits were photos of standing stones too large to move, but there were still plenty of physical items. She spent a good deal of time in front of a great example of some Scottish Townie. The highly decorated ceremonial stone balls were wonderfully detailed and preserved. But Samantha was right. Even taking time to pause and study, she had made it through the room in a short time.

Laurel checked her watch. She still had about twenty minutes before she had to meet Beth. Time for the gallery room.

She walked across the hall and entered another large open room. Making her way around, Laurel studied the portraits of men and women from ages past to present. It was a nice collection, especially since the art were works of their native countrymen. Paintings weren't her specialty, which was more in the artifact range, but she could appreciate them, and of course had come across some amazing portraits in her line of work. There was always something to admire, no matter the painter or style.

She was about to leave when she noticed a side room off the main exhibit. What the hell, she still had plenty of time. She entered the room and was drawn to a painting above a small table. Studying it, she cocked her head to the side. It was small compared to some of the other portraits, just two foot by three. A man in military dress sat astride a powerful bay horse. His dark black hair was pulled into a tight queue, and light gray eyes staring out of a striking face trapped her gaze. The man clasped one hand to the hilt of his sheathed Calvary sword, while the other stroked the neck of his steed, reins casually dropped, yet the horse seemed to still be in his control. The artist had brilliantly captured the moment. It looked as if horse and rider were on the verge of exploding into action, just waiting for the call to arms and the bugle to sound. But it was the man's face in the painting that seized her attention. There was something about the portrait, some sort of *déjà vu*.

And then it came to her. The man in the picture bore an uncanny resemblance to the man who had rescued her on the plateau. The clothing was different, but the face was eerily exact. She'd never forget those piercing silvery eyes and his jet-black hair. It was a striking resemblance.

"Ah, there you are. I see you've found him. Drop dead gorgeous, is he not?"

"Who is he?"

Samantha laughed. "Everyone asks that when they see him. I think it's his eyes. Let me introduce you. The beautiful man before you is Captain Simon MacKay of

His Majesty's Royal Army."

Laurel felt her jaw drop to the ground. She had to be kidding. The coincidence was just too amazing. "Simon MacKay?"

Samantha began telling the tale of Captain MacKay describing the tale Laurel had heard from Alex and bits from Beth. "He had a short but illustrious career before having to resign his commission. He fought Napoleon. Rumor has it that he was a bit of a spy and an assassin. His home is up north, in Cleitmuir."

"I know. I'm staying at his house. Cleitmuir Manor."

"You know…they say his ghost roams the manor."

Laurel knew the rumor of course, and by the looks of his portrait, she wouldn't mind a ghostly visit. Too bad nothing's happened so far. She just shook her head then looked at her watch. Oh crap, she was going to be late. "I'm sorry, Samantha, thank you for talking with me, but I've got to go. I was supposed to meet my friend five minutes ago."

"No worries. It was a pleasure to meet you."

"And you. Don't forget to use my name if you get to Chicago."

"Absolutely. And if you run into Captain MacKay, say hi for me."

Samantha's laughter followed Laurel down the stairs.

Chapter Twelve

"Have you made much progress?" Grant studied Alex, who was staring out the large bay window. His question was met with a shrug.

"Which progress are we discussing?"

"I don't know. How about any?"

Alex turned his back to the window and faced Grant with a slight smile. "She took the bait, hook, line and sinker. I didn't even have to ask her. She offered. In no time, we'll have the location of the treasure. I can taste it. For once you gave good advice."

He bit back his much desired sarcastic reply, knowing it wouldn't get him anywhere. "Well, Beth does go on about her. I feel I know the woman inside and out." He shook his head. "I wish we could have gotten her to come over any time but the festival. That will complicate matters, MacKenzie."

Alex waved a hand at him. "You and your old-fashioned superstitions. There's no ghost, Grant."

"Aye, there is, Alex." He frowned. "Too much weird shite has happened inside Cleitmuir. He's around."

"I'm not going to debate this with you, Grant. MacKay is long gone dead. My however-great grandfather made sure of that. Alistair MacKenzie's journal was clear."

"*Pish*. I know Simon MacKay's dead, that's what

has me worried. What sort of powers does he have? How do we know he's not in this very room listening? What if that meddling spirit finds it first? We're cocked-up."

"Listen to yourself, man. There're no such things as ghosts. If you're so concerned, bring in a priest or some stupid arse ghost hunters to get rid of him."

Grant heard the frustration in Alex's voice and knew when to back off. He may look like some Hollywood actor, but Alex had a mean streak, and a permanent means to ridding himself of those who failed or annoyed, or simply got in his way. There was no coming back from death. He hadn't known about MacKenzie's cutthroat murdering streak. If the money for this scheme weren't through the roof, Grant would never have joined up with him. But he desperately needed the income.

He'd sunk pounds into Cleitmuir Manor and it hadn't turned over the profits he had expected. His and Beth's future was sketchy. It would be a delicate balancing act of bowing to MacKenzie, yet getting the payout he very much needed. Grant had to show Alex he was no pushover, while treading carefully. MacKenzie wasn't going to get off so easily.

"Speaking of that godforsaken journal, it's useless. You think it's the Holy Grail, but I can't see how it's helped us these past months. We're getting nowhere, just like ol' Alistair."

"Have faith, friend. With Laurel's research skills and the knowledge I've already discovered, we're closer than my namesake ever was. We'll find it soon. I feel it in my bones."

"Shite. You've been saying that for months now. I

want the future you've promised."

Alex laughed. "You're in a bit of a snit today. We'll find the prize that will put all treasures to shame and every dream we could possibly have will be ours. We're in grand shape. We know the hidden chamber is somewhere on the manor's property. We've narrowed it down to just a few acres from all of Scotland. I have no doubt we'll find it. Laurel Saville is just our ace in the hole."

"More partners we don't need."

"You worry too much. I have the matter well in hand."

"Ha, no doubt." Grant rose and picked up his jacket. "You'll have your fun first, I'll bet."

Alex grinned. "I had a bit of a taste last night. And I must say, that I've developed an appetite."

Grant shook his head as he slipped on his coat. "Just don't let your wee brain overpower your big one."

"Aye, no worries, mate. When the time comes, the American won't be a problem."

Grant walked to the door and paused, just as long as Beth and himself were safe that was all that mattered. He didn't trust MacKenzie to keep his word in the end, but then, he knew where Alex's skeletons were. "I'm counting on it. We're just running out of places to hide your *solutions*." He opened the door and walked out of Sinclair House.

****

Cleitmuir's renovated stables were dark and shadowy in the rear of the barn, perfect for Simon's ghostly figure to lurk. An insubstantial shadow among shadows. The smells of hay, leather, and horseflesh surrounded him. It gave him comfort, a little reality in his unreal life. The horses always knew when he was there. Whether it was his solid body passing for human or his invisible spirit as now, they all sensed him and amazingly enough didn't fear him. As with cats, dogs, and every animal, all greeted him as friend. He came here often in the days allotted him. It was nice to be recognized.

What little peace and solitude this afforded him, however, was shattered when that woman invaded his territory once again. Three times now, first, on the plateau above the cave where he died, next in his own bed, and now in his only sanctuary.

If he still believed in God, he might wonder if this was a message being sent to him. But that was foolhardy. There was no God, and he was cursed.

Simon glared from his corner as he watched her run a loving hand over the gray mare standing in the crossties. Apparently she planned to ignore his advice and go riding. Maybe she'd fall off a cliff again and wouldn't torment him any further. He could only hope.

He edged his invisible-self closer, pulled by her presence. The mare turned her head, focused her mellow gaze on him and nickered.

"Anxious to go, girl?" The woman gave the horse another pat, before digging in her zippered breech pocket. "You'll get your wish. I think I'm late." She pulled out her cell phone and flipped it open. "It's dead? Impossible. I just charged it last night. Damn, maybe it's just off."

Simon watched her fiddle with the phone, but she must not have gotten any results by the anger marring her face.

"It better not need a new battery. It's less than a

year old." She stared at the useless phone than sighed and slipped it back into her pocket. "Well, Gale my girl, I guess it's only minimal grooming. I'm pretty sure I'm late and I definitely don't want to keep Mr. Alex MacKenzie waiting." She laughed and grabbed a brush, giving only a cursory pass over Gale's back, knocking off any dirt that might be trapped under the saddle pad. "He promised me I could look over his research. I know I can help him. How cool would it be if I found the lost gold? Step aside, Indiana Jones, there's a new girl in town!"

Simon's hands clenched, and his fists turned white when the woman laughed anew as she flung a saddle pad onto the mare's back.

Alex MacKenzie. Not that wanker. She couldn't be riding to meet him. And gold? What the hell was she into?

She slipped the bridle on and led the mare from the barn.

Glaring, Simon followed and stopped just inside the opening. He watched her mount and guide the horse onto the path leading to Sinclair House.

He swore under his breath as she picked up a ground-eating trot. The lass was an accident waiting to happen, and now she was involved with MacKenzie. She was trouble, yet Alex was worse. Way worse. The girl had no idea the danger she was riding into. It served her right. He didn't care about one wayward, difficult, chit. Her destiny was in her own hands. He had his own problems.

Simon stepped back into the barn and started to pace the aisle. So agitated, puffs of dust were disturbed by his immaterial passage as his anger took on physical form. The remaining horses poked their heads out, watching him. He paused, spun around, and manifested into solid shape, expending the energy he had unconsciously gathered around him.

He was so close. All he needed was the key to the chamber. Then he'd be able to protect the MacKay's legacy and lay down his burden of a cursed half existence. The elusive peace he coveted would be his. Yet, his mind kept going back to the reckless lass and the danger she was in. She shouldn't matter, he needed to ignore her, but he knew he wouldn't.

MacKenzie was using her. That's what all MacKenzies' did, what his whole family had done. He needed or wanted something from her. The gold was shite, just a flimsy excuse.

He hated the arsehole and his entire family, the murdering, scheming lot. If MacKenzie wanted the lass, Simon was obliged to see that didn't happen. It was his turn for revenge.

Tomorrow was the opening picnic and ball. It was also the anniversary of his own murder by a MacKenzie. It was time, Simon thought, to do a bit of party crashing.

Chapter Thirteen

"Are you sure you don't mind the boots?" Laurel looked guiltily around the finely decorated sitting room. The large bay window let in the bright Scottish sunshine, warming the room, and highlighting all the expensive looking antiques and Oriental rug. She didn't know where to sit, let alone move, in fear of leaving dusty footprints from her battered boots or grime from her well-used riding clothes.

"Och, no. I was the one who suggested you ride over," Alex smiled warmly. "It was a beautiful ride, wasn't it? Just as advertised?"

"Yes, lovely. I guess I just didn't think of the obvious consequences." She gestured down at her bedraggled self. "Besides, you have a huge crew of workers cleaning and prepping the house for the ball tomorrow. Maybe I should go? I'm not only in the way, but I'm surely making more of a mess for everyone."

"The decorating for the fancy ball is on the other side of the house. This sitting room is far off from the chaos. And as for yourself…you'll never be in the way, especially since you're helping me out. Besides, a little bit of dirt never hurts. That's what the cleaning crew is for. Have a sit on the couch and you can start flipping through those files on the table while I get us some tea."

"Well, if you're sure..."

She was already walking to the couch, drawn to the

files, completely forgetting her trepidation. What kind of research had Alex gathered? Was the answer to the missing Jacobite gold here, just waiting for her to solve the puzzle? She sat down and grabbed the first folder and flipped through the pages, deciphering them as shipping ledgers from the *Hazard*. She placed the folder down next to her on the couch.

She scrutinized the pile of records on the coffee table then shot a quick glance out the door Alex had disappeared through. She felt certain he wouldn't mind her reorganizing things just a bit. She didn't know how he could find anything in this mess. Once everything was in order, surely a pattern would be revealed. Patterns usually pointed to a trail, missing info that led somewhere. She was great at spotting patterns. Without another thought, Laurel slid off the couch and onto the floor and grabbed the next folder. A brief perusal had her recognizing a family tree. She placed that on the floor to the right and reached for the next file.

As she snatched the folder, she jarred some folded documents, and one fell to the floor. Dropping the file, she collected the fallen paper and curiously opened it to find a terrain map. Laurel quickly identified the North Atlantic and Scotland and realized it was a map of the local area. Her gaze focused on a hastily scrawled circle around Cleitmuir Manor and its property. It looked like there might be underground caves in the area. She folded the map, wondering if Alex had checked out the caves or not. She put the map aside and grabbed another folder, quickly losing herself in the work.

"Should I be concerned about my record-keeping, or just happy you've made yourself at home?"

Laurel jumped and banged her knee against the low

table at the surprise of Alex standing just a few feet beside her. "Ouch! I'm...sorry...I...you startled me. Here, let me help you." She leapt to her feet, feeling her face warm.

"It wasn't a criticism, Lori. I don't mind. Tea?"

"Um, yes. That would be great." Looking at the folder stacks, then back to Alex, she asked, "Haven't you been gone for a while? Or is this some extra special hard to prepare tea?"

He laughed. "No, I forgot about a phone call I had to make," he gestured to the ornate chair by the fireplace, "take a break and let me play host. I rarely get any company."

"Ah, sure." She met his blue eyes, before looking once more at the piles of folders stacked on the couch, floor, and table. Nervous, she found she couldn't quite make herself sit quiet in a chair, so she wandered over to the fireplace.

Glancing over her shoulder, she watched Alex put the silver tray with tea service down on the table, before her attention returned to the mantel of sturdy polished old oak. There were several famed photos—idly she picked up a picture. It was a lovely outdoor shot, of Alex with an older woman in a garden.

"That's my mum," Alex said as he arrived at her side. "She lives in Bristol now, North England. I get down when I can."

"She looks lovely," Laurel replaced the photograph on the mantel. Her eyes were drawn to another picture. This one was Alex with what looked to be a twenty-something girl in what had to be the Scottish Highlands. "Your sister?"

Alex shook his head. "Elizabeth. Just a friend." He

snagged her hand and gave it a tug. “Come, the tea’s getting cold.” He led her over to the chairs.

Laurel sat and watched as Alex’s long fingers wrapped around the pot’s handle. He poured from a hand-painted teapot into two china cups sitting next to a bowl of brown and white sugar cubes and a small carafe of cream.

“Cream? Sugar?” His voice, warm and smooth, rolled over her.

“Just black.” She looked over to find him staring at her. He had a look in his eyes, one she hadn’t ever seen before. Derek never had looked at her this way. Possessive? Hungry? She wasn’t sure, only it had a slight edge, and she found she was holding her breath. It wasn’t until he looked away to pick up her cup and hand it to her that she relaxed.

She watched as he poured a bit of cream into his cup, and took a seat in the matching chair on the opposite side of the small table.

“I’m sorry about the files. It’s a habit. It’s my way of looking at things.”

“There’s no need to apologize, Laurel. After all, I did ask for your opinion.”

“I think I just sort of pushed my way in and you graciously conceded,” she offered sheepishly.

“If you hadn’t offered, I’d have certainly asked. Especially after seeing your credentials,” he smiled.

“You looked me up?” She wasn’t sure whether to be flattered or annoyed. She was probably just uncomfortable that she’d have done the same thing if their places were reversed.

“I was curious. I started with the museum’s website, then roved with the Google.” He took a sip of tea. "I saw you've helped the police. Several fraud cases, correct?"

"Oh, just a few. In the first, I was an expert witness when someone tried to defraud the Field museum. The detective in charge of the case and I got along well, and when he needed someone to help with facts on a couple of his other cases, he asked me."

"It sounds exciting."

"Not really," she shrugged and drank some tea. "It wasn't like field work or anything. Mostly I just sat in my basement office, surrounded by books and my computer. Not glamorous at all. Not like you."

"Me?"

"Please… A treasure hunter? It's the age-old difference of the field operative versus the deskbound intelligence officer. The spy has all the glamour and excitement."

Alex barked out a sharp laugh. "I'll try to keep that in mind next time I'm stuck in a cave, smelly, dirty and lost." He placed his empty cup on the tray. "Besides, I'm an intelligence geek, too. I'm just too greedy to hire someone else to do the dirty fieldwork. You know, no partners or assistants, you don't have to share the profits."

"Well, I'm glad you broke your rules and asked for help. I've never been on a treasure hunt. It'll be fun playing the spy for a change." She grinned at Alex.

He chuckled. "Looking through papers isn't very spy worthy, I'm glad you're so keen. As for partners, I feel if the gains are worth it, I'm more than willing to break rules."

"Don't worry about your rules. You're still safe. Think of me as a silent partner. I'm in it more for the fun and the new experience. I don't need a cut of the treasure."

"That's most generous of you. You don't even want a small percentage?"

"No, not really. I'm good," she replied. "Though…"

"Oh here it comes," Alex goaded.

"It's just a thought. If these really are Jacobite era coins, maybe you could donate a few to the museum?"

He chuckled. "I suppose I could. It's the least I could do if we actually find the treasure." Alex stood and reached for her cup. "More?"

"No, I'm good. Thanks." She passed over her cup and stood. "I should probably stack things a little better than I have. You've amassed a lot of research. Hopefully a clue or two will appear and we'll find those coins of yours."

Laurel walked over to the couch and knelt. She gathered a pile and leaned over to place them on the table.

"How's it organized?" Alex wandered over, watching her. "No, leave the ones on the couch. They can stay there."

She looked up at him. Gesturing to the couch, "those stacks are historical documents referring to the gold. You know, ledgers, memos, orders, and such. The papers near this end of the table are genealogy and histories of the MacKays. The ones near you, I haven't a clue. I haven't gotten to them yet."

She glanced over to the mantel clock. It was nearing seven. She still couldn't adjust to the weird Scottish sunlight, she didn't realize how late it had gotten. Studying the mess of folders surrounding her, she realized there was no way to fix the clutter in time to get back to Cleitmuir before the late dinner Beth planned.

"I've got to go and I've left things a mess." She fiddled with a folder, not wanting to meet his eyes.

"Lori, it's fine. I don't mind. Besides, it's a perfect excuse. It looks like you'll just have to come over another day."

A hand appeared before her face and she grasped it. He pulled her to her feet, and now was suddenly standing quite close. Her heart sped up, remembering the last time she had stood so near to him. She met his eyes, and they stood there silently, gazing at each other.

"There is another possibility," Alex's voice came soft and low. "You could skip dinner at Cleitmuir, stay, and be early to work in the morning." His hand released hers and rose up to trail lightly down her cheek, across her throat, until it cupped the back of her neck.

Her pulse raced as she watched him tilt his head down to hers. His lips found hers. With only a slight pressure and the barest teasing tip of his tongue, she found herself opening for him. The kiss deepened, warm and sensual. She pressed against him, thoughtless and breathless once more.

She clutched at his shoulders and Alex's other hand moved to the small of her back, holding her tightly against his obvious interest. His mouth left hers, and he started trailing kisses down her neck, only to pause at her rapidly pounding pulse and suck hard. Her breath caught and she heard his murmured "Och, Lori."

His mouth captured hers again, and the gentle hand cradling her neck, pushed deep into her hair, gripping her, trapping her as his mouth fed ever more hungrily.

She tilted her head, to snatch some air when her hair snagged.

"Oww." He ignored her, in fact, held her tighter. "Alex, stop," she muttered against his mouth. Her pleas fell heedless. A cold chill raced down her spine, squashing her building passion. She moved her hands flat against his chest and shoved. "I said stop!"

Caught by surprise, Alex staggered two steps back, his hand falling from her waist, but his other hand was still caught fast in her hair, pulling her head to an awkward angle.

"Alex! That hurts!"

"Oh, Christ. Lori..." Alex stepped forward to release the pressure on her hair.

"Something's—"

"My ring. I'm so sorry. Hang on."

He must have slipped his finger out of the trapped ring, because his hand fell away, but a weight still clung stubbornly to her hair. She reached up and clutched it.

"Here, let me—"

"No, I've got it." She took a few steps away and fiddled with her hair, when the ring suddenly released and plopped into her hand. She briefly met his eyes before staring down at her open palm.

A man's ring, large, thick, and gold, ornate. The crowning piece a bright sparkling sapphire, faceted as an octagon. The jewel rested in a sharply riveted band of gold, almost looking like tight cogs to a watch. This was what had snagged, by evidence of a few wispy strands of her hair still caught between the small grooves.

"It's a family heirloom." Alex explained as he closed the distance and stood next to her.

"Is that writing?" She picked up the ring and held it up to her eye. Letters were etched inside the heavy band, nearly worn down, but still visible.

"Aye, Gaelic. *Bi Tren.*"

She looked up at Alex expectantly. He shrugged, and a small smile tugged at the corners of his mouth.

"Um, I don't speak the Gaelic, well, only a little and only common small phrases."

"You're kidding, right? This is your family's ring and you don't know what it says?"

"Well, I'm sure someone did at one point." He shrugged again.

"It can't be hard to translate. It's only two words."

Before she could close her hand, Alex plucked the ring from her and slipped it onto his finger. "It's not important, love." His hand briefly caressed her cheek. "I'm sorry I hurt you," he paused, "and for getting a wee bit too enthusiastic. It was completely uncalled for."

She swallowed and stared into his eyes, then shook her head. "It's okay, but I really can't stay. Beth's expecting me, and I just barely have enough time to ride back, take care of Gale, and be ready for dinner."

Laurel took a step away, creating a wider distance between them. "And I doubt I'll be able to work on the research tomorrow. Remember the garden party? We'll have to make it another day."

"Right. I completely forgot, so I guess it's off to the stables then." He took her hand and led her from the room. "I have to admit that I'm crushed. I'm sure it would have been a fabulous evening and a grander morning."

She gave a weak smile, embarrassed. "Alex, I—"

"No worries. It gives me something to look forward to." He shot her a winning smile, "and the chance to improve my manners."

Chapter Fourteen

Simon stared at the festively decorated Sinclair House which bore flickering torches lining the gravel drive, to the modern floodlights highlighting the House's architecture, all set off in the Scottish gloaming. The dance was starting fashionably late in the now setting sun, allowing revelers to nap and recoup after the garden party earlier that afternoon.

He sighed, garden parties were a bore, but he absolutely hated balls. Oh, aye, he could dance, and he didn't need to worry about the matchmaking since he had been all but engaged since the cradle. It was the superficialness he despised—the excessive politeness, the political posturing, and aye, the dressing up. It had felt fake when he was alive, and now he had over two hundred years worth of the sham.

At least his traditional ball had turned into a party, a costumed event. Making it much easier to blend in, and oddly, over the years, one of the rare places he felt nostalgic. After all, these people were mimicking the era where he had been in the prime of his life. It was ironic how an event he so despised in life became one he now cherished. Sinclair House hadn't changed much over the years, just the people and he admitted, himself.

He stood off the gravel path and watched from behind the flickering torches, suitably historic, his ghostly presence unseen. The celebrants were arriving faster now, but the one person he searched for remained absent.

Strangely, he felt excited. Was he actually looking forward to meeting the lass again? She'd been trouble ever since he laid eyes on her—falling off cliffs, sleeping in his room, getting involved with MacKenzie. Yet, he hadn't felt so alive since his death.

His eyes narrowed as he watched a Range Rover he recognized stop at the entrance. Grant, the current owner of his home, got out and took the valet receipt. A second attendant opened the passenger door, helped Grant's wee wife, Beth, out, and then opened the rear passenger door.

He tensed as a silk encased leg emerged followed by the rest of the lass. His breath caught. She was stunning. She sparkled in the glow of firelight, a glittering gem among the flatness of pearls. He couldn't make out the exact color of her gown, something golden. Bronze? Which ever it was, the torchlight complimented and highlighted her. The dress was authentic, an empire waist that displayed her breasts and a curve-hugging sheath that caressed down the tall length of her. With her upswept hair, she would have every male in the vicinity eyeing her.

He exhaled as he studied her walking behind Grant and his wife as they entered Sinclair House. Aye indeed, he would enjoy himself tonight. Smiling, he turned away and walked to the rear of the house, stopping in the shadows below the steps to the ballroom's terrace.

With little effort, Simon willed himself solid, manifesting as his body particles bonded and reformed, giving him human appearance and substance once more. He stepped into the light and strode up the stairs to the landing. He was in his element. Everyone else was pretending tonight, but for him this was real, a part of his history. He sauntered through the French doors, and the room opened before him. The modern light was dimmed in exchange of the old-fashioned gas lamps illuminating the space, revealing the guests crowding the party.

He listened as the orchestra tuned, planning his strategy for the evening. His mouth curled upwards and Simon nodded. Aye, he was going to enjoy tonight.

****

Laurel's gaze swept the ballroom as she stepped into the large room, just managing to stifle her sigh. The garden party this afternoon had been fun, but this? The white, cream, and yellow flower arrangements coordinated with fabrics artistically draped, and the beautiful old-style lighting gave the room a romantic element. It was all lost on her. It made her feel more awkward, and truthfully, dismayed her more than ever. As she heard the orchestra warming up, a boulder settled in her stomach.

She felt so out of place dressed in a costume gown and heels. She knew it was only a matter of time before she tripped and fell on her face. How had she let everyone talk her into this? She didn't dance. Plus, the feeling beautiful she'd experienced in the store while trying on the gown had fled. She now felt like a gangly giraffe in pajamas. How could she make it through the evening?

Beth stopped and took her hand, giving it a squeeze. "Would you relax? Wipe off the 'deer-in-the-headlights' look. You look gorgeous so enjoy yourself."

"I think I'm going to be sick."

"Nonsense," Beth frowned. "You're being ridiculous. Have fun. You don't know these people. No pressure. If you make an ass of yourself, you'll never see them again. Well, you won't once you're back in Chicago." She chuckled.

"Gee, Beth, you always manage to say the sweetest things."

"Oh, lighten up. Again, have fun. That's an order." Beth paused, her expression thoughtful. "Your not thinking about Derek, are you?"

"No, of course not."

"Well, good. Especially since you have a hot, hunky, Highlander interested in you."

"Yeah, Alex is pretty hot…" She softly replied.

"Hey, wait," Beth brows furrowed as she placed a hand on Laurel's arm. "Is everything okay between you two? I thought I only imagined the tension at the picnic this afternoon."

"No…We're good…It's just…" Laurel wasn't sure what to share. She could tell Beth anything and usually did, but how could she put into words the uneasiness she felt last night in this house? Especially, true to his word, Alex was nothing but a perfect, wonderful, amazing, gentleman today. It made her doubt her conflicted feelings.

"What?" Beth asked.

"It's nothing. It's just this stupid ball. You know how I hate dances. I didn't even go to most of the school events. How am I supposed to get through this evening?"

Beth gave her a quick hug. "You'll be fine. Go find Alex. Let him sweep you off your feet."

"Sure, as long as I don't take him down with me," She joked.

"Live a little. Turn that frown upside down," Beth ordered. "Besides, I'm ditching you. Unlike you, I love a good parrrr-teee." She turned toward Grant, who'd been chatting with another couple and called out, "Honey, let's dance."

Grant made his excuses then stepped to her side as he gave a sweeping bow with a large grin. He gave her a smoldering kiss, and to Laurel it looked like he reluctantly released her. Taking Beth's arm, he led her to the dance floor.

Laurel watched them go. They were so in love. She was happy for Beth. But standing here alone, her nervous jitters made a reappearance along with her loneliness. She missed having Beth as her wingman.

What she needed was a drink. There had to be alcohol somewhere. She scanned the room and noticed a large gathering near one wall, mostly men, sent to get drinks for their dates, or just searching out some liquid courage of their own? Either way, the bar had to be located near the mob.

Finally finding a true smile, Laurel pressed into the room, threading her way through the crowd to reach the vicinity of the bar. She got no further because a wall of costumed men blocked her goal.

Damn. She could hear the clinks of glass and ice behind the human barricade. *So close, yet so far*.

"Laurel?"

Double damn. Turning around with a smile plastered to her face, she faced Alex. "Hey."

"I've been searching for you."

No doubt. "Well, you found me. So cleverly hiding

by the bar."

"Come my beauty," Alex took her hand. "The opening set is about to start."

"Alex, I told you I don't dance. Or at least, not until I'm very drunk. Hence the bar," she gestured behind her.

"No excuses. You'll be fine. It's simple. Just follow and do what everyone else is doing."

As he dragged her to the center of the dance floor, she noticed while wearing heels, she was now a few inches taller than her escort. Maybe she could take him? Wrestle him off the dance floor? Or maybe she could pick a fight? No, she couldn't do that to him. Besides, it was too late now, they had arrived on the dance floor, and she could clearly see two lines of people fanning out to face each other. All thoughts fled her head.

Dear God, what kind of dance was this? Please don't let it be "period". She couldn't dance, not modern, and definitely not period. How the hell would she be able to perform the freaking minuet?

"Quit frowning, love," Alex gave her hand a squeeze. Did people think crushing her hand would really make her feel better?

"It's just a country dance. We always open the ball with something authentic."

"News flash, Alex. I. Do. Not. Dance. Which I've mentioned about a bazillion times. And now I'm expected to figure out some ancient thing?" She might have been able to stave off her embarrassment dancing "Debbie-dumb" style, but not some real dance. There was no hope.

Alex halted when they reached the first line of people, and positioned her between two women. He stood in front of her, grinning, before giving her a quick affectionate kiss that just brushed her lips.

"It's easy," he said, backing away from her. "Just follow what everyone else is doing."

"Great, I'm sure that'll transform me into a ballroom dancer."

Alex barked out a laugh and took his place in line opposite her. Separated by a mere six feet, it was easy for Laurel to catch his wink. She willed herself to relax and offered a small smile back to him. This was supposed to be fun. How hard could it be? Everyone kept telling her it wouldn't be a problem.

Laurel took a deep breath as the orchestra began to play. After ten bars in four/four time, the women in her line all stepped forward. A beat behind, she joined them.

It went all downhill from there. She did everything late and backwards. It was worst than the Macarena which she'd been forced to attempt at her boss's son's bar mitzvah. Now when she was supposed to link arms with a partner and spin right, she reached for the wrong man and found a woman already on his arm. Then when she was supposed to take a step back, inevitably, she stepped forward or to the side. Any direction but the correct one.

Her dancing finally reached the level of absurd when she collided with a parading couple. She couldn't help herself any longer and started to laugh. The startled couple linked arms with her, and they became a parading threesome.

All the dancers, and she assumed most of the audience, were laughing when the song came to an end. At least she thought so, until she spotted Alex frowning at her. Laurel barely noticed the fond farewells and congratulations of the departing dancers as she watched him approach.

She smiled brightly at him, and shrugged her shoulders. “I told you I didn’t dance.” She had to bite her lip to keep from laughing again.

Alex reached her. “I thought you were exaggerating.”

“Nope.”

“Well, let’s remove you from the dance floor before you cause any more carnage.”

He took her arm and escorted her off the floor toward the open French doors.

“I really am sorry. I did warn you.”

“I should have taken you at your word. No worries, there was little damage done, unless you count a few toes, some of which were mine.” He gave her a brief smile. “However, you’ll have to excuse me. I need to find a partner. As the host, I should be out on the dance floor. There’s one more country-dance, then a waltz, to finish the set. I won’t be gone long.”

“Please, go. Don’t worry about me. I’ll stay over here or at the bar and watch the action from a distance. Everyone’s feet will be safe.”

“You’re a good sport. See you later, aye?”

“Absolutely. Now, go.”

Alex gave her a quick kiss on the cheek before dashing off. He really wasn’t such a bad guy. A smile curled up her lips. She wouldn’t mind watching, especially knowing her participation was over for the evening. She could finally relax and enjoy herself. Alex was movie star handsome tonight in his indigo blue jacket, snowy white cravat, and tight black pants, which showed off some rather droolable assets. Laurel would have a fabulous view for the rest of the event, and with a good single malt scotch in hand, her night couldn't get better.

Chapter Fifteen

Simon stepped out from behind the potted palm where he'd been lurking, keeping an eye on Laurel. The lass really was a danger to everyone around her. He had no idea anyone could possibly dance that poorly. Maybe he should leave her with MacKenzie, there's a good chance with her klutzy, accident-prone streak, she may injure him.

But that was wrong. MacKenzie was like a cockroach, impossible to get rid of. Simon highly doubted she'd even be able to harm him. But MacKenzie could certainly hurt her, or something much worse. He needed to warn her, she didn't deserve what the bounder was capable of doing. If she listened, and he thought that might be a big if—MacKenzie would lose the girl, keeping her safe. And foiling MacKenzie's plans, fit perfectly within Simon's world—anything to screw the fecker.

He prowled closer, careful as always to never reveal himself to the key players. It had gotten easier over the centuries as those he knew and loved died. He supposed he was lucky with even his portrait gone from Cleitmuir, no one on earth knew who he truly was—but he couldn't fight the wave of bitter loneliness. Everyone thought him a greedy, cursed kin-slayer. The irony didn't escape him that MacKenzie was the only one who knew the truth, and MacKenzie was the heir of his sworn enemy. Everyone thought Simon long dead. His body had disappeared well over two centuries ago, and his spirit shredded by the intervening years. There was little left except the longing for peace.

He approached Laurel who shivered. The temperature change near him couldn't be helped. There was always a chill when he materialized. With enough time spent solid, the levels evened out, but there would always be that telltale sign to herald his arrival.

Stopping directly behind her, Simon followed her gaze to MacKenzie, who was out on the dance floor with a vibrant red head. He cringed as time blurred watching this MacKenzie as he had the other with Fiona. What was it with MacKenzie's and redheads? At least this lass before him had brown hair.

"Jealous, are ye?" Simon asked.

If she was startled by the sudden voice behind her, she hid it well. The lass didn't move, except to turn her head and look over her shoulder. Her eyes narrowed and her lips thinned.

"Excuse me?"

He fought to keep a grin off his face. He irritated her, which was fine, because she was a bothersome chit. Still, he couldn't help teasing her. Her feisty responses and her willingness not to back down from him was a small light in his darkness. He rarely got to interact anymore and realized how much he missed the human contact. He'd make the most of it. "You were staring at MacKenzie," he taunted. "Do you wish you were in his arms now?"

"For the love of—" She stopped herself, faced forward shaking her head. "For your information, I danced with Alex already."

Simon snorted. "If you can call it that."

She whirled around glaring. "At least *I* tried. I didn't see you out there." Then, like the sun breaking through storm clouds, she smiled up at him. "What the hell, I suppose you're right. It was pretty horrific. I never could dance. You should have seen me at my senior prom."

He stared at her, mesmerized for a moment. She was a lovely lass, especially when she was laughing at herself. A rare gift, indeed. "Maybe it's not you? It does take two."

She shook her head. "Not likely." Her smile grew larger. "Why is it our conversations turn into arguments? I never met someone who pushed my buttons like you do, and I don't even know you. You have a special talent."

He shrugged.

"Let's clear the slate. I'll start. I'm actually glad to see you again. I wanted to thank you once more for saving my life, but I realized I don't even know your name."

He stared down at her for a moment knowing he couldn't give her his real name, but then again, that's what middle names are for. "Cole, ah, Robert Cole."

She raised an eyebrow at him. "Not MacKay?"

He tried for puzzlement, but wasn't sure if he achieved his goal. "What makes you say that?"

"I was in Inverness the other day, in a museum. They had an exhibit of portraits by Scottish artists."

Oh, shite. She was staring at him oddly. Of all the people to see his painting. He waited for the axe to fall.

"Has anyone ever told you that you look a lot like Captain Simon MacKay? I have to say the resemblance is uncanny," she trailed off, leaving her statement as an unasked question.

"Aye, that it is," he gave her a smile. "Distant relative, mother's side." He glanced over her shoulder and noticed the dance coming to an end. Perfect, a much needed distraction. "You haven't introduced yourself."

"Oh, of course. I'm Laurel. Laurel Saville."

"Lovely, American?"

"By way of Chicago."

Simon heard the first note of the waltz strike. "Will you settle an argument for me?"

"Argument?"

"Aye, ours. The one where I blame MacKenzie for your dancing."

"What?"

Before she could anticipate his move, he grabbed her right hand, pulled her close, and eased his other hand to her waist, before whirling them out onto the dance floor.

Chapter Sixteen

"What are you doing?" Horrified, Laurel tensed and backed away. She didn't make it far. His grip remained strong and confident as he swept her in amongst the other twirling couples.

"Proving a point."

"Let go of me! It'll be a train wreck!"

"Och, no," he grinned down at her.

Her hold on his shoulder tightened, turning her knuckles white. This was insane. Any moment now they'd collide with another dancing pair or she'd trip and crash them both to the ground. She was tired of making a spectacle of herself. She glared into his eyes. "You are the most arrogant...you need to stop before something awful happens."

"Perhaps, but I think I'll take the chance. Besides, I've proven my point."

"I have no idea what you're taking about." Her mind reeled and she had trouble following what he was saying. She didn't enjoy making a fool of herself, and he had the temerity to actually laugh at her, causing her to stiffen in his arms.

He leaned in and whispered into her ear. "Relax. You're dancing."

The realization hit her and she stumbled. Robert Cole was there, his hold tightened and steadied her. She took a deep breath, stunned. "Holy shit, I am!"

"That you are," he continued to smile at her. His hand at her waist moved to the small of her back, pulling her closer. Effortlessly spinning, Laurel felt his controlled power as he guided them around the dance floor, steering, reversing and turning her. She held tight, amazed.

She was dancing and loved it. She couldn't stop her laughter and knew she was grinning like an idiot, but it didn't matter.

Looking up, she was trapped in his gray gaze. His eyes glowed a luminous silver, and his smile disappeared. There was something primeval in his look, a seriousness. All thought vanished and her laughter died. He tugged her closer yet, embracing her, as the world spun in six-eight time.

Her breasts brushed his storm colored jacket while his muscular thigh pressed between her legs. His hand burned at the small of her back. Her temperature rose as she became intimately aware of his masculine presence held there in his embrace.

Her world narrowed and she couldn't look away from his intent stare. Hips and thighs, brushed then parted as they revolved through a turn. The waltz's rhythm held an explicit promise.

Dear God. Laurel now understood why the waltz was once banned from the ballrooms of London. *Holy cow.* She could see why people thought this dance scandalous.

She broke off eye contact, to stare at one broad shoulder, feeling the flush heating her cheeks.

****

Simon fought the urge to smile when Laurel demurely dropped her gaze and blushed prettily. It was such a feminine response. He felt a surge of satisfaction and pure male possessiveness. The feelings fled as realization slammed into him. He wasn't alive. He'd never have a woman of his own—never know love. Laurel could never be his. But regardless of his unholy situation, he wouldn't leave her to MacKenzie. He had to warn the lass.

The music came to a swirling end, and he realized the doors to the terrace were a few steps away. Before she could gleam what he was doing, he whisked her from the ballroom and escorted her into a dark corner of the patio.

He watched as her awareness returned and she glanced sharply around. Taking a step back, her hips struck the railing, and her hand grasped the beam. She took a deep breath, causing him to admire the neckline of her dress. He reluctantly dragged his gaze away and back up to her face, where he met her questioning glance.

"I thought we both could use some fresh air."

She looked away before meeting his eyes once more. She swallowed and a small smile curled up her mouth. "Yes, well...that was, um—"

"You're welcome."

She laughed. "Thank you. It was...amazing. I had no idea." She shrugged. "I can see now why people love to dance."

"All you needed was the right partner."

Her smile grew larger. "If you say so."

"Indeed." He studied her for a moment. "I need to speak with you."

She raised an eyebrow and waited patiently for him to continue.

"It's about, MacKenzie."

"What?"

"He's not the gentleman you think he is."

She pushed away from the balustrade, all relaxation gone from her demeanor. "Excuse me? I must not have heard you correctly."

"I'm just trying to warn you. MacKenzie's trouble. Stay away from him."

"Kettle. Black." Her lips thinned, and her eyes narrowed. "At least he isn't constantly picking fights with me, or deciding I'm some accident-prone idiot. He credits me with intelligence." In obvious disgust, she tried to leave.

"Listen, Laurel," he grabbed her arm. "He's a dangerous man. He's only using you." Like Alastair MacKenzie used Fiona, history was trying to repeat itself.

She shrugged out of his hold. "What are you talking about? He's not *using* me. I volunteered to help find the gold."

Gold? What the blazes is she—

"Lori?" Beth's voice called across the terrace and Laurel broke off in the mid tirade to stare past his shoulder.

Damn. Simon couldn't reveal himself to too many people. Time to disappear. He stepped off to the side while she was distracted.

****

"Lori? Are you out here?"

She watched Beth exit the ballroom. "I'm over here." Laurel waved and then shivered as a chilled breeze washed over her. She turned to face Cole, but he was gone. Vanished. She shivered again as icy fingers crept up her spine. Where had he gone? How had he disappeared so fast? It was just like on the plateau.

"Hey, where've you been? I lost track of you and wondered if you chickened out and ditched without telling me," Beth said. "What's wrong? You look like you've seen a ghost."

Laurel stepped away from Beth and walked the few strides to the darkest corner of the terrace. *Maybe I have?* There was no way for Cole to just disappear into thin air. There had to be an explanation. And there it was, stairs leading into the garden. No ghosts, here. She looked for Cole, but if he was there the shadows hid him.

She continued to stare at the garden as Beth reached her side once more. "What's going on?"

"Did you see the man I was dancing with?"

"You were dancing?" Beth stared at her incredulously. "Nobody died or was injured?"

"Beth, now is not the time," she shook her head. Her friend could never pass up an opportunity to tease her about her two left feet. "Yes, I was dancing, and the waltz, no less." She couldn't help the smile that lit up her face.

"Wow. Who was this brave dancing instructor?"

"That's the point, you didn't see us? What about just now on the terrace? He was standing right next to me."

Beth raised an eyebrow. "No. There wasn't anyone with you."

"Really? How could you possibly have missed him?" Exacerbation laced Laurel's question. "He's huge, like six-four, tall."

"I'm telling you, you were quite alone lurking in

the murkiest corner of the balcony," she replied. "Though it was dark… Is he handsome? Was he hitting on you? What's his name?"

"Get your mind out of the gutter," she let a frustrated sigh escape. "The name he gave me was, Robert Cole. Do you know him?"

"Nope, never heard of him. But there are a lot of strangers in town for the festival. Was he cute?"

Laurel frowned. "Seriously?" She thought for a moment and smiled. "He was more than cute, he's in the ruggedly handsome category, and I really wanted you to meet him." She turned her back to Beth and stared into down into the gardens, searching for her mysterious dancer partner.

"Bummer, sorry I missed him," Beth replied. "No worries though, if he's here for the festival I'm sure your paths will cross."

"I hope so, because you'll never believe this. He's the spitting image of Simon MacKay."

Chapter Seventeen

"You're kidding, right?"

"I'm not." She spun to face Beth. "Remember the portrait I told you about while in Inverness? It was downright eerie seeing Robert Cole tonight. I was staring at the same man, even though I *know* it's impossible."

"Did you ask him? I mean, it's not like he wouldn't know about MacKay since that clan originally started this festival. It could be the reason he's here."

"I did." Laurel sighed. "He kind of blew me off and changed the topic. All he'd admit to was some sort of distant relation on his mother's side."

"Well, that makes sense. After all, his last name is Cole not MacKay, and the surviving line was Simon's mother and sister."

Laurel gazed intently at her best friend. "And there's something else… He warned me to stay away from Alex. Pretty much said Alex was dangerous."

"What? That's ridiculous!" Beth denied. "Sounds more like jealousy to me. Maybe he isn't here for the festival at all. Maybe he's a competitor, a fellow treasure hunter."

"Really? Looking like Simon MacKay?"

"Well, the gold was from their clan. Maybe he's hoping to reclaim it? Warned you off so you couldn't help Alex succeed before him."

"I don't know…Damn, it," Laurel brushed aside a tendril of hair off her face. "I wish you'd seen him."

"Since I didn't see the painting, I have only your word to go by anyway."

"But I just don't understand his disappearing act." This is twice now. Something weird was going on. How come she was the only one to keep seeing him?

"Maybe he's afraid to meet me? Afraid I'd rat him out to Alex."

Laurel snorted. "Doubt it. It's not like he told me he was hunting the gold, so there was no reason for him to tell you."

"I suppose you're right," Beth replied.

She shook her head. "Hey, you were looking for me. What did you want?"

"Nothing much really. You disappeared and I saw Alex making time with Kyla, and I thought an intervention was necessary. What did you do? Piss him off?"

"Hardly, just danced with him." She walked to the doors with Beth pacing at her side. "Kyla? Is she a redhead?"

"Yup and fake boobs. You're losing your hot highlander," Beth tossed out as she entered the ballroom before her.

"He's not mine," Laurel muttered. She shot one last glance at the garden below before following Beth inside.

****

Simon stared after the women from the shadows below the terrace. *Too close by far*. Not that Laurel's friend would have recognized him, but he didn't need more introductions just now. He also didn't need to be on speaking terms with the wife of the current owner of his manor when he returned next year, or hell's curses, the year after that.

No, damn it. By all he held dear he vowed his final rest was at hand. There would not be a next time. He would find the key to the hidden chamber. And nothing, not even a fiery, accident-prone, American lass would distract him.

But damn the girl. It had been so long since he talked, let alone teased another human being. Even longer since he had held a woman in his arms. He closed his eyes and was vividly transported back to their waltz. Her warm soft body pressed against him, the citrus scent that floated lightly from her hair, her smile…

A spot deep in his chest began to ache. How had this woman touched him so deeply and in such a short time? Anger grew in Simon. He wouldn't let feelings of desire or loneliness sway him. It was gobshite that his emotions decided to surface now at the end of his trial. No more, he promised himself. Much easier to be cynical and bitter than to let any other feelings enter. He had enough pain without opening his heart. His resolve grew. He would do everything in his power, use anyone, hurt anyone, and even abandon the girl to MacKenzie if he had to, in order to achieve success. End game. He would not fail this time.

****

Laurel's fingertips brushed her lips. They still tingled from Alex's goodnight kiss. After he finished the dance with that redhead, Kyla, he'd kept his word and stayed at her side all night. A perfect gentleman. He had been attentive and funny, making her laugh at his insights about the people around them, and he had made her feel beautiful. Tonight really had turned out fabulous.

It was hard to believe Cole's warning. Alex was smart, charming, and incredibly sexy. Beth knew her all too well, Alex was everything she'd been looking for. He even treated her like an equal and he was interested in her. He couldn't be more perfect—just what the doctor ordered to heal and distract her from her breakup.

She pulled the tight black tank-top over her head and smoothed it down so it touched her yoga pants. Brushing her hair behind her ears, she wondered if she made a mistake in declining Alex tonight. She burned with a weird energy and chalked it up to sexual frustration. It was way too long since she last got laid, with all her moping around since Derek. Maybe that would explain her jumping hormones for two completely different men.

Robert Cole, the mysterious Scotsman who was a dead ringer for MacKay. How could she be attracted to such an irritating jerk? Argumentative, arrogant, and now he was trying to break her away from Alex. How had she let Cole under her skin especially since she had the undivided attention of Alex? She lifted the gown draped on the platform bed and smoothed out the wrinkles. With a slight frown, she walked to the wardrobe and hung the dress up. She should have stayed with Alex. She could be having wild monkey sex right this minute.

Instead, she'd gone back to the manor, and then consumed a pint of triple chocolate ice cream while she and Beth gossiped about people back home. Laurel told

Alex she wanted to spend time with her best friend. It wasn't even an afterthought, or a hesitation. After all, she had traveled all the way from Chicago because she hadn't seen Beth in well over a year, and between the festival and everything else, Laurel felt like she still missed her friend. Tomorrow was an "off" day. She planned to spend the entire time with Beth. But if she had the whole day with Beth tomorrow, couldn't she have had the night with Alex? Laurel blew out a frustrated sigh.

Thank God, Alex had graciously understood but said he couldn't help but be disappointed. Now she couldn't help being a bit disappointed herself. Oh well, it's not like she could turn back time, and she didn't regret time spent with Beth.

She walked out of the bedroom and into the suite's main room to curl up on the window seat, clutching an over-stuffed pillow to her chest. But why was she anxious and restless? She should have been exhausted with the long day, but she wasn't. Leaning her head against the chilled windowpane, Laurel stared into the darkness. Finally the sun had drifted below the horizon. It was well after three in the morning. Hard to believe it would be making another appearance in just few hours. The nights were incredibly short this far north.

Robert Cole. What was his story? And why was it when she closed her eyes, instead of the lovely blue of Alex's eyes, she glimpsed silvery-gray? She tried repeatedly to banish Cole from her thoughts, but he stuck there like a moldy fungus in a damaged museum text. No matter how carefully you tried to cauterize it, the fungus just kept returning. It's why she didn't go to bed. She was worried what her dreams would hold.

Damn, the man.

With a disgusted sigh, she threw the pillow she clutched to the floor and stood. Striding across the room, she vowed she'd get some sleep. To hell with him and his warnings. To hell with his mesmerizing eyes. She flung herself down on the bed and closed her eyes. She'd banish him from her thoughts, count sheep, do algebra, or catalog the Field Museum's artifacts—anything to get him gone.

But as she slipped into her dreams, it was Cole's face she spied intently staring down at her. His arms wrapped around her in a tight embrace. His warm breath brushed her cheeks. She spun and twirled as the waltz's refrain haunted her dreams, just as the man haunted her thoughts.

Chapter Eighteen

St. Brendan's Church
October 1795

The church bells rang causing Simon to glance sharply up and stare out the stained glass window. His da would be coming soon. He swallowed and scuffed his muddy, booted foot on the stone floor. It was just a bit of joke, he and his friends, Dougal and Byron, decided to play. It was supposed to be grand fun. The Priest hadn't agreed.

Lord Sinclair had already arrived, and after delivering a loud tongue lashing that blistered the twins' ears, he followed it up with a good ol' highland thrashing. The twins had given the Priest an apology then followed their Da home. The lads probably wouldn't be able to sit for days with their sore arses. Simon would be so lucky.

Bloody hell. His own Da, Murdoc MacKay, wasn't a shouter, but that just made it worst. He'd talk with his son calmly and quietly, showing only disappointment and sadness on his weathered seafarer's face. What he wouldn't give to have his Da shout at him and beat him. Simon sighed. He looked at the altar, studying the wooden crucifix and said a silent prayer.

Lord, I know you're a wee bit angry with me, but it was only meant as a jest. You made man, so you certainly must understand boys. After all, we're made in your image. You had a son. Surely he had fun as a lad, didn't he? Simon scuffed his boot across the floor again, glancing down and away. *Well aye, you're probably right, he was your Son so he must have been perfect. But I'm just a lad. I didn't mean any harm. Please let my Da understand. I hate seeing him so sad. I try hard, but I always seem to disappoint him. I don't mean to—*

His stomach lurched when the church doors opened behind him. The wind howled, blowing dry leaves over the granite floor, mingling with the solid booted stride of a man. His Da had arrived. Simon swallowed again.

Without turning, he listened as his Da closed the doors and was joined by Father Colin McPhee. Low voices rumbled behind Simon as he portrayed an avid interest in his boots. Why was he so stupid?

"Thank you, Father. I apologize for my son. Simon will understand the seriousness of his mischief, you needn't worry." His da's voice rose loud enough for Simon, no doubt, to intentionally hear.

"Aye, I know ye will. The MacKay's have a long standing with the Church. I'll leave the lad to you, sir."

His da's steps came down the aisle then turned into the pew before him. The worn wooden bench creaked as he sat.

"Simon, lad. Look at me." His father's request was couched in a calm and quiet manner.

Simon's stomach lurched again and soured. He might as well get this over with. He looked up and met his father's sad, gray gaze.

"Son, you're ten and one now." It wasn't a question. "A man almost grown. You should be taking on responsibilities, no' acting like a wee lad in short pants." His da pushed aside the escaped black strands of hair from the tight plaited queue off his face. He seemed more than just sad and disappointed, almost disturbed.

"There are things..." His da shook his head. "*Bi Tren*, be true, be valiant. You're a disgrace to the Clan. I thought I taught you better. Where is your respect?"

"Da, it was just some stupid statues—"

His father's hand struck blindingly fast in a stinging slap that brought tears to Simon's eyes and left his cheek burning.

"Where? Where is your faith? How will ye—" His voice choked off and he tore his angry gaze from Simon to stare down at his hands.

Confused, Simon watched his father finger the large signet ring on his right hand. The sapphire winked in and out of view as it turned and spun. "I had hoped," his da's voice no more than a whisper, "to leave you the family legacy. It goes beyond the mere position of Earl. A responsibility that canna be measured. But time and again, Simon, ye have proven yourself unworthy." His father raised his head and pierced him with his gaze. "When will ye grow up? I keep waiting, yet ye lark about never understanding that there is more to life than earthly pleasure."

His father stood, towering over him. "Apparently I have been too indulging and kind. No more. It's time I remember our clan's motto: *Manu Forti*. Aye, a strong hand is needed. Listen carefully, Simon. It is time to put your childish ways away. It begins tonight.

"I've spoken with Father Colin. You will go to the Angels' shrine and clean it—"

"But why just—" The slap was as stinging as the first, grinding Simon's interruption to an abrupt halt.

"It was *your* plan. Byron and Dougal are followers. *Ye* will take responsibility for your actions so ye learn there are *always* repercussions. When Father Colin deems the statues pristine, ye will then kneel before them on the stone floor, and pray for their forgiveness. Ye will pray for their intercession on your soul, and then ye will meditate on your past actions. Pray for enlightenment. Pray ye understand what is needed to be a man of honor and a member of the clan MacKay."

He had never seen his father so angry, his face set, lips thinned and eyes cold. There was a deadly seriousness to him that belied the dressing up of a few statues. More was going on. Simon feared his life was about to change, forevermore. His certainty was reinforced at his father's next stern command.

"Ye will keep this vigil on your knees until the bells of Lauds are rung. By dawn, my fondest hope is that ye will have grown up." MacKay laid his hand gently upon Simon's shoulder and then raised the other so the signet ring was level with Simon's eyes. "*Bi Tren*. One day this key will pass to ye. Ye must be ready and worthy."

He lowered his ring hand and squeezed Simon's shoulder. "I do this for your own good." The MacKay exited the pew and walked up the nave's center aisle to the doors. He never turned and glanced back. He just opened the doors and walked out into the stormy night.

Simon stared after his father, confused, angry and hurt. He didn't understand what was going on. So lost in his thoughts, he never heard the Priest approach until Father Colin cleared his throat.

"Get on with it, lad. And don't think to be cleaning all night in order to save your knees. I'll be checking in on you and notice if you're stalling."

"Aye, Father." He hung his head, hiding his rebellious expression from the old Priest. He shuffled out of the pew and headed for the shrine. He was in for a long night.

Chapter Nineteen

St. Brendan's Church
July, Present Day

Standing in the chapel of St. Brendan's, the angels stood in a semi-circle before Simon, staring impassively down at him. Nothing had changed in two hundred years. The shrine to the seven Archangels remained exactly as it had from that long ago stormy October night. St. Michael stood in the center, with Raphael on his right and Gabriel on his left. The remaining Archangels, Uriel, Raguel, Sariel and Remiel formed the rest of the half-circle.

This was where it had all started and now apparently, ended. On that cold and windy night, his youth fled as he knelt before the angels' judgment. His father thought to teach him a lesson, yet, it was the wrong one he took away. Though he had been a mischievous lad, the true start to his rebellion began that night on aching knees tormented by hard granite. The stone had seeped into his heart. The relationship with his father spiraled rapidly downward, culminating in Simon shunning his duties as heir and joining the army—all against tradition and rational responsibility.

With that final act of rebellion, Simon never had the chance to reconcile with his father. His da was murdered and left in the cold, ocean's grasp, the legacy lost, and his family torn apart. It had taken a few hundred years of personal torment for Simon to realize what a fool he'd been. Just as on that Halloween night, a part of him wished he could turn back time and understand what his father had tried to tell him so he would have emerged from his vigil the man his da wanted him to be. But, as with then, there was no turning back, only forward.

Simon glared at the angels before him. For everything the MacKay's had done, he thought some intervention would have been allowed. He prayed his family was at peace, and one day, he'd be able to join them.

"Well, old friends," Simon greeted the silent statues. "The time has come. I will honor our clan's legacy. *Bi Tren*." He sighed. "A little help would be appreciated, though."

Simon crossed himself and tried to find some inner calm as he prayed.

"St. Michael, smite my enemies. St. Gabriel, the messenger, send me a sign. Uriel," he growled out the name, losing all patience. "You bloody know...tell me, show me..." He glowered at the stony stillness staring down at him. "Damn you all! You do nothing and expect everything. Fine. This is the end. I'll see it done."

Simon turned his back on the Archangels and stormed out of the shrine. The candles flickered and gutted in his violent unseen passage, leaving darkness in his wake.

****

Laurel pulled open the heavy door to St. Brendan's and stepped inside. She paused, letting her eyes adjust to the interior's darkness. She had spent the morning with Beth as planned, but the afternoon became a wash. Beth confessed she had a surprise for her, planned well in advance of Laurel boarding her flight to Scotland. It was Beth's early birthday gift to her. Grinning, her best friend left after preparing lunch, making Laurel promise if she went out, she'd be back by five. Suddenly having the afternoon to herself, Laurel thought she'd get in some research that might help Alex.

St. Brendan's, the local area's church, had been in existence for centuries. It had withstood wars, clan fighting, and the harsh northern weather. Ever vigilant. The perfect place to house old records and clues for the missing gold. She spotted a priest lighting candles on the far side of the transept and walked to him.

"Excuse me, Father. I called earlier and spoke with a Father Campbell."

"Ah, yes. You must be Ms. Saville. I'm Father Campbell." He smiled warmly and offered his hand. She was surprised by his youth. He looked to be about her age.

"Laurel, please," she shook his hand. "Thank you for taking the time to meet with me, especially at the last moment."

"It's no problem. I'll be with you in just a moment." The Priest went back to lighting the votives.

"I thought your parishioners were the ones to light the candles."

"Och, well, I'm just re-lighting the ones that blew out. They're meant to stay lit until the candles burn out, but I think the angels are playing jokes on me."

"Angels?"

"Aye," he gestured into the alcove next to him.

"`Tis a shrine to the Archangels, and these candles are the only ones that keep blowing out. I seem to be re-lighting them every summer. None of the other candles within the church are affected. I think they like my company." He chuckled and placed the lighter down. "Now, lass. I understand you wanted to discuss local history? It's a rare, bonnie day, why don't we go outside and chat?"

Laurel followed Father Campbell as he led her to a door near the altar. They exited into the bright sunshine and followed a graveled path to a small cemetery. He gestured to a stone bench beneath a leaning tree. She sat as Father Campbell joined her.

"Now, Laurel. What can I do for you?"

"I'm trying to help an acquaintance of mine. Alex MacKenzie?"

"Aye," the young Priest paused. "I know him."

"Has he been through St. Brendan's records?"

"No, he hasn't. The only times I've spoken or seen him were outside the church. He doesn't attend Mass. What is it you're after?" He watched her closely, his blue gaze locked intently on her face.

Laurel fidgeted under his scrutiny. "Is there a problem?" She was definitely picking up a vibe from the Priest.

"Frankly, I don't care much for MacKenzie." He looked up to the sky, then down at his hands folded in his lap. "Not very priestly of me." He sighed.

She stared at Father Campbell, torn, wondering why the Priest didn't like Alex, but squashed her curiosity. Maybe an opportunity would present itself where she could dig into his reason. But Father Campbell's discomfiture caused her to change tack. She wanted answers and there was no point in alienating the Priest. "I was hoping to learn more about the MacKay's. I'm visiting from Chicago and staying at Cleitmuir Manor. Beth Murray, my best friend, is chair of the festival committee." She didn't bring up Alex again, hoping to make the priest more receptive than when she first mentioned his name.

"Aye, Beth. She's a good lass. Fits right into the community. Grant was lucky when he found her." Father Campbell replied, his posture relaxing.

Laurel smiled from the obvious affection the priest had for Beth. Not mentioning Alex appeared to be the right approach.

"She is wonderful. I've missed her greatly since she wed and moved to Scotland. We've known each other since grade school. This is the first I've been able to leave Chicago to visit her."

"'Tis a shame for good friends to be separated so."

"Yes is it. My job, I work for the Chicago Field Museum, makes it hard to get away," she stated. "My work has made me a bit of a history nut. I've always wanted to visit the Scottish Highlands and now I'm here, surrounded by incredible history."

"That you are," the Priest replied with a twinkle in his eye. "Are you enjoying your visit?"

"I am," she offered him another smile. "It's been amazing. Especially staying at Cleitmuir Manor. The MacKay's have such a long history."

"Did you know the clan was descended from the Picts? Do you know about the Picts?" Father Campbell asked.

"Simplistically, the Picts are the earliest Celtic race of Scotland."

"Aye. When Christianity came to Scotland, the MacKay's were one of the first to convert. They've been closely involved ever since. The Earl of Cleitmuir is buried here." Father Campbell stood. "Let me show you."

Laurel followed the Priest as they wove their way through the graveyard. They stopped in front of a large ornate tombstone of an angel with its wings unfurled. The statue stood taller than her. She scanned down the granite angel to the tablet in its hands.

Murdoc MacKay
1767 - 1809
3rd Earl of Cleitmuir
Beloved Husband and Father
Bi Tren.

"Excuse me, Father. Wasn't Simon the last Earl?"

The Priest cleared his throat. "Aye, but his Da was the last of the MacKay's to be buried here."

"Did anyone ever discover what happened to Simon?"

"No, but never believe the stories spread about our young Captain. He may have had a wild history, but he'd never turn against his family."

"You seem so sure," she studied the Priest.

"Aye, well," Father Campbell turned a bit sheepish. "The MacKay's are a large part of this area, and St. Brendan's has journals from the Priests that stayed here. It started with the first Priest, Father Timothy. It's kind of a tradition that's carried on through today. No matter what might have been between father and son, Simon wouldn't have abandoned his mother and sister, especially during the unstable times of the Clearances."

"Clearances? That's the second time I've heard that word spoken in terms of a noun."

"Aye, well, it was another dark time in the Highlands. The English were evicting Highland families off their land for sheep and other more profitable means. They weren't pleasant about it either. At its height, thousands of families, a day, were forced to leave without notice, just simply told to get out or suffer devastating consequences. A lot o' people died because of the Clearances. If you ask me, it was just another excuse for English revenge against the Highlanders, just like banning the tartans and speaking the Gaelic."

"What happened to his family?"

"Och, Lady Cora and wee Jean were cast out. They lost everything. Cora MacKay, never fared well after losing her husband, grew sicker and died. It's believed Jean became an indentured servant and ended up in America." Father Campbell shook his head. "It was a sad time. The Highlands have gone through hell, but the clans kept their pride. Simon would never have left his family willingly."

"So you don't believe he killed his father?"

"Never! I think poor Simon suffered his father's fate." The Priest glanced back to the church. "I must return and prepare for *None*," noticing her confusion, he clarified. "Mid-day prayer. It starts at three. However, if you're interested, you may look at the journals left by Father McPhee, the attending Priest during Simon's life."

"Thank you. Thank you so much. I'd love too!" It was just the invitation she had been hoping for.

She followed Father Campbell back to the church.

He showed her into a small office and pulled down five leather-bound books.

"Here you go lass, have at them. I'll check back later to see if there's anything else I can help you with."

"Thank you, Father. Oh, just one more thing. What about the Jacobite gold?"

The Priest snorted. "You've been listening to folklore and MacKenzie. Gold?" The Priest stared directly into her eyes. "Smoke and mirrors. There's never been any gold."

Chapter Twenty

Laurel dashed for the steps, trying to avoid the large drops of rain splashing down on the manor's gravel drive. She was late.

As always, when immersed in history, she'd lost track of time. The journals were fascinating, reliving the era in the leather-bound books. From the stories about St. Brendan's parishioners to the simple lists of church stores, McPhee's voice rang through and transported her to another time. She especially enjoyed reading about a Halloween prank Simon and his friends had pulled when he was eleven. Apparently they had dressed up the angel statues. It made her smile until she read about his punishment. It seemed harsh, but was probably normal for the era.

Emerging from her cocoon, she found it was after five o'clock, and the previous brilliant sunshine gone. The ever-changing Scottish weather had taken a turn while she'd been inside the little office of St. Brendan's. A cold, northern wind had swept down, bringing clouds that threatened rain. They pressed down upon the land like a thick, charcoal blanket, echoing the thoughts bouncing around in her head.

She'd read nothing about the Jacobite gold, or even any hints or codes that could be about the elusive treasure. Father Campbell might be right. There could be no gold. Was Alex chasing nothing more than a rumor? It was hard to believe considering he made his living by finding treasure. Maybe the earlier church's journals held the key?

What was going on? Her inner sense tingled, just like it did when she researched artifacts for the museum and found them to be fakes. Something was off and she just wasn't seeing it.

Laurel raced away from St. Brendan's, ahead of the storm, while her mind shifted through the possibilities. She reached Cleitmuir just as the rain started falling and concluded the church had been a dead end. Hopefully, Beth wouldn't be too upset with her. It was only now just past five-thirty.

Laurel opened the front door and was relieved when she heard Beth's laughter coming from the front sitting room.

"Yeah, you're right. Suitable weather, indeed," Beth commented to someone.

A low voice answered her and more laughter followed. Curious, Laurel shook the few drops of water from her hair before entering the room.

"Ah, there you are!" Beth bounded over to her, leaving two men standing by the fire. She grabbed Laurel's arm and dragged her over to the waiting men. "Let me introduce you. I'd like you to meet Steve Wright and Doug Kerr.

"A pleasure to meet you," Laurel shook hands with both men.

"Gentleman, meet your newest team member, Laurel Saville," Beth continued.

"Team member?" Confused, her gaze bounced between Beth and the men.

Beth couldn't stop the grin that lit her face. "Yup.

BAPS, the British Agency for Paranormal Studies. Surprise!"

Laurel stood stunned for a moment. "You're kidding right?"

"Hell, no," Beth answered. "We're having our very own ghost hunt. Happy early birthday!"

"Sweet! This is so cool. I've always wanted to do this," she hugged Beth and grinned. "I'm sorry I'm late."

"It's okay. We've got plenty of time. I showed the boys around and gave them a bit of history on the two active rooms downstairs. We even got the digital video cameras up and wired. Besides, it gave me time to remind our guests about the investigation and to point out which rooms are off-limits tonight when it gets dark. Not that many of them will be up and about at two in the morning, but we don't need to record a disembody voice only to discover it wasn't a ghost but a real human walking down the hall to the loo. No debunking my own paying customers." Beth laughed and hugged Laurel back.

"We were just waiting for you to get your room hooked up," Beth looked over her shoulder and crooked a finger. "Gentlemen it's time for the *pièce de résistance*. Follow me."

Laurel tagged after Beth as they walked to the main staircase with Doug and Steve close behind. "I can't believe you kept this a secret! Our very own ghost hunt! And, you didn't tell me you had other haunted rooms. You have more than one ghost?"

Doug chuckled behind her. "We've done some research since we were scheduled so far in advance. This hotel could be loaded with spirits. There have been a lot of deaths associated with Cleitmuir Manor."

"Oh, yeah," Steve agreed. "Not only both Murdoc and Simon MacKay, but there've been servants and people who were guests here. There's a plethora to choose from."

"Awesome, well not awesome people had to die, but you know what I mean," she said. "You've been holding out on me, Beth. And here I thought you were my best friend."

"Well, I only knew of the recent activity. You know, stuff missing or moved in the office, which used to be the study when it was a manor and not a hotel. We've also had occurrences in the kitchen and the stables."

"I can't believe you haven't said anything." Laurel glared at her friend.

Beth laughed, not intimidated at all. "It was a surprise. Of course I've held things back. Better to make things more exciting tonight." Her eyes gleamed with elation. Their mutual love of ghosts since childhood was going to finally pay off. At any moment she wouldn't be surprised if they started squealing and jumping around like they did when they were little girls.

"We've only rigged the office and kitchen for tonight," Beth continued breaking into her musings. "And of course, we'll be covering all of your rooms as well. If we get any action, we'll expand to a bigger investigation to include the entire property, probably during an off time when we can close the place entirely."

Beth paused outside Laurel's suite. "And now, for the most haunted room in our hotel." With a flourish,

Beth unlocked the door. "This suite once belonged to Simon MacKay."

Luckily, Laurel thought, she'd left the place tidy, with no embarrassing bits of clothing.

"So, Beth," Steve said. "Tell us about these rooms."

"Its history is kind of odd. First, we know for a fact this suite was Simon's. We only notice occurrences during the Primrose Festival. Or at least, it's the time we have reports or complaints. That's why we think it's Simon doing the haunting. After all, he disappeared during the festival, or at least that's what the folklore says.

"We've had everything from moved and missing objects, to feelings of paranoia and creepiness. Someone even thought they saw a figure."

"Was it a full body apparition or more like a shadow figure," Doug asked.

"Shadow, large and black. It crossed the room and disappeared by the fireplace."

"*Beezer*." Steve smiled noticing their confusion. "Excellent, or I believe you Yanks would say, cool?"

"That's a new one. I'll have to add it to my slang. Lets go to the bedroom," Beth suggested.

They crossed the expanse of the sitting area and crowded into the bedroom, where Beth continued with the briefing.

"In here, we've reports of the bed shaking, moved objects, missing personal items—particularly clothing. A few guests have reported hearing a voice telling them to get out."

"Could they distinguish if it was male or female?" Doug asked.

"Male."

"Interesting. Let's hope it is Simon," Steve commented. He walked over to the bathroom and poked his head into the water lover's paradise. "Wow. That's a hell of a bathroom."

Laurel smiled. "Isn't it? I love it."

"I bet. Any activity in there?" Steve looked to Beth.

"Not that I'm aware of. Especially since we've remodeled it."

"Huh. I still think we should put a recorder in there as well. You never know what we might pick up."

"Right. We've got plenty of cameras," Doug agreed.

As a group they left Laurel's room, descended the stairs, and walked into the main room. Laurel went to the window to watch the rain which had begun to fall in earnest, while Beth plopped herself down on the couch. The two BAPS hunters opened their suitcases and started pulling out equipment. They unraveled extension cords, assembled tripods, and started hooking up the digital cameras.

"So, Laurel," Steve said. "You've been here almost a week. Do you have anything to add?"

"Beth said they usually can't keep this room booked during the festival, and stopped trying all together," Doug stated. "You must have set some kind of record."

Laurel shrugged. "I feel like a loser. Nothing's happened, no odd feelings, nothing missing that I'm aware of, no disembodied voices. And I certainly haven't seen any figures, shadows or otherwise. Complete zip." She laughed. "And here I'm the ghost lover."

"Shame. I wonder if he's passed on. It'd be great if he has, at least I think it would be better if he has, but Simon's got such an interesting past," Doug commented. "The stuff we uncovered during research was fascinating."

"True," Steve agreed. "Simon, the only son of Cora and Murdoc MacKay lived here until the age of sixteen. He lied about his age and went to France to fight. What we could find about his military stint was sketchy but colorful." He passed a few cameras off to Doug, who went into the bedroom.

"He was in a cavalry unit and distinguished himself. He was then assigned to General Lord Edward Carlisle, who was the third son of the Duke of Elsmere," Steve continued. "After that, he mostly falls off the map. From some dispatches it looks like he became an infiltrator, or what we'd call a spy today. You know, working behind enemy lines.

"There aren't any details of this part of his military service. Just that he achieved the rank of Captain and his name was mentioned with distinction in the rolls. We can trace him returning home sometime in 1809, and then we lose him again. He completely disappears."

Doug emerged from the bedroom. "I've set up cameras in both the bathroom and bedroom. They're ready to rock and roll when it's time."

"Thanks." Steve gave his partner a thumbs up. "Anyway, we do know Murdoc MacKay died in 1809 under mysterious circumstances. Whether Simon killed his father we don't know. But there's certainly enough weirdness for ghosts to be around."

"And on that note," Beth stood. "Dinner should be

ready. Let's eat."

"Great. I'm starving. Thanks for feeding and putting us up, Mrs. Murray," Doug replied.

"Beth, remember? And it's my pleasure. When two a.m. strikes, I just hope we find ourselves some ghosts!"

Chapter Twenty-One

Simon watched. *Not again.* Invisible, he lurked in a darkened corner of the lobby of his manor. It was late, the sun had gone to bed below the horizon while a heavy rain lashed Cleitmuir, casting shadows throughout. His mood now matched the gloom. Another day gone and he still hadn't found the blasted key. And now this. A crack of thunder rumbled in the distance. Another bloody ghost hunt.

He hugged the wall, a shadow among shadows, and approached the little group consisting of two men, Laurel and Beth.

"It's magic hour now," the shorter of the two men said. "I think we should split up. There's not much nighttime this far north, so our time is limited before sunrise."

"All the equipment is turned on and running," the second proscribed ghost hunter confirmed. This one was tall and skinny like a reedy tree. "Here are your walkie-talkies."

"Thanks, Doug." Laurel took one of the small devices and hooked it to her jeans' pocket.

The man identified as Doug, passed another to Beth. "There's a digital recorder on the table in front of the couch for your EVP session, you know, to record any Electronic Voice Phenomenon. Oh, Steve, give 'em a K-II meter as well."

The short guy, Steve, took out a hand held device that had a series of lights in a line. When he waved his hand in front of the device, the bulbs lit in a sequence from yellow to green to red. Steve nodded and passed the meter to Beth.

"Are you okay with all this stuff?" Steve asked.

"Don't worry about us," Beth assured him. "We've got all the lingo and equipment down, years of study under our belts."

Laurel laughed. "I don't think watching the television show, *Ghost Hunters*, makes us experts, Beth."

"We might not be like Jason and Grant, plumbers by day, ghost hunters at night," Beth paused in order to mimic the show's intro. "But we know our way around a dark spooky mansion. Particularly when it's *my* mansion." Beth chuckled.

"We're losing the night, so if you're sure you two will be good on your own, we should start," suggested Doug.

"I know you girls will be alone in Simon's room," Steve added. "But there shouldn't be any cause for alarm. We've no proof he's a murderer or violent spirit. No one's gotten hurt. But if you get unsettled or anything, just call us on the walkie-talkie."

"We'll be fine," Laurel reassured him. "Come on, Beth, let's investigate."

"Back at ya. I've got a ton of questions right here," Beth tapped a finger to her forehead, "for my ghosts lurking in my house." She laughed again and by the light of their small torches, climbed the stairs toward the second floor.

Shite. They had to be joking. Did they really fear

him? Think him a scary, harmful spirit? True he had "chased" many a guest away who stayed in his room, but he never hurt anyone. If they wanted a true fright, all they had to do was enter room 302. Inside was Mrs. MacLeod. She'd died while bedding a sailor. She haunted all of eternity in a lacy teddy, all seventeen stones of her. Now that was terrifying. He chuckled to himself.

During his sojourn in this purgatory, he had noticed other spirits occupying Cleitmuir. He'd even hoped to meet his father, who if anyone had a reason to haunt, it was his da. But he never came across the late Earl, and Cleitmuir's other ghosts, though he could see them, never acknowledged him. Across the centuries he had wondered why. He could only surmise though he died, he wasn't like them, not a real ghost. Something else, something cursed.

Frustrated, Simon made up his mind and followed the two men into the old study. The hunters wanted dangerous, he'd give it to them. He'd spent years behind the French lines where one misstep meant his life, or worse, the lives of the soldiers fighting against Bonaparte. He liked danger, thrived on it, and in return became a dangerous man himself. This time at least, he needn't worry about dying. It was time he had a wee bit of fun.

He noted the fixed camera's position and waited to see what Doug and Steve were up to. The men had taken seats by the bookcase directly across from the camera and placed what they'd called a handheld recorder and the K-II meter on the table between them.

"Start EVP session, 2:30 a.m., Doug and Steve in the office," Steve announced and paused. "Is there anybody in this room with us tonight? My name is Steve and this is Doug. We mean you no harm. Can you tell us your name? Make a noise, move something, touch one of us."

Simon grinned and crossed his arms. Not bloody likely.

The silence in the room remained unbroken except for the rain pounding against the windows.

"I hope this weather doesn't mess with our recordings. Try the K-II," Steve suggested.

"Right." Doug waved his hand in front of the device causing it to light up. "This is a K-II meter. It detects magnetic fields. If you approach, you might be able to light it up. It won't harm you. It'll let us know you're here, and we might be able to communicate with you."

Simon frowned. Why would a ghost be afraid of harm? After all, they're dead not stupid, nothing could hurt them anymore. He walked over and stood by the device directly between the men, waved his hand across and all the LED's flashed on.

"Wow, did you see that!" Doug exclaimed.

"The video camera should have gotten it as well," Steve replied. "Let's see if that was a fluke. If that was you, can you please light it up again?"

He gave a mental sigh and waved his hand. The lights flashed on.

"It's a strong signal. Let's try questioning the spirit," Doug said. "Are you, male?"

Both hunters stared at the dark device. "Are you female?"

Simon smiled and waved his hand.

"Cool. Did you live here?" Steve asked. "Huh,

nothing. Oh, did you work here?"

Simon waved his hand again. The questions and answers went on until he had the two men convinced he was a twelve-year-old girl who worked in the kitchens. These hunters were choobs. That was until the tall one suddenly stuck out his arm, which passed right through him. Christ, that hurt.

"Steve, a cold spot. Get the thermal. It's subtle, but it might pick up."

Steve got up and went to the case sitting on the desk and began unloading the new camera. Simon waited. After two hundred years, he'd learned a trick or two. And with the tall sod sending sharp daggers through him with his touch, Simon deserved a little pick-me-up. He felt the contained energy in the thermal camera as it powered up. Before Steve could raise the lens to scan the room, Simon concentrated and felt the power from the battery surge across the room and flood into him. He stepped away from Doug's prodding arm.

"Hey, the camera's dead! This was a new battery. I know I charged it."

"Check the video camera, did it drain as well?" Doug asked. "The voice recorder is still fine."

"Hang on," Steve went to the camera and checked the recorder. "Nope, it's good. I'll just swap out for the spare."

Simon watched as the man juggled his torch and changed batteries.

I don't think so, smartarse. He felt the camera powering up, and with little concentration, just like before, the burst of energy hit him, draining the second battery dry. That was more like it. He felt stronger and more powerful after sucking the two batteries dry. At times like this, it was good to be a ghost. He felt ready to tackle anything.

"Damn, this one isn't working either. I guess we won't have any thermal this time around."

"Forget it. It's probably a great sign. Maybe there's another presence here. Let's do more EVP work," Doug suggested.

Right. Simon had had enough. He looked up as if he could see through the ceiling. He wondered what the lasses were up to.

****

"I guess we should probably start working instead of chatting," Laurel suggested. "As the boys at BAPs said, 'time's a wasting'."

Beth picked up the digital recorder and turned it on. "Okay, let's be official." She cleared her throat then laughed.

"Oh, yeah. That's professional," Laurel teased.

"Hang on, I can do this," Beth replied. "Start EVP session, Lori and Beth in room 208, Simon MacKay's room. If there's someone here, can you please tell us your name?"

Simon, having returned to his rooms, sighed. Not this again.

"My name's, Beth. Are you angry that an American owns your home?" She paused. "Are you pissed we've made it into a hotel?"

Laurel grinned. "I would think so."

Simon almost laughed. He wasn't happy his home was a boarding facility, but at least it wasn't abandoned and in ruins.

"All right, smarty-pants, ask away," Beth countered.

"Umm, thanks for allowing me the use of your room. I understand normally it's a problem for you." She glanced toward the bedroom and then let her eyes wander the sitting area. "Why are you still here? Is it the gold?"

"Oh, good one. Ask him where it's hidden!" Beth exclaimed.

"I think if Simon knew where the gold was, he wouldn't need to haunt the manor."

"You're probably right. Oh," Beth exclaimed. "I've got another good one. Did you kill your father?"

"No! It was the MacKenzie bastard." Simon froze when he realized he had spoken out loud, but when the lasses didn't react he relaxed. It wouldn't be the end of the world if the truth of his da's murder came out. Simon had nothing to hide. Maybe, his protest had recorded. He smiled. Wouldn't that disturb the young modern MacKenzie.

"Can you do something for us? Knock, touch one of us," Laurel requested. "Maybe turn on this flashlight? See, there's a button. If you push it once, it turns on." She pressed the circle and the torch came on. "Press it again and it turns off." The torch turned off. "I'll put it here on the table."

Simon walked over and stared down at the torch. He wondered if he'd be able to turn it on without manifesting. Well, he had some extra energy from the batteries he drained downstairs. He reached out and the torch turned on.

Beth yelped and Laurel jumped.

"Oh my God! The light turned itself on! Can you believe it?" Beth exclaimed.

"If that was you, Simon," Laurel asked. "Can you

turn it off?"

The torch went dark and Simon grinned when both lasses applauded.

"Do it again!" Beth requested.

He turned the torch back on.

"Oh, this is awesome. Call the boys, they have to get up here."

Laurel picked up the walkie-talkie. "Steve, Doug? Come in. We're getting some cool activity up here."

"This is Doug," the voice came over the speaker. "We're on our way up."

Within minutes, Steve and Doug walked into the room and sat down with the women. Simon backed away and settled into a dark murky corner to watch.

"Do you see that flashlight?" Beth pointed. "It turned on, then off, then back on again...by request!"

"Really?" Doug motioned to Steve. "Check the digital camera and make sure it's still recording. It's pointing right at it. If we caught this on video, it'd be grand."

Steve got up to check. "We're golden. Go ahead and ask the entity to turn it off."

"Simon," Beth said. "Can you please turn off the light, again?"

The group waited with baited breath, but Simon wasn't about to turn the torch off. They could all pass out with lack of air for all he cared. He was done. He hoped they'd leave and torment the real ghosts of Cleitmuir.

The hunters stayed for another hour, spending time in the bedroom and bathroom, trying to coax him into more circus tricks. Of course they couldn't, even when they were standing right next to him. The overhead lights were back on and the equipment was put away. They'd be leaving, finally.

"That was fun, guys. Wasn't it Lori?" Beth asked.

"Yeah, thanks." Laurel seemed distracted to Simon, something that was proven when she barely acknowledged her friend and the hunters leaving the room.

"Let me show you to your rooms," Beth gestured for Doug and Steve to follow her.

"Great. We'll get some sleep and then start reviewing the evidence later in the morning. 'Night, Laurel," Doug called out as he left.

Laurel gave them a brief smile, but she was already turning away before the door was even closed. He watched as she walked to the window seat and gazed into the stormy night. She shivered, then sat, tucking her legs underneath her and picked up a pillow, which she hugged to her chest.

Simon drifted closer, pulled by her.

"You're really here, aren't you?" her voice was barely a whisper, almost as if she was talking to herself, but he felt the words knife through him. It was centuries since anyone had acknowledged him. Treated him as an individual, a man, and not some phantom. It was laced through her voice. An understanding.

"Let me help you."

A simple statement, one he should have ignored.

Simon manifested.

"You canna, lass. It's my burden to bear."

Chapter Twenty-Two

Laurel blinked. Was this really happening? It was hard to deny when he stood directly in front of her. A ghost had just materialized. One moment no one there, then, a slight opaque mist quickly transforming into a man shape silhouette. A silhouette that turned solid right before her eyes.

Her mind raced as her brain tried to process what her eyes studied. He was the mysterious rescuer from the plateau and then the handsome ballroom dancer. It could be no one else. The man was etched into her brain. A throwback from the age of Heroes, he was tall, easily six-four, built strong with broad shoulders and muscular legs, just as she remembered him from her past encounters. Striking. His deep black hair hung in waves just past his shoulders and matched the slashing dark brows and long eyelashes that would be the envy of any woman. The palest gray eyes staring back at her caused a shiver to race up her spine. The man exuded power and virility long since lost to his twenty-first century counterparts.

Yet this folklore hero looked modern standing there, barefoot in faded jeans slung low on his hips and a tight, plain black T-shirt that clung and showed to great effect a chiseled upper body.

She swallowed and forced herself to close her eyes from the vision before her. Was she just tired and imagining things? Clutching the pillow tighter to her stomach, she inhaled once deeply then slowly exhaled. She could handle this. After all, she'd asked for it.

Her eyes opened and found him still looming large a few feet away, seemingly as mesmerized by her as she was by him. She cleared her throat.

"Captain Simon MacKay or," Laurel asked, "Robert Cole?"

"Both." He admitted, his voice deep with a hint of roughness that showed through the single word. It wasn't until he spoke again that the warm Highland brogue rolled out. "I suppose an introduction is called for. Captain Simon Robert Cole MacKay, fourth and final Earl of Cleitmuir," he finished with a mocking, courtly bow.

Laurel dropped the pillow and stood. She wasn't sure what to do or say next. She was talking to a ghost. Never in her dreams… Too many emotions collided inside her, excitement, fear, curiosity, and most of all wonder. She had always believed in ghosts, but deep down never thought she'd see one, let alone interact with one. She took a deep breath. It wasn't like this was the actual first time she had met him. She'd danced a waltz with him. He even saved her from falling to her death. She realized then that she liked him, even his argumentative arrogant side. Maybe more than liked him as she remembered her racy dreams from last night.

"You..." She took a couple of steps closing the distance between them, but stopped at arms length. "How..." She looked up at him and took another deep breath. "Hi."

This earned her a smile, erasing the grim lines that etched his face since his manifestation. She reached her hand into the empty space before them and was startled when goosebumps rose up along with the small hairs on her arm. The air was cold. Almost frigid, a good twenty degrees colder than where she stood.

"A cold spot!" Curiosity took hold and she walked a circle around Simon with her hand stretched out. The cold surrounded him in a two-foot circumference. As if reading her mind, he answered her unspoken question.

"Coldness…it happens when I first appear or disappear. Your ghost hunters were right. It takes energy. The temperature will even out with time."

She stepped closer. Simon was right. It wasn't nearly as cold as before. In fact, she could almost feel heat radiating off of him now.

"Is it intentional? The surrounding energy drain?" *That was her question?* She could kick herself. She had a ghost in front of her and she was babbling about science? Laurel guessed she really was a true geek unless it was just the researcher in her, coming to her rescue. Since her brain must have shut down in all the magical wonder that had suddenly appeared. Or maybe a defense to hide the true feelings she'd grown to have for him. She felt like an awkward schoolgirl.

"Aye, well no, at first, but now, at times I can direct the energy consciously."

She smiled. "Like draining camera batteries?"

Simon smiled back.

"You were here the entire time? Why didn't you make yourself known?"

He ran a hand through his hair, pushing it off his face. "It's better if people think I'm only a legend."

"Then why...Why are you here?"

Simon hesitated, not responding. His handsome

face marred by a frown. She could feel his frustration and sadness.

He shrugged. "It's a long story."

She'd try a different tack. "Why did you choose to appear to me?" Laurel waited for his answer, cautiously hopeful. Maybe her attraction was mutual? Can things like this happen so quickly? *Stop it*. He probably just needed her help and nothing more.

"I really don't know." His voice was low, a whisper that disappeared as he looked away.

Compassion rose inside her. No matter how fierce and strong this man may appear, he was breaking inside and was reaching out, whether he knew it or not. Help it was. Without thought, she closed the distance between them, stopping when their bodies were close to touching. She took his broad hand in hers. He was warm to her touch, but then she easily remembered his embrace as they had waltzed.

"I do. I know why you're here," her voice answered, soft and low, not wanting to startle him. A tone one used to calm a frightened animal. "It's been over two hundred years. I think you need someone to talk to. I'll listen."

He studied her, then reached up with his free hand and lightly stroked her cheek. Something filled his eyes at this gesture, but she couldn't identify the source.

"Aye, perhaps I do."

Laurel smiled gently then took a step back. Holding his hand she guided him to the window seat, where they sat side by side. She released his hand and pushed the throw pillow out of the way. She studied him as he stared out into the night. She was reassured when she caught his refection on the glass. Not a vampire at least, just a ghost.

Dear God, she was comforting a ghost! Staring at him, she silently wished he was real, a man she might get to know, spend time with, maybe even grow old with. She couldn't get over how attracted she was to Simon, how drawn and connected she felt to him. If only he would feel the same about her. But who was she kidding. He was a ghost. She waited him out, comfortable in the silence which gave her the opportunity to study him. High cheekbones, square jaw, a crooked nose, obviously broken more than once to achieve the lumps that interrupted the long profile.

"I'm cursed." He spoke so quietly she almost missed his words. She waited longer, but he didn't continue.

"It's the gold, isn't it?"

That got an electric reaction. He turned to face her, eyes flashing silver in anger, lips pursed to a thin line.

"Bloody hell! No! It's *not* the gold!" He tried to leap to his feet, but she stopped him with a hand on his thigh. He froze. His thigh muscle clenched and released as he stared down at her hand.

Again, with a calm voice she asked, "Then what is it about?"

He exhaled, removed her hand from his thigh, and leaned against the cold glass panes at his back. "I dinnae know where to start." His voice laced with emotion, caused his accent to thicken, making him hard to understand.

"Excluding the obvious cliché, how about your death? It's probably why you're still here."

This earned her a snort. "You have no idea."

Again he pushed his hair off his face. An

unconscious gesture, for nervousness or frustration, Laurel wondered.

"I was murdered," he pierced her with his gaze. "By Alastair MacKenzie, the oh-so great-whatever relative to your oh-so charming boyfriend, Alexander MacKenzie."

Laurel felt her jaw drop and quickly closed her mouth. "You can't possibly blame Alex for your death. He wasn't even alive then! Is that why you're still here? To take revenge on," she affected a Scottish accent, "Clan MacKenzie?" Her voice dripped with sarcasm.

"No!" He looked away and closed his eyes, leaning back against the window once more. "It's complicated."

"Then tell me!" Frustrated, she felt like smacking the close-mouthed apparition next to her. Why did they always end up arguing? She was yelling at a ghost! Pursing her lips, she admonished herself to stay calm. Getting into a raging argument with him wouldn't solve anything.

"Please tell me. I'd like to understand."

Simon opened his eyes and stared blankly into the room. "With my da's death, an...item shoulda passed into my protection. I was murdered before…" he trailed off. Before she could ask he raised his hand to stall her. "It wasn't the gold." He sighed.

"My da and I weren't close. Mostly my fault. This...legacy was handed down from father to son, until me. The MacKay had been waiting for me to," he ran a hand through his hair, again. "It doesn't matter. He was killed and I left France to come home. That's when the notes started."

"Notes?"

"Aye. Threatening. Telling me to hand over the

treasure, or else." Simon smiled slightly at the modern cliché. "Well, 'or else' happened."

"So you haven't passed on because of this lost item? You've been searching for two hundred years?" Laurel asked.

"Aye. Given only one month, then back to the cave." His voice dropped with the last, becoming hoarse.

"What?"

"I come back for a bit over a month, the length of the Primrose Festival, every year since I was killed. At first I had no idea what or why, but I'm dead, not stupid. I figured it out."

"Only a month? Why?"

"God's will? Fate? The Devil? Does it really matter?" Simon's disgust was apparent. "This is the last time. I won't...I canna go to the cave again and die." His voice broke, and he squeezed his eyes shut.

"Simon," she placed her hand on his thigh once more, needing to comfort him, needing to touch him, after hearing the agony in his voice.

Slowly he regained his composure, but he kept his eyes closed. With his voice soft, his accent thick, he told her. "I was going to Sinclair House, 'twas the first day of the festival. When I entered the stable to get my horse, someone struck me from behind." He took a deep breath. "When I awoke, I found my hands bound behind my back to a mooring ring anchored in solid rock. Though it was pitch black, I had other senses than my eyes. I felt the biting cold and could smell the sea. They had trapped me in a cave."

He opened his eyes. "The tide was coming in."

"Simon..." Tears burned her eyes.

"People say drowning is peaceful. It isn't." He swallowed roughly. "`Tis agony as you try not to breathe, but against your will, you do. Water pours in, burning, stinging. Your muscles clench then convulse. There's nothing but pain, until," he trailed off, his breath came fast as if he couldn't get enough air.

Laurel pressed her hand hard against his leg, trying to anchor him, to draw him out of reliving his death. He closed his eyes again.

"At the end of the time I'm allowed, the festival's duration, the month," his muscles beneath her hand tightened. "I find myself back in the cave...to die...again...and again every year."

Laurel gasped and felt a tear run down her face. For two hundred years? With little thought, she knelt and turned on the window seat. She embraced him, slipping her hands underneath his arms to wrap around his back, hugging him and buried her face into his neck.

"Oh, Simon. I'm sorry."

"I canna...I can't."

Laurel felt him bow his head, and his arms came around her. She held him as tightly as she could when she felt the tremors shaking his body. The torment he had suffered. How had he not gone insane? Whoever was responsible, be it God, the devil, or Simon's own guilt, the cruelty had to end. He needed peace. He needed to pass on.

She eased a hand from behind Simon, placed it under his chin, and tilted his head up so he was forced to face her. His cheeks were dry, but his eyes held the pain of centuries.

"Please, Simon. Let me help you." Silence greeted her. She knew Scots were stubborn, but this bordered on absurd. He needed help. "You showed yourself to me. Not once, but three times. You say you don't know why, so let me tell you. You're reaching out. You need help. Let me do this for you." She willed him to see beyond his pain and frustration. "Trust me, Simon."

His grip loosened and his arms dropped away. Once again he raised a hand and stroked her face.

"So long," his voice was gravel and the pieces sliced into her heart. "Alone. Forgotten. Reviled."

His hand slid behind her ear, then down, caressing her neck before spearing into her hair and clasping the back of her head. He pulled her close. His mouth closed over hers, at first gentle, then needy, demanding.

She answered and opened for him. His tongue plunged inside her waiting mouth. Warm, wet, with powerful strokes. He moaned and her breath became short.

He consumed her. He kissed her like a drowning man.

Chapter Twenty-Three

Laurel was lost, trapped in the depth of Simon's need. Swept away, all thoughts fled, only sensation remained. His hand buried deep in her hair, held her tight. His other hand smoothed past her shoulder, stroked down her side to settle on her hip. He tugged and answering his unspoken request, she slid a leg across his lap to straddle him. The moment she settled, his broad hand moved to cup her from behind and push her close against him.

Simon was hard and thick through his jeans, adding a pleasant pressure to already sensitive parts. She heard herself moan, and her hips twitched. Both of his hands tightened, then he suddenly stood. She wrapped her legs around him as he started to walk, never breaking the kiss. She couldn't think, until his strong arms released her and she fell.

Laurel landed, cushioned by the soft, downy comforter covering the four-poster bed. Opening her eyes, she found him standing beside the bed's edge staring hungrily down at her. Mesmerized by his gaze she waited with anticipation as he slowly leaned forward. His knee pressed onto the mattress between her legs, and his hands tugged at her shirt, moving it out of his way. Warm hands grasped bare skin at her waist. They stroked up her ribcage raising chills as Simon reclaimed her mouth, this time slow and languid, but equally passionate. Was this happening? It wasn't like her, yet with Simon, it felt right, oh so right. She let go of her doubts and plunged herself into feeling. His warmth enfolded her, the bold strokes of his tongue, as he tasted her and she him. His flavor was purely masculine, heady, and addictive.

His hands moved and cupped her breasts, and she heard his growl of frustration upon finding them covered. He rose up breaking their kiss and stealing the warmth of his body. She shivered as much from Simon's hungry gaze as the night's chill. One hand gripped her T-shirt while the other reached for her bra, he yanked, and the clasp to her bra popped opened as both offending articles were dragged over her head. She lifted her arms and the garments came free to be flung carelessly away.

Their gazes locked for a moment, before Simon's gaze slid away, pausing briefly at her swollen, well-kissed lips, to travel downward. She watched him inhale and hold his breath as he stared at her uncovered breasts. His hands once again were at her waist, pressed upward until he cupped her breasts, gently squeezing. Each thumb moved across her tightened nipples sending waves of heat downward.

He leaned forward, his hair fell concealing his face, and she arched upward in anticipation. First the caress of silken hair, followed by his warm breath, then his hot mouth closed over her breast. Laurel's gasp turned into a low-throated moan when his tongue swirled around her aching nipple, followed by a light grazing of his teeth. Once again she buried her hands in his hair.

One of Simon's hands went roaming when he switched his attention to her other breast. Her stomach concaved as his hand stroked downward. Reaching her jeans, he deftly popped the button and lowered the zipper. Thank God he was familiar with modern clothes. He teased her first by cupping her outside her underwear, pressing the heel of his hand to her mound. She raised her knee and placed her foot flat on the bed, giving her added leverage to push back against the sweet pressure his touch built inside her.

Simon chuckled and released her breast, capturing her again with his gaze.

"Greedy." His accent thick, making the single word long and drawn out. Staring intently at her, his finger slipped past the elastic of her panties to teasingly touch her, finding her wet and needy. There was no way to hide or deny her attraction to him.

Whispering, "Simon," she barely recognized her own voice. She wanted more. Now. For once she'd allow herself to live in the moment, no second thoughts, no guilt, just indulgence.

He stood in one fluid and dexterous movement and stripped off both her jeans and panties. Her socks and shoes lost long ago that evening helped to speed things along. She should have been shocked, even embarrassed, laid bare before him, but just the opposite happened. She felt beautiful. How couldn't she when Simon gazed upon her with such hungry eyes? His expression and his body told her everything he didn't verbalize. Standing bold before her, his erection stiff and bulging behind denim, his eyes devouring her. Any awkwardness vanished as she stretched her arms toward him, slightly rising from the bed as her hands greedily reached for the snap on his jeans. She wanted to touch, to feel, to return the pleasure he gave her.

A slight smile curved his mouth, as he shook his head and gently grasped her seeking hands. He leaned forward, using his body to press her deeper into the mattress and stretched her arms above her head. His lips caressed her forehead, and he kissed his way to her ear and whispered, “not just yet, lass.” His hot breath tickled her lobe.

“I’ll be needing you good and ready.” His graveled words held an erotic promise.

Simon released her and stood between her legs. His hands gripped her thighs as he dropped to his knees at the edge of the bed. In seconds, her legs were draped over his shoulders. A squeak of surprise escaped her throat. His mouth pressed an intimate kiss to her inner thigh as agile fingers caressed upwards, reaching where she most needed him. He trailed kisses upward, until his mouth replaced fingers in the most carnal of kisses.

Laurel didn’t want him anywhere else but there. The man knew what he was doing. Apparently this art form had been around a long time. He teased and tantalized her with his tongue. Her hips twisted and his hands moved from her thighs to cup her bottom, lifting her, trapping her against him. A whimper escaped her as she tried to move, her body wanted to answer the ancient rhythm instilled deep in her DNA, but he wouldn’t let her.

His tongue passed her swollen folds and pierced her. Her hips bucked within his tight hold. When he sucked her nub into his mouth Laurel moaned. She clutched the comforter with both hands. Her breaths came short and fast, and she felt a familiar pressure begin to build.

Finally Simon released his tight grip, and she could

move her hips, grinding and pressing, desperately seeking her release. He added his finger as he continued to suckle, and she exploded.

She shouted as the orgasm threatened to pull her under, and she arched up off the bed, hips bucking. White lights glittered behind tightly closed eyelids. He kept her there, spiraling in the heavens until she thought her heart would burst.

Laurel collapsed onto the bed, eyes closed, panting. That had been the most amazing orgasm of her life, and he hadn't even been inside her. All her muscles loose and warm, she didn't think she'd be able to move any time soon. Any thoughts of Derek or Alex were wiped clean from her mind. Simon was all that remained. She could see herself falling in love with him. Hard on the heels of that thought, she realized the danger she was in. How much further could this go? He was a ghost. She heard his quiet chuckle and felt the soft caress of his hands, pass her hips and down her thighs, leaving her when he reached her knees which draped limply off the bed.

"Simon." She needed to talk with him. Her breathing slowed and she shivered when a brush of cold air stroked her legs and canvassed the rest of her naked body.

What should she say to him? That she was in love with him? That this could go no further? Laurel wanted him, but it was impossible in her mind. She didn't know what to do. And he stood there without saying a word.

"Simon?" She struggled up onto her elbows and finally opened her eyes.

The room was empty. Simon had disappeared.

Chapter Twenty-Four

Sinclair House
July 1809

Simon was done with games. Deciding on the direct approach, he rode to Sinclair House to confront Fiona. The threatening notes and harassing crimes had gone on long enough, especially now with the last threat's deadline less than a week away. If his betrothed held the identity of his mysterious tormentor, he would get it out of her. Enough was enough.

Cantering to the stables, he pulled his horse up and dismounted in a single fluid motion. Before he could take a step, Billy, the stable lad, was at his side taking hold of the reins.

"Will you be staying long, my lord?" The young boy's question squeaked out.

"Unsure," he replied.

With a quick nod, Billy led the horse into the stable, leaving him standing outside, alone.

"Simon?"

Hearing his name, he turned toward the house and saw Dougal Sinclair. Fiona's older brother strode down the stone path heading in his direction. It was once a rare sight to see Dougal by himself, but since his twin, Byron married last year, it was now a common occurrence.

"Aye, Dougie."

"Byron's arrived. He and wee Catherine got in last night. Are you here for a visit?" Dougal asked reaching his side.

"Nay. I'm looking for your sister. Do you know where Fi's at?"

Dougal glanced away. "Ah…not sure. Both Byron and Cat mentioned this morning about going to Cleitmuir to visit. You're here now, why not come in the house?"

Simon's inner alarm went off. Dougie was never a good liar, it was Byron who had the gift. "I need to see, Fiona."

"Umm," his friend trailed off. "Really, you should just come in."

"Dougal."

His friend's face filled with guilt. Simon waited him out, silently.

"Simon, you don't need to see her right now," Dougal evaded.

"Aye, I do. Quit havering and tell me what's going on. Spit it out, man."

Dougal shook his head, then met his gaze straight on. "She's in the garden. I'm sorry Simon, she's not alone."

He quirked an eyebrow as he watched Dougal brush his hair off his face, clearly uncomfortable.

"Alastair MacKenzie."

MacKenzie? Fiona wasn't fond of him.

"How long?" Anger tinged his question. It wasn't from being cuckold, but more about MacKenzie. It didn't fit. Was Alastair behind it all? Had he been responsible for his da's death? Anger boiled into rage.

"About when your da disappeared… Fi was heartbroken. And when they found the Earl's body, well, you weren't here were you?" Dougal's arrow struck home.

Aye, he'd been off fighting someone else's war, doing everything in his power to avoid the issues with his father. Well, he got his wish. He'd never have to confront his da again, and Simon hadn't been there for his remaining family or friends. Guilt washed through him.

He shook his head, needing to focus. He couldn't change the past, but he could do something about the future. Protecting his family was paramount, and if Fiona was being used, whether she liked it or not, he would protect her as well. He needed to find out if MacKenzie was guilty. It was an easier idea than Fiona plotting alone against his family. Simon spun on his boot heel and strode off to the garden.

He only made it few steps before Dougal grabbed his arm.

"Simon, stop. You can't go charging in there. She's my sister. Please don't shame her. I know she should have told you, but—"

"Enough." He turned and faced his friend. "Do ye think me a monster?"

"Just don't…hurt her," Dougal pleaded.

He stared at his friend in disbelief. Did Dougal really think him capable of such action? Had he changed that much since his time on the Continent and his father's murder? There were moments he felt he had, war changes a man, especially when he went off as a lad with an ego too big for his body. He had grown up while fighting Napoleon, it had taught him the lessons his da had tried to instill in him. His thoughts went back to that fateful Halloween night, and all the times he had been foolhardy and rebellious up to then, and realized just how childish he had acted. Regret rode Simon like a constant companion. He met his friend's worried gaze.

"Don't fash yourself. I'll not hurt her. I just…" He shrugged. He didn't know what he'd do—only that he needed answers and to stop the threat to his family. It'd be easier if MacKenzie were to blame. He'd never liked the dandy Highlander.

Dougal dropped his hand away from Simon's arm with a sigh, and nodded. Simon turned from his friend and went to the garden hoping his answers lay within.

What he found wasn't what he expected. Silently, he slipped behind a hedge affording him a clear view of the couple, but hid him from their sight. He stared as emptiness consumed him.

MacKenzie gazed down at Fiona with adoration and love. Two emotions he dinnae think the man owned. Alastair genuinely looked besotted. Fiona sat on a stone bench while MacKenzie stood by her side. Simon couldn't hear what they discussed, but Fiona's agitation was clear by her wringing hands and the frown marring her pretty face. Words were exchanged, then MacKenzie opened his arms, and Fiona leapt to her feet and into his embrace. A sharp blade twisted in Simon's guts. Would he ever have this kind of love? Watching the two lovers, he felt the agony of his loneliness pierce right through him.

He must have made some sound or unconscious movement, because next, he was meeting MacKenzie's sharp blue gaze. Fiona looked up from Alastair's embrace and gasped.

"Simon?" Fiona stepped out of the man's arms, but not before Simon noticed the possessive reluctance on MacKenzie's part to release her. He was clearly staking his claim.

Having nothing to lose at this point and only information to gain, he strode the gravel path to stop in front of the couple. "Fiona," he greeted, and then nodded to MacKenzie. "Alastair."

"Oh, Simon," Fiona's hand rose to cover her mouth. Both guilt and sorrow glittered in her green gaze. "I…never—"

"Hush, Fi," MacKenzie interrupted. "This is for the best." He wrapped an arm around Fiona's shoulder and tugged her close. "It's time this was in the open."

Simon studied the couple. He noticed Alistair's fierceness, but more, he took in Fiona's slight trembling and watched as she leaned into MacKenzie for support. A support Simon had never given her, never even offered to her, a support that should have been hers for the taking. He felt disgusted with himself. He should have treated her better, never thinking twice about jilting her, or how she would feel. He had been such a bounder, and oh so selfish.

Ignoring MacKenzie, he asked, "Do you care for him, Fi?"

She swallowed hard, but the inner strength of a Highland lass came through as she straightened her spine and stared him dead in the eyes. "Yes, Simon. I do. I love him."

Her words slammed into him. Would a lass ever say those words to him? He pushed his hair off his forehead with a frustrated sigh. "Fi, you could have told me. I would—"

"When?" Her redheaded temper struck. "When you first arrived, almost a month after your da died? Or when you locked yourself away in your study? I know!" She exclaimed as if discovering a brilliant idea. "I could have spoken to you on any of our outings." She flung up her hands in disgust. "Oh, wait, ye cancelled most of those. When Simon? Ye no' been there to speak to."

It didn't surprise him to see the smug expression on MacKenzie's face, but it made Simon uneasy when the mask of concern dropped easily in place when Fiona turned to MacKenzie for support. Games within games? His gaze narrowed in suspicion.

"You'll release Fiona from the betrothal, MacKay," Alastair stated. "Find ye honor. Take the blame and break your engagement. Leave no mark upon her."

Fiona's pleading gaze met his eyes. "I didn't mean to hurt you, Simon."

That was the hook. She hadn't hurt him. At least not in the manner she thought. She hadn't left him broken-hearted. He hadn't loved her, and she hadn't loved him. Simon cared for her deeply, like a sister. It was obvious now. That's why it hurt him to look upon the couple so clearly in love.

"And I, didn't mean to hurt you, Fi—" It was Simon's turn to open his arms. She came to him gladly, and he held her. Softly, for her ears only he whispered, "Do you really love him?"

She nodded her head against his chest. "Then my answer's easy. You're free to go, free to choose." A realization tore within him. Had he but tried, perhaps,

Fiona would have loved him as she did MacKenzie. He had never made the effort. Was something broken inside him? Or was it just not meant to be? Loneliness cut through him. He gave her a hug and pulled her slightly away to drop a kiss upon her head. "If you need me for anything, know I'll be there for you. Always."

Simon looked up and glanced past her shoulder to MacKenzie who wore a contemplative expression, his eyes, calculating.

"Fiona," MacKenzie called.

She left his side to return to Alastair's.

"If you hurt her, MacKenzie, you're dead," he warned.

The man chuckled. "I won't, unlike what you have already done."

"Alastair," Fiona admonished.

MacKenzie gave a kiss to her hand he held. "Hush, Fi. We're only marking our territory."

"Men!"

MacKenzie laughed again and pulled Fiona tight against him, before turning them away to stroll further into the gardens, but not before he shot a menacing glare at Simon.

Simon stared after the couple, thoughts churning. He didn't like MacKenzie, the weaselly cur, but if he made Fi happy he'd stay out of the way. However, if he were using her to get to him or his family, nothing would stand in Simon's way of taking his revenge.

Chapter Twenty-Five

Outside Cleitmuir Manor
July, Present Day

Simon watched in his ghostly form, as history repeated itself. Laurel and the modern day MacKenzie walked hand in hand. However, this time he was more invested than in the past. While he had cared for Fiona, loved her as sister, Laurel had somehow gotten under his skin. Ironic, since currently he was a ghost with no flesh. He was drawn to her, quickly becoming obsessed by her. He vividly remembered the feel of Laurel in his arms, her taste, the comfort she had afforded him, even in their arguments.

Had it all been a ruse? Was she playing him as Fiona had?

"Will you be at the festival's brunch?" Laurel asked as she walked next to MacKenzie.

MacKenzie smiled at her and squeezed her hand. "I don't think so, I have a meeting. But I'll make the sailing. Have you been out on the water yet?"

"No."

"Well, then," MacKenzie replied as he stopped next to his white Mercedes SLS AMG.

It was an ostentatious vehicle for an ass of a man, the doors didn't even open properly. They opened upwards, like wings flapping on a bird. The car looked fast though, Simon thought. It was one thing this century had over his, he envied the new version of horsepower.

"You'll find our Scottish waters bonnie indeed. I look forward to sharing the experience with you." He pulled Laurel close, one hand on her hip and the other cupped behind her head. He leaned in and kissed her. Long and lingering.

Simon's muscles tensed, and he had the sudden urge to materialize and yank the devil away from his woman and beat him to a bloody pulp. He grimaced. History wasn't going to repeat itself. This time he wouldn't let a MacKenzie take what was his. He'd fight for her. It had taken centuries to feel this way about a woman, and he wasn't about to lose something he'd never thought he'd feel. Laurel was his.

****

Laurel took a step back as Alex closed the gull-winged door of the sleek-shaped Mercedes. She hadn't realized cars still had doors like a DeLorean. Instead of the Flux-Capacitor kicking in, it was the throaty growl of the AMG's engine. With a smile and wave, Alex shifted into gear and drove away. She wrapped her arms around herself as she watched him leave. She was so confused.

First there had been Derek. A relationship of three years, where she had felt herself in love, but found it one-sided, her judgment sorely lacking, making her distrust her instincts.

Then, Beth had introduced her to Alex. She was excited a man so handsome and successful would be interested in her again. She had doubted at first, thinking back to Derek and her severe misjudgment, but

Alex, aside from looks, had acted completely different than Derek. Alex thought her intelligent, cared about her opinions, and treated her as if she were equal and yet special. It was night and day from her last relationship. She should be on cloud nine, but then there were moments she questioned herself again. Alex hadn't responded to her "no" during their kiss or again when she didn't want to go out on the dance floor. There were reasonable excuses for both instances, but her gut still roiled at the thought of a man who didn't respect the word "no".

Then there was Simon MacKay. A tormented ghost, over two hundred years old, who was irritating, over-bearing, yet had an inner strength and honor that kept him sane through the centuries. Handsome in a different way than Alex, more rugged, a warrior of the past, he drew her to him. It was hard to believe how the attraction had grown in such a short amount of time. It wouldn't take much more before she'd be in love. But what good would that do her when he was dead? There would be no marriage or children in a relationship with a ghost.

With a heavy sigh, she dropped her arms to her side and started walking, careless in her direction. The bright blue Scottish sky and the northern chilled wind, didn't even register more than a passing consideration. Lost in thought, she didn't know what to believe anymore. The trust in her instinct whittled to nothing.

How had this happened? Logic was her God. She could puzzle through anything given enough time. She always found the answer, but now, she just felt adrift. Laurel should be ecstatic that two handsome men were interested in her. Her gut told her she would pick Simon over Alex, but he was a ghost. Was Simon's hatred and warnings about Alex just a long held clan grudge? Or was Alex, an actual living, breathing man, exactly who he appeared to be? A successful, self-made individual who was attracted to her.

Who should she believe? Alex, the modern day treasure hunter or Simon, the out-of-time soldier? Who was telling the truth? Both would set her against the other, well if Alex knew of him.

She continued to wander as her thoughts meandered. Last night with Simon had been incredible. It was hard to believe it had happened. She wasn't one to have adventures. Boring and mundane, was her life. It was why, she admitted to herself, she had stuck with Derek all those years. He had been safe, a known quantity. Yet, she had ignored the voice in the back of her mind telling her something was wrong. Three years and no proposal? In hindsight, she wasn't particularly surprised to find out Derek had been cheating on her, just more shocked seeing it with her own eyes. What did that say about her?

Laurel found herself at the stable and entered. Gale poked her gray head out and nickered at her approach.

"Sorry, love. I don't have a treat, but how about some attention," she said as she reached out her hand and stroked the mare's soft nose. "Too bad you can't talk, I desperately need some advice. I'd talk with Beth, but would she believe me about Simon? I begin to doubt it myself."

Had she actually encountered a ghost? Not just once, but three times? And last night… Was that even her? She barely kissed on the first date, let alone allowed a man, a stranger, be that intimate with her.

Laurel couldn't explain her actions.

Except, there had been this connection. She felt she knew Simon, understood him. No explanation really, just a little voice telling her she was safe with him. It had felt like meeting another piece of herself. A missing piece she hadn't realized was gone.

"What am I going to do, Gale?" She sighed and gave the mare a final pat before she left the barn. She stared at Cleitmuir Manor and the distant cloud-draped mountains behind it. She wanted to believe Simon, wanted to trust him. Was Alex really dangerous? It was so hard to believe. Were the doubts Laurel felt about Alex, planted by Simon, or was her subconscious trying to tell her something? How could she trust herself? She needed answers. She wanted to talk to Simon, but had no way of contacting the recalcitrant ghost, damn him. She had a few words for him after the way he had just disappeared last night and, of course, questions, hundreds of thousands of questions.

Well, there were other options while she waited for Casper the friendly ghost to show himself. She wasn't helpless or stupid. She just needed more information—proof would be preferable. Answers were her specialty. As with the historical treasures she was trusted to authenticate, she'd treat both Alex and Simon the same. Laurel would prove what was real and what was not.

Chapter Twenty-Six

The door opened with a long ominous creak, causing Beth to giggle while she stuffed the key ring into her battered jeans' pocket. "That was completely appropriate for an entrance leading into a creepy attic," she gasped out between chuckles. "Maybe we should have had our ghost hunters stake out up here."

"More like Molly Maids, or should I say *MacMaids*," Laurel countered as she followed Beth into the thickly layered dust-filled room. The attic ran the length of the house. The room was easily tall enough to stand upright, the broad support beams lost in the vaulted ceiling. Small octagonal windows with chunky period lead glass were evenly spaced to allow some natural light to leak through. Though the room was big, there was little space because the area was crammed with objects—furniture, boxes, and an odd assortment of junk. No laid out pathways, just a haphazard piling of things lending the attic a tunnel-like maze. Truly a treasure hunter's paradise. "How long since you've been up here?"

"Ah, never?" Beth pulled the lamp chain hanging from the wall light. As the bare bulb flickered on, a cloud of dust descended, sending her into a coughing fit. "I had no idea there was even a 'here' here until you brought it up to Grant this afternoon. And, I had no idea it would be quite so dusty."

“Creature of habit…dust happens. I really appreciate you letting me poke around,” Laurel apologized.

“Oh, what’s a little dirt between friends,” Beth answered. “Besides, I haven’t spent as much time with you as I’d like. I thought it would be fun for you to visit during the festival, but now I’m realizing it’s just in the way. Stupid planning committees.” She walked over to her and gave her a dusty hug. “It feels like I’ve barely seen you since you arrived.”

“Nonsense. You’ve made plenty of time for me,” she hugged Beth in return.

“Hmmmf. We’ll agree to disagree. So, what are we looking for?”

“I don’t really know.”

“A woman without a plan. I just hope we find something super valuable up here. Wouldn’t that be awesome? Maybe I’ll be able to go on one of those how-much-is-my-junk-worth shows.”

“I wouldn’t get your hopes up, Beth. But then again, this is an old house, you never know what you might find,” she reassured her friend. “Just start digging around. If you find anything interesting, shout out.”

“Will do. How fun, our own treasure hunt, on the heels of our own ghost hunt. I can’t wait for their report. Maybe I should stop feeding them? They seem more interested in Cleitmuir’s offerings than their analyzing.”

“I’m sure it’ll be worth the wait. The video of the flashlight will be amazing.”

“I need to light a fire under their asses,” Beth joked before she knocked into a box and sent another dust cloud flying. After a severe case of coughing she continued, "I just wish our treasure hunt was in a slightly cleaner environment, perhaps with champagne and a massage? I don't know how Alex does this for a living." Beth grinned before randomly picking a pathway and disappearing behind a large walnut wardrobe.

Laurel brushed the loose strands of hair off her face then strode past a column of stacked boxes, noting the lighter coating of dust and modern cardboard, she easily dismissed them as too new. She needed something old, like a steamer trunk or an old-fashioned writing table. She wanted diaries or letters, preferably a signpost that read, "this is the man you should trust."

She sighed as she wove through the maze. Why couldn't anything be easy?

They searched for well over an hour. Though it was dirty and a somewhat drudge worthy task, they had fun. Beth started reminiscing about high school and the stupid embarrassing situations they'd gotten themselves into. She had always managed to get Laurel into trouble, harmless, but awkward trouble. During their afternoon attic search, she came to realize just how much Beth meant to her, and Laurel promised herself she wouldn't let so much time pass between visits. Beth was family, the sister she never had.

"I still can't believe I fell for that."

She heard Beth's laugh across the attic. "Oh, you were sooo easy! I know you wouldn't have spoken to Keith on your own, no matter how much you were crushing on him. There was no reason you couldn't just speak to him."

"Easy for you to say, oh Miss Cute, Bubbly and Petite."

"Pah. Keith was perfect for you. So it was easy to figure out when he was going to be alone in the library and send you to him."

"Yeah, but you lied to me when you said he wanted help on his history paper and was too chicken to ask me."

"A technicality. It worked out in the end after all, didn't it?" Beth asked.

"Oh sure, only after I realized he had no idea what I was talking about," she pushed her bangs off her face. "I was so embarrassed and felt like an idiot."

"But it did get you two talking," Beth responded. "And a date, not long after."

"I still don't know how you can get me in all these embarrassing situations, yet I'm never angry with you. I'm surprised our friendship has lasted as long as it has."

"It's a special talent—Oh! Found something," Beth cried out. "Get over here."

Laurel zigzagged through the maze and reached Beth's side. Bingo. It was an old desk covered in such a thick layer of dirt you couldn't tell the original color of wood. Beth held up a yellowing piece of paper.

"It's from Sinclair House. Apparently someone from Cleitmuir, but I can't make out the signature, bought the desk." Beth handed the receipt over.

Laurel couldn't read the name either and placed the paper aside when she saw Beth struggling to open the single desk drawer.

"Damn it. It's stuck." Beth slapped her hand against the stubborn wood.

"Here, let me help, we'll pull together."

They both tugged on the tarnished brass handle, but

all they achieved was the desk sliding toward them.

"Right. We need more leverage," Laurel stated, then promptly sat down on the floor and braced a foot high on the desk and wedged her other foot at its base. "On the count of three. One. Two. Three!"

They both pulled in sync.

With a large crack, the drawer suddenly yanked out, causing Beth to dance backwards to catch her balance and if Laurel hadn't already been sitting, she probably would have landed on her ass.

"Well, that was dramatic," Beth exclaimed. "There better be something good in there."

She offered her hand to Laurel and helped her to her feet. They both looked into the offending drawer sticking out of the desk and saw nothing.

"Gosh, that's disappointing," Beth pointed out.

"Hang on, the drawer was stuck on something or it would have pulled entirely free," Laurel replied. She jiggled the drawer, trying to slide it out of its track and remove it from the desk. "Hmm, still not coming out." She squatted down and peered into the drawer.

"See anything?" Beth asked.

"I think," she reached a hand inside until her whole arm disappeared up to her shoulder, "there's something wedged in the back." She contorted herself sideways to try and lengthen her reach. "Got it!"

She stood and pulled out a square cloth placket tied with a faded blue silk ribbon. She placed it carefully on the desktop.

"Wonder what it is?" Beth asked.

"Don't know, but let's see."

Laurel untied the bow and gently unfolded the cloth. "Perfect! It's exactly what I was hoping to find.

They look like letters."

Carefully she unfolded the top vellum in the stack, as Beth peered around her side. Neatly spaced cursive handwriting was revealed, easily readable.

My Dearest, Fiona, Laurel silently read the first line with growing excitement until Beth interrupted.

"Damn," she cursed causing Laurel to focus on her friend instead of the tantalizing treasure.

"What?"

"I've got to go. I'll just barely have time to shower before making another stupid meeting."

"It's okay, we made a great find. Well, you did." Laurel refolded the letter and cloth, securing it with the old ribbon, and then scooped up the placket. "It's probably the best we'll find so far, but if you don't mind, I'd love to keep searching just in case."

"Please, be my guest. Though why you want to hang any longer in this dusty, nasty attic is beyond me."

"Yeah, I know, but I don't know when we'll have time to search up here again and I'd hate to miss something."

"Suit yourself, but I'll only be gone a couple of hours. Don't make me drag your skanky self out of this attic."

"I promise I won't be much longer. I even guarantee I will shower and have read these letters before you get back. Maybe I'll have some interesting stuff to tell you."

"Well, I'm sure it'll be more interesting than my meeting will be," with a sigh, Beth patted some dirt off her jeans, gave Laurel a quick hug, and headed for the attic entrance.

Laurel watched Beth leave while lost in thought.

What would the letters contain? Who was Fiona? Was there something else hidden away in the attic just waiting to be found? There was still too much unknown and she didn't know whom to trust.

Chapter Twenty-Seven

Freshly showered and dressed, Laurel entered the common room of Cleitmuir. Glancing around, she saw there were only a few guests in the room—no doubt the majority were enjoying the bright Scottish afternoon. Happily, she found a couch to herself and curled up in a corner with plump pillows cushioning her body. The only thing that would have made it perfect was a cup of tea. Maybe later, she thought, as her curiosity of the letters could wait no longer.

She slipped the faded ribbon from the placket and unfolded the linen cloth. Opening the first letter, she let her mind focus as she began to read.

My Dearest Fiona,

It saddens me to read the dreadful news you have written. My deepest condolences to the MacKays. You are well aware of my feelings of the former Earl of Cleitmuir, but my admiration of him changed, at least slightly, on the day he let you go with honor. Having the MacKay declared formally deceased after his disappearance ten months ago, leaves the family with reputations intact.

However, Simon MacKay, I truly believe, isn't dead. Finding no future in his betrothal to you, he shirked his duty, abandoned his family, and most likely took their fortune as well, though Cora MacKay would never admit it. I am not singular in this dark belief. The timing of his disappearance with the announcement of the broken engagement was too coincidental. He was ever a selfish man. A tiger never changes his stripes.

I know the truth is hard for you to read and I am truly sorry if this saddens you, but you are a strong woman of good character, whom I love dearly. MacKay was never worthy of you. I have hastened to end my business in Edinburgh and will attend to your side in this time of grief. Look for me by the end of the week. I only wish I could grow wings and fly to your side sooner. You are always in my thoughts. Until we meet again...

Your Loving Husband,
Alastair

Written on this Fifth Day of May in the Year of Our Lord, Eighteen Hundred Ten

Jackpot! Laurel's pulse raced. So the rumor of Simon's greed had started immediately with his death. And he had been engaged! She wondered who Alastair was. Obviously the winner of fair Fiona's hand no doubt, but who was he? Perhaps the answer lay within the stack of letters. She carefully refolded the vellum and put it aside. Picking the next off the top of the stack, she eagerly wondered what it would contain.

My Dearest Fiona,

In joyful words I write what I am unable to speak. You have made me the happiest of men. On the morrow, we will be made one, man and wife joined in the eyes of our Lord. I have long awaited this day. That one so beautiful and fair could see any worth in me, has struck me as if Zeus himself had fired his lighting bolt and scored a direct hit. I will forever be your servant in this life and in the next for your gracious acceptance. You do me great honor.

Fear not, leaving your family and Clan Sinclair. Though I am a mere humble man, know you join into a great Clan of enduring history. The MacKenzie's will greet you with open arms, though I am loath to share you. You will forever be protected and provided for and I shall worship at your feet.

Thank you from the depths of my soul for choosing me, you will never regret a single day of our blissful joining.

Your Faithful Servant,
Alastair

Written on this Seventeenth Day of September in the Year Of Our Lord, Eighteen Hundred Nine.

Laurel stared blindly at the page before her, the wheels and cogs of her mind churning. It was so obvious now. Simon wanted her away from Alex because almost two hundred years ago he lost his finance to another MacKenzie. Were Simon's warnings spouted solely from jealousy? She needed to keep reading.

Almost an hour later she reached the last two letters in the placket. The common room was mostly deserted now, except for a male guest using the hotel's complimentary computer. The earlier bright sunlight streaming through the large glass-paned windows was now absent as dark billowing clouds from the North Atlantic flooded the sky. The saying if you didn't like the Scottish weather, wait one minute and it would change, held true. She never knew if it would be raining, windy, sunny, or just cloudy from one hour to the next. Laurel may not know how to predict Scottish weather, but she had learned a few things after reading the many letters. First, Alastair MacKenzie didn't have a high opinion of Simon and took every opportunity to share it with Fiona Sinclair. Second, it was also quite obvious the man was completely besotted with Fiona. Alastair genuinely seemed in love.

Laurel opened the next to last letter and saw that it was the shortest to date.

Fiona,

I beg you, please meet with me. If your feelings for me still are true, we must talk. Some disheartening information has reached me about your betrothed and you must be told. I plead for your forgiveness in advance. I never would hurt you intentionally, but I vowed to love and protect you, even though you may disagree.

If you still hold even the slightest kindness in your heart for me, meet me this eve at the fountain in the center of the hedge maze by ten of the clock.

A.M.

Damn, no date. Sighing, she folded the short note and placed it on the stack of read letters then opened the last vellum in the packet.

Dearest Fiona,

It has now been several months since MacKay has returned from the Continent following the Earl's untimely death. This silence between us must stop. You know he cares nothing for you and only I have given you my love. Nine years ago he selfishly left you and his family without word. He defied all honorable conventions being heir and first born to join the army, a lowly profession beneath his status. Since his return, he has barely paid you heed. These are not the actions of a gentleman.

It burdens my heavy heart to write these ugly, but truthful, words to you, but you have left me little choice since you refuse to speak nor even write to me. You know my love for you, my fairest, Fiona. It was I who have stood by your side and helped you through your grief. It was I, by your side, when you needed help and advice. It is I, who has sworn myself to you. Are you willing to throw this all away? For what? For a betrothal from the cradle? Do not let our love die a callous death over a selfish man.

Please, dearest Fiona, please contact me. I live in hell, suffering the fires of the damn with our isolation. Save me. Save us.

With All My Love,

A.M.

Written on this Second Day of June in the Year Of Our Lord, Eighteen Hundred Nine.

It appeared Fiona had stopped her cheating ways

when Simon returned from France and stonewalled Alastair. What had MacKenzie told her to change her mind? How had the engagement been broken? Laurel folded the last letter and placed it with the others. She gathered the yellowed linen back around the pages of vellum and once more tied the blue silk ribbon around the placket.

Her attention was drawn to the hotel guest at the computer as he stood. He noticed her watching him and gave a genial smile before leaving her alone in the common room. There was so much to ponder. Were the warnings about Alex purely from a jealous ghost holding a grudge? The letters certainly gave that impression of Simon. Yet, there were untruths in them, too. She already knew Simon hadn't abandoned his family and stolen the Jacobite gold. Instead, there had been threatening notes and his agonizing murder in a dark cave. How sad to think his family might have believed he had betrayed them. There had to be more going on.

She eyed the computer across the room. There was always more than one side to every story. Maybe it was time to do a little research on Alex. He had googled her after all. She stood and stretched then walked over to the computer. Placing the letter placket on the table, she tapped the keyboard and woke up the computer.

She launched the web browser and Google's page popped right up. Perfect, it was already set as the homepage. Placing the cursor in the search box, she thought a moment before typing in her request: *Alexander MacKenzie, Scotland, Treasure, Rare Antiquities.*

Surprisingly, the page filled with results. Now it

was just a matter of finding her Alex MacKenzie. She clicked on the first two links and easily ruled them out, the first being too old and the second a fictional character. Scrolling further down, nothing looked promising, and then she remembered Google's images. It would be much easier finding the correct MacKenzie if she saw a picture of him.

She clicked on the images button and the screen quickly filled with columns of pictures. Scrolling down the page, she saw lots of photos, but none of Alex. She thought she'd struck out until the second time she selected "more" and he popped right up onto the page.

Alex stood in front of the Scotland National Museum in Edinburgh. The side column bar held the direct link to the site where the photo was taken. Clicking on it, a website for an online news site popped up, along with a bold and screaming headline.

Grieving Family Blames
Modern Day Indiana Jones

What the hell? Right below the headline was the photo of Alex at the museum. Holding her breath, she read the article.

> *The Carver family seeks justice denied them by Scotland Yard against modern day treasure hunter, Alexander MacKenzie. Elizabeth (Ellie) Carver, 26, a graduate student from St. Andrew's University, was assisting MacKenzie on his quest to locate the mysterious Knights Templar's cave supposedly hidden on Sciehallion.*
>
> *Ms. Carver disappeared more than two months ago while working alongside MacKenzie. He had run into town to resupply*

and when he returned, she was gone. Her backpack along with climbing gear were also absent.

Rescue parties along with MacKenzie searched the area for over a week, but found no trace of the missing woman. The Carver's blame Alexander MacKenzie, a successful fortune hunter, believing he is responsible for her disappearance. They now think, since there has been no word from Ms. Carver, she must be dead. The family has pursued this line with Scotland Yard.

Laurel stared shocked. There was a picture of the missing girl. It was the same woman in the photograph on the mantel in Sinclair House. The girl she had mistaken for Alex's sister.

The Yard refused to press any charges, claiming there is no evidence of foul play. In their opinion, the woman must have succumbed to a hiking accident or possibly arranged for her own disappearance. "With a solid alibi, Mr. MacKenzie has been cleared of any wrong doing," stated the lead investigator, Inspector Trent.

The Carver's disagree. Considering it was just MacKenzie and their daughter alone together in an extremely isolated spot, their daughter could have been killed at anytime. They only have MacKenzie's word that Ellie Carver disappeared when he was in town. It is extremely suspicious in their opinion, considering the subsequent Templar treasure found in a cave where they had both been searching.

After all formal pursuits against MacKenzie have failed since their daughter's disappearance, the Carver's are now willing to try other avenues of justice convinced of MacKenzie's guilt.

"We will not give up," vowed the father of missing Ellie Carver. "My daughter would never be out of touch with the family for this length of time." Mr. Carver feels his daughter deserves the justice Scotland Yard has denied his family.

Laurel had to stop reading. She couldn't believe Alex had been accused of murder. It was shocking. Her mind reeled. Was that why he had the picture of the poor missing girl? A reminder of a colleague he had lost?

She scanned back up the article. Not a colleague, but an assistant. Yet, she remembered Alex had said he worked alone. He hadn't liked to share in the profits. Unless the article was incorrect, Alex had had an assistant at least once. Was it after this horrible time, he had decided to work solo?

Laurel checked the original date on the article and found it was only a couple of years old. It didn't make sense. Alex had been at his lucrative career for years. She needed more information, but how in the world to find out if he lied? Why would he lie? Why keep a picture of a girl he murdered? A trophy? Or had it been some horrible accident, and she'd just been a friend and he wanted to remember her?

Getting an idea, she scrolled down to the bottom of the article. Most online news sites had assorted links relating to the story. Maybe one of them would point her in the right direction.

She lost herself within the Internet. Following inner hunches and her knack of finding what she needed on the web, another hour flew by and she stared in disbelief at the two other articles she had managed to track down in the buried circuits of the computer.

Three. There had been at least three missing or dead assistants. Two too many for a man who claimed he worked without partners.

Besides the missing, presumed dead, Ellie Carver, she found Shaun Ryan. He died in a supposed diving accident during the discovery of the sunken ship *Gibraltar* in the English Channel. Alex had made a hefty profit from finding the steam and sail cruiser that had originally been used by the American Confederacy during the Civil War. Ryan's death preceded Ellie's by a good three years.

After more searching, she also found Eric Rosemount. He had been Alex's climbing partner when they found a cave on a rocky precipice in the Highlands of Scotland. Rosemount had fallen to his death, while Alex made a small fortune on the well-preserved Jacobite artifacts from the lucrative cave.

Sick to her stomach, Laurel stopped searching when she read about Rosemount. Two accidental deaths and one missing person, probably dead as well? Granted, all three events were years apart and obviously the places Alex went to were high risk, but what were the odds? And profitable treasure to be gained in all instances? Afraid to find out more, she stopped reading as a shiver chased up her spine. Three? Two dead assistants might be a coincidence, but three? She checked the date on the newspaper article. It was older than the other stories. Were there more?

Her gut clenched. He told her he didn't use assistants. He didn't have partners. Yet here was proof he lied. Did he stop using assistants because like the poor drummer in *Spinal Tap*, they just kept dying? Or was Alex a murderer? What if the climbing and diving accidents weren't so accidental? What had happened to that poor girl? Her instincts screamed at her in a way all the slanderous writing about Simon hadn't.

Were Simon's warnings about Alex to be believed? If so, she was working with a killer.

Chapter Twenty-Eight

Leaning against the piling of the battered yet still functioning pier, Alex wondered what was keeping everyone. He had been waiting at least twenty minutes. He closed his eyes and let the ocean breeze caress his face. The day was starting to warm now the sun had broken through the cloud cover and the wind was starting to pick up—a bonnie day to go sailing.

"MacKenzie! Are you daft? Where the hell have you been?" The shout echoed down the beach to him.

Alex opened his eyes and pushed off the piling and saw Grant striding through the sand toward him. He frowned then walked to the head of the pier waiting for him to arrive.

"I've been trying to reach you," Grant said, breathing hard as he reached his side. "Why haven't you called?"

Alex narrowed his gaze. "I had things to do. Where's everyone? We were supposed to start sailing at one."

"Aye. That was the plan, we're just running late. The girls are right behind me. We haven't much time," he exclaimed.

"What are you nattering on about?"

"Christ. You should have called me, and now there isn't time." Grant shot a look over his shoulder back down the beach making sure no one was around yet.

"Just spit it out, Grant."

"The ghost is real!"

"Bloody hell," he swore. "Not this tripe again."

"It's true. My wife had some ghost hunters out a few days ago. Today they revealed their findings and had evidence of Simon MacKay. I've seen and heard the proof."

"Get a hold of yourself, man. You're acting the two-year old."

"The torch. It turned itself on and off by direction."

Alex couldn't help himself. He laughed. Grant was coming unhinged and that would make him another liability, which was enough to end his mirth. He really didn't need this right now. "You're afraid of a bloomin' torch. It's just a light, Grant. What do you think he'll do, blind you? Not that I believe a ghost is involved. Find your spine. We have enough problems without you adding spooks to it."

He wished Grant would drop the haunting thing. What could a ghost possibly do against two live men?

"Was that all?" He let the sarcasm drip.

"Alex, I know I'm not convincing, ye, but it's the truth. There was a voice," Grant swallowed hard. "The voice clearly said 'no' to the question if Simon killed the Earl."

"Who cares? The murder happened over two hundred years ago. No one gives a bloody hell. Right now," he kept his voice a low whisper. "You should concern yourself with me. I am much more dangerous than a flickering light or a subliminal noise a mass hallucination has conjured into words." He draped an arm casually over Grant's shoulder and turned him to the group that was now a few yards out.

Adding in a voice pitched only for Grant to hear, Alex threatened. “If you’d like to join MacKay, it can be arranged.” He felt Grant stiffen under his arm and was satisfied when a shiver chased close behind.

He dropped his arm and put on a warm smile when Beth and Laurel stopped in front of them. The rest of the soon to be sailing merry-goers were still approaching.

“Grant was just telling me I missed the excitement,” he greeted the lasses, first giving Beth a hug and a peck on the cheek, then took a hold of Laurel’s hand. “Sorry I missed brunch.”

“No worries,” Beth replied, pointedly looking at their joined hands with a big smile. “You’re welcome to come over any time to review the evidence. Laurel can keep you company if you get scared.”

“I might have to take you up on it,” he smiled broadly. “But first, to the sea!”

A small cheer went up from the crowd as the revelers started to disperse down the pier to various sailboats.

“Lori, you coming with Grant and me or…” Beth trailed off.

“She’s with me,” Alex insisted. “Unless that’s a problem for either of you, lasses?”

“Not me,” Beth grinned and grabbed her husband’s hand yanking him down the gangplank. “Come on, Grant.”

Alex watched them disappear along the pier before turning his attention to the American at his side.

“Let me show you the coast. I’m sure you’ll find it lovely.”

“All right.” Laurel darted a glance at the retreating

Beth and Grant.

He didn't miss the slight hesitation to her reply. Why the pause? He firmed his grip on her hand and gave a small tug. Laurel let him guide her to his skiff. He helped her aboard then grabbed the mooring line and jumped into the boat, releasing them from the pier.

"Have a seat. I'll row us out of the inlet than we can get some canvas up."

As he settled the oars in the guide rings, from the corner of his eye he watched Laurel settle in. She was blindly staring at nothing in particular.

"You're awfully quiet. Is everything okay?"

He saw her shake her head, setting her silky, high-set ponytail swinging.

"I'm fine, just tired. I didn't get much sleep."

"Oh, aye. I bet you lasses gossiped through the night. It must be grand to have such a close friend. Were you speaking of the ghost of Cleitmuir?" He chuckled as he maneuvered away from the dock and started rowing.

"I take it you don't believe in ghosts," she replied, shading her eyes with her hand in order to see him.

"In all of my travels, be it to sunken ships, dark caves or archeological sites, I have yet to come across a spirit, or even a supernatural echo. I leave that stuff to the movies. You'd think with some of the tragic places I've been, a wee ghostie or two would have made themselves known. So no, I don't believe in ghosts," he finished with a hard pull to the oars and a charming crooked smile. "And I take it you do..."

She shrugged and looked out to sea. "I guess I always have. It's hard to believe in an afterlife and not think about some poor souls who might get lost. I just haven't had any personal experience."

"That is, until the other night," he cajoled.

"What?" Laurel snapped back around to stare at him, a shocked expression on her face.

"The ghost hunt," Alex said wondering why she was so startled. "The torch, the mysterious voice?"

"Oh," she gave a short laugh. "Of course. You're right." She gripped the seat with both hands. She gave him a sheepish smile than turned her gaze back to the water.

Alex mused the American certainly had odd moments about her. No matter, he had her well in hand. He'd be between her long legs before the day was through and then have her undivided attention with finding the treasure.

"Alex," Laurel continued to scan the water ahead of the inlet. "Are there any caves around here?"

"Aye, the area is riddled with 'em."

She swiveled to look at him. "Can we go inside any?"

"Sure, though most aren't verra exciting," he thickened his accent trying to keep her attention on him. Don't lasses like watching men row? She barely seemed to notice him. In fact, since she walked up to the pier, she's been distracted even distant. Well, he'd change that and a cave was just the place for a seduction, private and out of the way.

"But you never know, some of these caves were used for smuggling. Maybe we'll find some treasure."

"Maybe," she gave him a tentative smile.

They reached the head of the small inlet leading into the ocean. Luckily the swells were small for this part of the Atlantic.

"Help me get a sail up."

"Um, I've been sailing, but only as a passenger. I don't know what to do." Laurel shrugged.

"Well then, it's time you learned."

He gave her instruction and the two of them got the canvas raised, the wind catching it with a loud snap and shooting them forward. He coaxed her to his side so he could teach her how to steer. Any excuse getting her close. He'd certainly take every advantage to lean up against her and wrap his arms around her from behind in order to show her how to handle the boom. She relaxed against him and even laughed a time or two as she tackled the current and swells while trying to remain on course. Aye, a cave was a grand idea.

Chapter Twenty-Nine

"There. You see it?" Alex pointed as Laurel sighted down his finger. "The black smudge. Tack a little more to the right."

She adjusted the sail, and the boat skipped across a wave, spraying them with blast of cold water. She squealed, but held tight to their course.

"Just a moment more...now. Lower the sail," he commanded.

Their movements were sharp and fast and the sail dropped. He reached for the oars and locked them into place.

"We'll row from here on out. It's safer. Though I've known a few crazed souls who shoot the caves, blazing in with their canvas up. Suicide if they miss at speed."

Not ten minutes more, Alex rowed them into the dark entrance of a sea cave.

"There's a torch in the box next to you."

She rummaged through the equipment, pulling out the light and snapped it on.

A large channel greeted them with limestone outcroppings on either side well above their heads. The cave was deep, the light of the torch not reaching the far end, but it still showed crusty stalactites clinging to the roof.

"See if you can find a place to tie off."

"Will that do?" She pointed the light to an overhanging branch of stone a bit ahead. It almost looked like an arm to Alex.

"Aye, that'll do."

He rowed, luckily the current helped and they reached the outcropping in short order. He released an oar and jammed it into a crevice. "Lass, toss a rope around and tie us off."

Laurel scrambled off her seat, grabbed the mooring line, and efficiently looped it around the stone. She made a quick slipknot and turned back to him.

"How's that?"

"Great." He put the oar back in the skiff and stood, walking carefully to her side. "Let me give you a boost." Alex cupped his hands and started to lean over.

"Are you sure? If I jump, won't the boat pitch?"

"Don't jump. Just start climbing while I lift."

Taking his suggestion, she placed her foot in his hands and reached for the limestone, finding handholds were no problem in the pitted rough rocks. As she started to haul herself upwards, Alex straightened, aiding her ascent. She gained the ledge and leveraged her arms up.

"I'm good," she called down.

He released her and watched her feet gain purchase then pull herself onto the ledge. Sitting with her legs dangling over the edge, she looked down at him.

"Need a hand up?" She offered while extending her arm. "I'm not a professional like you or your assistants, but I'm sure I can lend you a hand."

"Nay, I'm good. Just clear me some space," he replied. "I'm use to doing things on my own, remember? I don't need partners, too complicated."

She got out of his way and without much effort Alex scaled the stone face and reached the ledge. He double-checked the mooring line before swinging the rest of the way up. He stood dusting himself off then reached behind him and pulled out the torch he had shoved in his back pocket.

"Right then, ready to hunt for some treasure?" He grinned at her.

She didn't answer him immediately. The American was actually frowning as she looked around the cave, instead of making eye contact. That wouldn't do.

"Scared? There's no reason to worry. You're with an expert. I practically live in caves," he chuckled then closed the distance separating them, taking her hand, and giving it a squeeze. "You're safe with me."

She stiffened at the contact before relaxing, and then shook her head. "It's not that. I know you wouldn't let anything happen to me. Or at least I hope not," Laurel said as she finally looked at him. "It's just...Oh, never mind." She squeezed his hand back. "Show me the money," she chuckled at her own bad joke.

"Aye, indeed. This way."

Alex gave a gentle tug to get her moving and started to survey his surroundings. He needed just the right spot. Shining the torch ahead, he spotted it. There was another ledge in the limestone that was perfect, a little higher than bench height, it was deep as it was long. It would easily fit two adults. He smiled.

"And here we are."

"Where?" Laurel looked around. "I'm not seeing any gold or jewels. Some treasure hunter you are."

"Ah, but you're not looking in the right place."

Before she could respond, he backed her against

the ledge. When her legs hit the stone, she abruptly sat. Alex lifted his hand and cupped her chin, raising her face so he could look her in the eye. "The treasure is right before me."

Her face flushed. "Alex."

"Hush, lass." He leaned forward and kissed her. Her lips were as full and soft as he remembered. Licking them, he urged her to open for him. He slid his tongue in slowly, relishing the taste of her, sweet and fresh, but warm like honey. His hand slid around to cup the back of her head, her long ponytail teasing his skin.

He laid the torch next to her and with his newly freed hand placed it on her knee and coaxed her legs apart. He stepped between them, and in a slow gentle caress up her thigh to her hip, he tugged her closer to the edge. His blood stirred and pooled, making his jeans tight. It was then he noticed she wasn't kissing him back. There was no passion from her. He broke the kiss, but didn't release her.

"What's wrong, Lori?" His voice was rough with his arousal, but he tried to temper it, not wanting to spook her. His hand gently stroked her hair. "Tell me, lass."

"Alex...I," she shook her head and dropped her gaze.

His hand left her hair and cupped her chin once more, tilting her face upward. "You know I'm attracted to you. I thought the same of you. Has something changed?"

"No. Yes. I don't know, maybe it's just this place."

Alex backed away a few steps, his arms dropping to his sides, giving her the space she so obviously needed. What the bloody hell was going on?

"I don't understand, Laurel."

"I guess it's just the atmosphere," she slid off the ledge and gained her feet. "I can't seem to get it out of my mind."

He stood mute, waiting for her to continue. He had no idea what she was nattering on about. His frustration grew. All he really wanted to do was lay her down on the ledge, strip off her jeans, and plunge himself deep inside. Have her cry out her passion as he did. He knew it would be good, if not better, than his tormented nightly fantasies.

"All I keep imagining is being trapped inside here, with no light, no hope. Dying alone."

It took a moment for his lust-addled wits to catch up to her words. What the bloody hell? How could she...

He stepped close, invading her space, trapping her against the ledge. He raised his hand and gently gripped her neck. "What made you think of that?" His voice was low and soft, and he never took his eyes from hers. It had to be coincidence, nothing more. There was no ghost.

"I..." Laurel tensed. "I don't know."

He unconsciously tightened his grip on her neck. "I think you're not telling me the truth, lass. Who put this idea in your head?" It had to be Grant. He was the only one beside himself who knew how MacKay had died. Grant would be joining MacKay shortly if he was the one telling tales. He needed the American on his side. She might very well be the key to finding the treasure.

"No one. Alex, you're hurting me." Her voice gained strength as she stiffened her spine. She tried to move away from him, but he had her effectively pinned by his body and the hold on her neck.

"Tell me."

"Let go." She managed to get her hands between them and shoved.

He was ready for her and didn't budge an inch. "Who told you about dying in a cave?"

"No one. Damn it, Alex. Let me go, you ass." She shoved again with the same results. He felt her start to tremble. There was no hiding it when he was pressed against her. Good. She realized she couldn't get away. Maybe, finally, he'd get the truth from her.

"Alex, please." Her voice was a whisper.

He released her and stepped away. She sagged against the outcropping and took a deep breath.

"I'm sorry if I frightened you, Lori," he looked away trying to hide his frustration. He couldn't completely alienate her. "I don't like the thought of anyone scaring you. You can tell me. If it was Grant, I'll just have a few words with him." Some he'll never forget. "He shouldn't have scared you. There's nothing to be afraid of in these caves."

He turned back to face her. He found her staring at him with a hand to her throat, massaging away the pressure left by his grip. "Forgive me?"

She finally met his gaze. "It wasn't Grant," her voice was timid but grew in strength once more. "I have an active imagination." She straightened and stood tall. "Don't touch me like that again, Alex." The threat was clear.

Inwardly, he was amused. Feisty bitch, he'd touch her in any way he'd like and she'd soon learn that. But not yet.

"I think I'm done with caves. Take me back,

Alex." She grabbed the torch and strode past him, heading back to the skiff.

Oh, yes. He liked a challenge and bringing this American to heel would be his pleasure.

Chapter Thirty

Hot water sluiced over Laurel's head and enveloped her body. She stood inside the granite and glass shower with her head bowed and arms wrapped tight around herself—letting the heated water and thin mist sink into her bones. She wasn't sure if she'd ever feel warm again. This afternoon had scared her, quite like nothing had before. She wasn't use to feeling powerless.

For the first time Laurel began to take the warnings about Alex seriously. He'd lied again about his work when she tried to get him to slip up about having assistants. When he kissed her, she had felt nothing. The passion she had for Alex was gone. It was hard to be attracted to a possible killer. And later…his reactions had been scary. He hadn't harmed her, not really, but she could still feel the iron grip of his hand around her neck. There had been this quiet, intense menace about him. She didn't buy for a minute he had been concerned that Grant had frightened her.

Alex had kept something tightly reined, and that was what had freaked her out. Worry of what he was withholding, what he was truly capable of. Trapped by him in the cave, she had no trouble imagining him murdering his assistants. It had been way too easy to visualize. She wondered if there had been more than just three bodies in his past.

She shivered and fought back tears from the aftermath the adrenaline rush had left behind. Dinner had been a disaster with Alex next to her. Beth, thinking she was doing her friend a favor with the seating arrangements, just made her want to scream and rip off Alex's façade and expose him as the mongrel he was. She'd quickly excused herself claiming a headache. She felt guilty lying to Beth, but in truth, by the time she reached her room there was a pounding behind her eyes threatening to turn into a migraine. She hated the fact she was shaking. Laurel climbed into the shower hoping to gain control of her cart wheeling emotions. She was a strong, independent woman and could take care of herself, but today, inside the cave, she wondered if that was true.

Was Alex a murderer? Maybe she was letting her imagination run away with itself. She just didn't know, but she did know she never wanted to be as scared as that ever again.

Laurel wasn't sure what made her look up, but startled, she glanced up and saw Simon. He stood a few feet away from the shower, frowning at her, dressed in his usual jeans, T-shirt and bare feet. She didn't think, only reacted. A sob caught in her throat as she opened her arms out to him. He didn't hesitate.

Within a long stride, he reached the shower, opened the door, and stepped into her embrace—completely uncaring he was still clothed. His arms wrapped about her as she clung to him and buried her face against his chest. He held her tight without saying a word. Hot water doused them as the warm mist swirled in the cubicle. This was real. The only thing that mattered.

Simon reached his hand up and stroked her hair. "What is it, *mo leannan*? Tell me what's wrong?" He pressed a kiss to the top of her head.

She couldn't tell him. He had enough tortures and didn't need to hear her fears, possibly imagined suspicions. And God only knew what he might do if he thought Alex had actually harmed her. She just wanted Simon, only him. Laurel realized just how true it was. There wasn't a choice at all. The connection she felt that day on the plateau, being in his arms when they had waltzed, and their kiss, had only grown stronger. She felt safe with him. He was deep within her blood. It must be some Highland magic, because she couldn't explain it. Didn't care.

She released her hold on him and grabbed his T-shirt, tugging it from his jeans. She pulled it upward, but stopped when his hands closed about hers.

"No, lass. Tell me what happened?"

She shook her head and met his silver gaze. "It doesn't matter."

She tugged on the shirt again and he relented, letting her pull it over his head as he raised arms. She flung it away. It smacked the glass wall and slid down to splat onto the stone tiling. It barely registered. Her attention was riveted on the man before her. Pressing her palms against his broad chest, she fingered through the slight dusting of dark hair then followed the trail downward as it disappeared underneath his low-slung pants.

Grabbing the button of his jeans, she was stopped once again. His large hands closed around her fingers, but not before she slipped the button free.

"Lass. Laurel," his voice was low and rough.

"No," she glanced briefly up. "I need you."

His hands loosened and she yanked his zipper down, slipping her hands inside and finding only him. *Dear Lord.* He hadn't been hard when she started, but grew so beneath her hands. She let out a satisfied sigh and tightened her grip. She was rewarded by a choked moan. Naked. She needed him naked.

Laurel reluctantly released him and started pulling his jeans down. It wasn't easy with the wet denim, but he took pity and helped. In short order the jeans were off and kicked to the side. Laurel got her first good look at him. His proportions remained true. He was large. All over.

"Simon," her voice came out husky and she reached for him, plowing her fingers deep into his long black hair and pulling his face down to hers. Their mouths collided in a slow gentle touch, and she sucked his tongue into her mouth as she pressed herself against the full, hard length of him.

He growled his approval, and his hands went to her hips, pulling her closer still. Their kiss was unending, and she grew light headed. She moved against him, wanting, needing to be closer. His response was to walk her backwards until she felt the uneven granite tiles of the shower's wall. The stone was rough against her skin, but she was heedless of the discomfort as warmth, hotter than the water pouring over Simon and onto her, filled her.

"Simon," she groaned into his mouth.

His hands left her hips and traveled upward to cup her already swollen, sensitive breasts. She arched into his hands, pressing her hardened nipples into his calloused palms. He broke the kiss only to start trailing his mouth downward, kissing her chin, sucking on her rapidly pounding pulse, licking the hollow of her shoulder.

"Laurel, *mo leannan*," he rasped out before his mouth closed on its prize.

She moaned and her hands flew to his head, holding him tight to her. Desired flooded her. Stroking down his back, her fingers trailed across his hips, and she reached between them. Her hands were filled with the thick hardness of him. She caressed and explored, feeling him, getting to know him.

His head jerked up with a sharp inhalation as below he jumped in her hand. She smiled just before he claimed her mouth, plunging boldly in, taking possession.

His hand moved purposefully downward, stroking her thigh then grasping her knee. He lifted her leg, placing her foot on the bench beside them, spreading her wide. His hand left her knee, brushed the inside of her thigh, then cupped her. Her head fell back against the wall as she gasped and rose to her toes on her standing leg. Oh, her nerves were on fire. Her breath came in short pants as he stroked her swollen folds, then a shout was ripped from her as he plunged two fingers inside.

She rode his hand, feeling herself close to flying apart, but it wasn't enough. She craved him. She didn't want him disappearing again before she felt him fill her. When Simon started to lower himself she stopped him by the easiest means in reach. She held his erection tight in her hand as she massaged him. His gaze flew to hers as his hand slid from her body.

"No more, Simon. Now. I need you now."

"I dinna want to hurt you," he replied, his voice heavily accented as his hips began to move in rhythm to her hands.

"You won't. I'm not fragile."

Laurel rose up on her toes and moved her hips forward until he was at her heated entrance. That was all that it took and Simon's control snapped. In a single swift motion, one hand grabbed her wrists, raising them above her head and pinning them to the wall while the other gripped her hip, and with a single powerful thrust ploughed inside her. He rooted himself deep, completely filling her. Wide, thick, and hot, there was no more room. Stretched tight, her inner muscles clenched at the intrusion, setting off a chain reaction when they found no give. She shouted as her climax caught her.

His mouth descended, swallowing her cry, devouring her. He released her wrists, as he needed both hands to cup her bottom, lifting and dragging her away from the wall. He pulled out only to thrust again, past clenching muscles to fill her once more. He repeated, getting faster and rougher. Her hands flew to his shoulders, clinging, her fingernails digging in, trying to hold on when her world continued to spin wildly out of control. She was flying and thought she knew what heaven was until Simon's head flung back with a cry and final thrust. He exploded inside her, sending her spiraling again as she climaxed higher still, joining him in echoing pleasure.

His head bowed as he rested his forehead against her shoulder gasping for air. The shower's water continued to roll down his back. Bright lights flickered behind her closed eyelids as she rested her head against the granite, trying to slow her racing heart and catch her own breath as her muscles continued to tremble and clench.

She had never experienced anything like what had just happened. She could never remember coming just from being entered. Let alone a never-ending climax which continued to grow when she thought there had been nowhere else to climb. She doubted she would ever be able to move again. Her mind was a much-needed blank. *Holy heaven.* If this was an example of what ghostly loving was about, she doubted a mere mortal would ever fit the bill again. A smile curled up her lips, but disappeared when a moan escaped her throat as she felt Simon slip from her and gently lower her leg back to the shower floor. With her body still so sensitive, the friction of his movement set off more tremors. His hands moved to her hips where his thumbs gently stroke her heated skin. He finally raised his head to look at her. The anguish and guilt that filled his silvery eyes shocked her.

Chapter Thirty-One

What had he done? He had rutted like an animal, careless and rough. It wasn't how a gentleman acted—especially to a woman he might love. He should have been tender, careful with her. Shame flooded him. He had hurt her if that last groan was any indication. At a loss for words, he stared into her eyes. How could he have harmed her?

His hand reached up and stroked her cheek. Her eyelids fluttered shut.

"Laurel. *Aingeal…*" His hand dropped back down to rest on her hip, his gaze following. "I'm…forgive me." He felt her shudder under his hands. Lord, what had he done? "*Mo leannan*, tell me, are you all right?"

She started shaking and he jerked his head up and found her biting her lip. "Christ, Laurel."

And then it happened. She broke out laughing. He stood there dumbfounded, watching her mirth, her eyes sparkling.

"I'm grrrreat," she replied, rolling her r's in an exaggerated Scottish accent. "Though in truth, I don't think I'll be able to move. Ever. My muscles are Jell-O."

Jell-O? He was stunned, not quite believing. Laurel managed to lift her hand to his neck and gently tugged him toward her. She kissed him then rested her forehead against his.

"Thank you," she whispered. "That was completely and utterly amazing." She sighed.

The foundation to his centuries old fortress surrounding his heart shuddered and crumbled. Her acceptance of him shattered the solid walls he had created, revealing feelings he'd long since hidden. Emotions thought lost forever. How was it possible? How, after all these years, in this time and place? His feelings for her earlier were possessive, he realized. He knew he had wanted her, but hadn't expected this gift. He thought to never feel like a man again. This woman had touched him, blended into his soul like no other, and somehow gifted back his life. He felt human once more.

He felt fragile and exposed, unsure of how to explain in words the riot of emotions crashing through him. It was too new, too raw, but he knew how he could show her.

Simon shut off the water. Steam swirled around them as he bent and scooped Laurel up into his arms. Her eyes flew open.

"Simon?"

He didn't answer, except to steal a kiss and give her a smile, before turning and kicking the shower door open. He strode out, both dripping water from their bodies as he left the bathroom and entered the bedroom.

He laid her gently down on his bed. This time it would be slow. His lovemaking, an extension of his feelings, making words unnecessary. A way a man showed his woman how much he loved her.

"Simon," Laurel opened her arms to him.

An embrace he was more than willing to fall into. *Mo aingeal*, his angel, his savior. She had reclaimed his soul. Her arms closed around him as he gathered her close and kissed her. Slow and heated, he took his time, relishing the contact he'd been missing, even before his death. This is what it truly felt to be loved and return that love.

Her hands began to move, trailing down his back in soft strokes. He deepened the kiss and rolled onto his back, taking her with him so her weight straddled him. Her hands buried deep into his hair as she sucked his tongue, taking control. He allowed it for the moment, enjoying her initiative and boldness. Without breaking the kiss that was turning more passionate by the moment, she began to slide her body downwards, trapping his hard arousal between her legs. His muscles clenched, and his blood surged to the point of contact causing him to groan.

She hummed her contentment into his mouth as she moved, rubbing him. Her own arousal more obvious by the moment as her warm essence smoothed and glided her intimate caress. When she broke their kiss, raised her head with eyes closed, breath turning short, her hips pressing harder and faster, he knew he had to take control or he would embarrass himself. Simon grabbed her hips, holding tight and flipped her onto her back. He knelt between her thighs, keeping her still as he caught his own breath.

"No, *aingeal*. Slowly this time."

"Simon, please."

"No."

He leaned forward and placed a kiss to her stomach, which quivered at his attention. Smiling, he trailed a line of kisses upward, until he reached her breasts. His hands were filled with the soft, large, globes. The hardened peaks of her nipples drew his gaze. God, she had beautiful breasts. He bent and worshipped them. Her breathy gasps turned vocal and heat flooded him at the sounds of her pleasure. He had never wanted a woman more, needing to please her, satisfy her, and make her his own.

Her hands spiked deep into his hair once more, but instead of pressing him closer, she tugged. He looked up and with a cry of his name on her lips, she claimed his mouth in a searing kiss, piercing him with her tongue, scalding him. He groaned against her invasion.

But she didn't stop there. One of her hands wormed its way between them. She held him tight causing another moan to escape him. He reached for her, but she was faster. Her tormenting hand released him and found a softer part of him. With a gentle rake of her nails, she sent him over the edge.

He cursed in Gaelic, gripped her hips lifting her. With a well-placed thrust he was deeply rooted in her welcoming hot tightness.

"Yes!" She shouted her triumph, egging him onward.

All thoughts fled as she clung to him and cried out her pleasure. He pushed past her greedy muscles, setting a fierce rhythm that had them both gasping and reaching for release from the pressure building deliriously higher.

With a twist of his hips, she found hers first. Laurel shouted his name as she soared. He gritted his teeth, determined to send her higher, stroking deep. He lasted only a little longer when his own sudden release took him by surprise. His back arched, and his hips jerked, once, twice, and on the third he fell back to earth.

Gasping, Simon rested his weight on his elbows, trying not to crush her. She lay beneath him, her eyes closed, breaths short and muscles trembling deep where he was still buried. He treasured her—her passion, her utter abandonment of self, her honesty. A gift across time, unsought, unexpected, but greatly appreciated nonetheless.

He pressed a kiss to her mouth and felt her smile.

"Gotcha," she murmured.

He laughed and shifted his hips, causing a moan to escape from his *aingeal* beneath him.

"Not fair."

He laughed again, before slipping from her and cradling her to his chest. She lay limp in his arms. He couldn't remember the last time he had laughed, or the last time he felt contentment. *Aye, a gift, indeed.*

Her finger traced small, light circles on his arm. "Once could have been a fluke, but twice? I'd have to say you're an amazing lover, especially when you've been so out of practice."

Suddenly she lifted her head and pierced him with her tiger gaze. "You have been out of practice, right? You haven't been taking advantage of some unsuspecting tourists, have you?"

"Nay, *mo aingeal*. I haven't been tooping the tourists. You've been my only one. My first lover, for a very long time, as my handling of you as no doubt proved."

She frowned. "Handling? Have you heard me complain?"

"Nay, but I shouldna be so… rough. I've acted like a mindless beast with ye."

Laurel chuckled and then rested her head back on

his chest.

His hand on its own volition rose up and trailed down her back, across her hip to her thigh, then back in a mindless, satisfying rhythm. She snuggled closer, sighing her own contentment.

"I want to tell Beth. I want her to meet you."

His languid caress stalled as he took in her words. "Laurel, it wouldn't…I can't. I—"

"Please." She caught his hand and squeezed. "She's my best friend. Beth might be able to help. Besides," she looked up at him once more, leveling him with her gaze. "Beth will stop trying to push MacKenzie on me."

He sighed and closed his eyes. She had a point. He didn't want his woman involved with MacKenzie. History wasn't going to repeat itself. Besides, the man was dangerous all by himself in this time. The past didn't need to come into play. He wanted MacKenzie out of her life. He wanted her safe.

And happy. He knew he would deny Laurel nothing. Joy had re-entered his life when he revealed himself to her. What could happen if one more person knew? What else might come to pass?

"Aye, lass. For you."

He was rewarded with a kiss. "But you need to tell me what was bothering you earlier." He opened his eyes and pinned her with his glare. "You were upset. What happened?"

She froze then shook her head. "Nothing."

He didn't say a word, waiting her out.

"Really, it wasn't anything. I promise."

He didn't believe her, but he wasn't going to force it and ruin the ties that were beginning to bind them. He would find out. He learned patience across the centuries and would bide his time. He closed his eyes and released her.

He heard her sigh as she settled back into his embrace. Simon turned on his side, draping a leg over hers, curling her into his body, shielding her, protecting her from her unspoken fears. He held her as she fell asleep. He didn't need to sleep, though he would have to dematerialize eventually as his stored energy ran out. But in the meantime, Simon held fast to his illusion of humanity, holding tight to the woman he loved and for the first time, prayed in earnest.

"Thank you, Lord, for returning hope to me. We haven't been on good terms, but for this, I'm eternally grateful. I'll retrieve the relic. And it will be protected once more."

Chapter Thirty-Two

"What's going on in that head of yours?" Beth asked. "You've been picking at your salad for the past ten minutes."

Startled, Laurel met her friend's concerned gaze across the table. "Sorry, just lost in thought."

"It's too early for you to be going through the change, so what's up with the mood swings? You come bouncing down the stairs all aglow and running late, which I might add, you never are, late that is, and chatted at me the entire drive to Brora," Beth fixed her with a knowing stare. "Now, when you're in a four star hotel having an amazing lunch while awaiting an afternoon at the spa, you clam up." She shook her head. "Lori, I know you like a sister. Fess up."

Laurel went for a delaying action. She stabbed a piece of lettuce, took a bite, and chewed slowly. How to tell her? What would Beth believe? She really hadn't understood either until Simon appeared out of thin air. That kind of removed all doubt, for her, but how to make Beth understand what was bouncing around in her head when Laurel didn't get it, either.

"Stop stalling."

Caught, she took a deep breath. "I'm not sure where to begin…you'll….damn…I've met someone," she finally spat out.

"I'm going to assume you're not talking about

Alex?"

"No," she shook her head and took a quick swig of her wine. Liquid courage. "God, this is going to sound so crazy. I've just met the guy, but…"

She couldn't say it. Admitting it out-loud would be like making it real. It couldn't be real. She had actually slept with a ghost, not to mention how fast she had fallen into bed with him. She just didn't do things like that.

Beth tilted her head, "but…"

Laurel sighed. Her friend would never let up. "He's swept me off my feet. I can't believe I just said that."

"Oh. My. God!" Beth exclaimed in a hushed whisper. "That was after-glow sex! You slept with him. You, oh Puritan, had sex with a guy you just met. I think I just saw a pig fly past the window. I want details!"

She felt her cheeks heat and laughed. Of course that would be the first thing Beth would say. Some things never change. "That's not the point I was trying to make, but, in fact, he's rather amazing."

"Wow, I can't believe it. It must be true love for you to have given it up so soon. Ah, love at first sight. How romantic," Beth quipped. "Thank God he's fantastic, or you'd be second guessing then sabotaging yourself right out of what might be a great thing."

She couldn't meet Beth's eyes, so she toyed with her salad. Great thing? How could this be a great thing when she was in love with a ghost? It's not like they could move in together, make a family, a life.

"Don't you dare think too much. I won't let you," Beth scolded. "Especially not when this is the first wonderful thing you've done for yourself in years."

Laurel felt her eyes sting and blinked rapidly before looking up. “That’s just it. I… I think I’m falling in love. It’s insane…too soon. It can’t be love.” She sighed. “I mean, there’s Derek. I just broke up with him. I need time to get myself back together. I wasn’t looking for this. I…how can I possibly trust these feelings? I’m so not the love at first sight kind of gal.” She shook her head.

Beth reached for her hand and gave it a squeeze. “Oh honey, is it two week vacation love or moving in love?”

She already knew it was the moving in kind of love, that’s what made her so crazy. There was no way Simon and she could have a life together. Her heart squeezed painfully. “It’s all too fast, too impossible.”

“Nothing’s impossible, let’s look at this logically. Your brain is wired for it. So, aside from the big ‘O’, how does he make you feel?”

“Of course, feelings.” She whined. “Like I can trust those. I thought I loved Derek, and look where that got me.”

“You are so not going there. Yes, you loved Derek. Your judgment may have been off where you placed your heart, but the feeling wasn’t wrong. It wasn’t a fault on your end. It was him. Derek didn’t love you. I’ve got a question for you. Does this modern day Don Juan feel the need to prove how smart he is by belittling you in front of his friends?”

“No.” But would Simon behave like that if he *had* friends? Damn it, no. She wouldn’t start distrusting him when all he had been was amazing.

“Then he’s no Derek,” Beth replied echoing her own thoughts. “I still can’t believe you managed to sneak a guy past me without me knowing. I need to meet this mystery man. How about tonight?"

"Um..."

Beth stared her down. "It's Grant's poker night, so he won't be home 'til way late. I'm all yours. I'm dying of curiosity."

"I, uh, guess so. I just don't know if he'll show on such short notice. No promises."

Hopefully, Beth wouldn't drop dead from shock when Simon manifested. She wished he hadn't disappeared again. It marred the excitement that had been building since she first met him. She vowed to buy every battery source in a hundred mile radius so he could remain at her side, forever, if that's what it took to keep him. She felt connected to him, a feeling that only Beth had held until now.

Love? Her heart raced. How had this happened? It was so unexpected and yet so powerful. Dear God, she was in love with a ghost! How could this go anywhere?

"Hey, Lori, what's with the frown? Stop doubting yourself."

"Beth, it's just, I can't see this lasting. It'll never work. I just don't see how."

"Look," Beth replied. "At the worst, it's a vacation romance. Those can be great. There's no chasing, no complications 'cause it's short term. Have a fling for once and turn your over-active brain off."

Laurel grimaced. How could she possibly stop thinking? Her simple vacation was turning into some kind of Hollywood movie. At first she almost started a relationship with a killer, and now she was sleeping with a ghost. How had she gotten into this position?

"Stop it! If this is real, love will find a way. Cliché

but true nonetheless. Don't worry about it being a long distance relationship. It'll work out somehow. Look at me and Grant. Quit second guessing, come on," Beth stood. "It's time for our massages. Self-indulgence, here we come."

She smiled and followed Beth out of the restaurant. Beth was right. For once in her life, she wasn't going to plan out every second of her future. She'd take the here and now, whatever time remained. She'd help Simon find his treasure so he could move on. She'd let him go. He deserved peace. Knowing he reclaimed his soul would be enough. But why did that leave her heart pounding and a sudden sense of doom creeping up her spine?

Chapter Thirty-Three

Laurel paced. It was getting late and Simon was a no show.

"You're wasting a wonderful massage and a fabulous gourmet dinner not to mention lunch. Will you please relax?"

She shot Beth a look over her shoulder and continued pacing. Damn it, he would be here tonight, he had to.

"Really. Please sit down. You've been fidgety all afternoon. If you got something to say, then just tell me."

"You're right," she joined Beth on the couch. "There's something you should know about… him. Something I haven't told you."

"No kidding? You haven't even told me his name, or even how you met. No matter how many times I asked, or even when I threatened you."

She chuckled. "I really wanted to tell you, but it'll be much easier this way. You'll understand when you see him."

"Soooooo? What's up? Can't you tell me anything?" Beth's smile disappeared and concern filled her blue gaze. "He's not married, is he?"

"Oh, God, no, nothing like that." She shook her head. "He was engaged, but that was a long time ago. Anyway," she took a deep breath. "Remember the night of the ghost hunt?"

"Well, since it was less than a week ago, of course."

"That's when I met him. Well sort of. I inadvertently bumped into him when I had gone out riding the first day, and then I also saw him at the ball, but it wasn't until later that I really knew who he was."

"No way," Beth exclaimed. "You hooked up with one of those geeks?"

"Ah, no," she felt her face flame. "It was more like the guest of honor."

It took Beth a moment for it to dawn on her and when it did, her expression was priceless—a cross between disbelief, excitement, and shock. "Shut up! You don't mean…"

"Yes, really. He was in my room."

"Technically, it's my room."

Laurel didn't need to turn around to realize Simon had materialized behind her. It was written on Beth's face. Her friend had turned sheet white, and her chin practically hit the ground. The expression "just seen a ghost" was aptly apparent.

"Holy shit!" Beth voice warred somewhere between terror and giddiness.

Laurel felt the chill of Simon's approach before his hands came to rest on both of her shoulders. A kiss caressed the top of her head and a whispered, "*mo aingeal*" lilted to her ears. She leaned back against his chest and felt his hidden laughter rumble through him.

"Knock it off, ghost boy. She has every right to be spooked."

"No pun intended, I'm sure." He released her and stepped around to stand in front of them, once again wearing low-slung jeans, this time a pale blue T-shirt with his bare feet. He didn't look like a ghost from the 19th century. It was good Simon just poofed into existence in front of Beth, or she might have thought they were trying to prank her.

Laurel stared greedily at him, already missing his physical closeness, but her attention was drawn to her best friend as she saw Beth had recovered from her initial shock.

"Beth Murray, let me introduce you to your ghost, Captain Simon MacKay."

Simon caught up Beth's hand, gave a small bow over it before pressing a kiss to her fingers. "A pleasure to meet you."

"Get. Out." She squealed.

Simon abruptly dropped her hand and took a step back.

"No, wait!" Laurel leapt to her feet and grabbed his arm. "It's an expression. She doesn't want you to leave. Honest. Beth," she nudged her friend with her foot.

"Oh, yeah. Right. Sorry about that. I guess you wouldn't be familiar with modern day slang, would you?" She apologized.

"I've picked up some, but not all. And don't ask me to text, it's like a foreign language, besides the phone would just die anyway."

Laurel smiled up at Simon and squeezed his arm in approval, happy the two most important people in her life were meeting at last.

"Ghost sex! You had ghost sex," Beth shouted then slapped her hand across her mouth.

Laurel closed her eyes and willed herself to disappear. Of all the times. She felt Simon's muscles tense under her hand.

“Shit! Filter, Beth. You have to filter,” Beth admonished herself.

Laurel’s face heated, and she was praying for Beth to shut up when Simon started laughing.

Chapter Thirty-Four

Alex tossed his cards down in disgust. He had no luck tonight. "I'm done. Deal me out."

Grant said nothing from his seat across the poker table. It was Roger who uttered the words bouncing around inside Alex's own head.

"Aye, mate. Good call before we wiped you out. Your luck's all dried up."

He glared at Roger then picked up his glass and slugged back the rest of his whiskey. Without a word, he walked to the bar and slammed his empty glass down. Taking the half empty bottle of single malt, he poured himself a stiff four-fingered dram. Damn, what was happening to drive him to get pissed faced?

He wandered over to the window, glass in hand, to blindly stare out. The poker game continued in the background, but he ignored it. His thoughts were lost in his quest, hell, his family's quest. He wasn't going to fail. The treasure would be his. He'd get the American to tow the line. He knew she'd been doing research, he'd press her for any discovery, maybe even drop a hint or two he wasn't looking for gold, but a priceless artifact. Anything to get more momentum going. He wanted that relic. He would succeed where his ancestors had failed.

Alex took a thoughtful sip of scotch. And if there really was the ghost of Simon MacKay haring about, he'd deal with that too. MacKay may have out maneuvered old Alastair, but that wasn't going to happen to him. There were ways to deal with the dead and Alex had vast experience. He had the bodies to prove it. He'd enjoy putting MacKay into the grave. This time permanently.

Chapter Thirty-Five

Simon consciously willed his hand to uncurl from the fist it had formed. Silently he counted to ten, before replying. “It’s not about the gold. It’s *never* been about the gold.”

Since manifesting himself to both Laurel and Beth, everything had been going along smashingly. For once, he thought there’d be no repercussions in revealing himself to the living. Both lasses were taking it in stride and he was about to tell them of the legacy, when Beth had to bring up the fecking Jacobite gold. It was always about the gold. For the past two hundred years, when people thought of Simon MacKay, they associated the name with a thieving greedy bastard who cared nothing for his family. It was the furthest thing from the truth. Lies spread by the MacKenzie clan.

“Beth,” Laurel interrupted with the patience of a Saint. “Why not let Simon explain?” She looked to him. “Go on, throw it out there.”

He pushed his fingers through his hair, brushing it off his face and sighed. “I’m not sure if you’ll believe me.”

She laughed at him. “You mean it’s more unbelievable than ghosts?”

“Aye, well, possibly.”

Beth decided to chime in. “Is there something more real about it than say, supernatural? Maybe you could start there…"

Bloody hell. There wasn't a good way to go about this. He'd already jumped into the deep end. He might as well seriously commit himself now and start swimming, because Lord knows he hated the thought of drowning.

"It's a religious artifact."

"Wow, that's so hard to believe," Laurel didn't try to hide the sarcasm in her voice.

He glared at her and then smiled. "We'll see about that, lass."

Simon started to pace. The women were eager, wanting to help, but could they? Would he be putting them in danger? Too much was unknown. He might as well get it over with. He stopped and faced the lasses.

"The MacKay's, our family branch in particular, were given a legacy to protect and guard. The secret had been handed down generation after generation, until mine," he sighed. "It's a long story, so I'll sum it up. When I was young, my da and I didn't quite see eye to eye. He died before telling me of our heritage."

"But what is it?" Beth interrupted.

"Aye, well, it's known as the Orb of St. Uriel or the Fiery Stone, depending on how religious you're being. It's valuable in itself, without the, uh, its other properties," he paused before blurting it out. "It's a single, solid, yellow diamond. Big," he spread his hands apart giving the women an idea of size. "It stands about twenty-five and a half centimeters tall. The stone is shaped in a three-dimensional teardrop. At the base it's a good fifteen centimeters wide, tapering to the top at five, and weighing a solid two kilos, smooth and rounded, no sharp edges."

"Holy cow! I'd love to see that rock," Beth exclaimed.

"Hush," Laurel admonished. "Yes, that's impressive, but somehow I don't think Simon's been horribly cursed over a huge, rare, diamond."

"You'd be right," he sighed. "Legend has it, the Archangel Uriel crafted the stone and imbued it with special abilities. He gave it to a handpicked individual to act as a seer. The stone grants its holder with prophetic knowledge and foresight. And therein lies its true value."

"Wow," whispered Beth.

Laurel appeared just as surprised, but neither of the women looked shocked or disbelieving.

"Alex knows about St. Uriel's Orb?" Laurel asked, getting straight to the point.

"Aye. History is repeating itself. The Orb was stolen from Uriel's chosen Seer and used for destructive purposes. Uriel decided it was too dangerous to leave it in mortal hands and he couldn't unmake the stone, so he gave it to the MacKay's to hide and guard it, never to be used again. The MacKay's gave their oath."

"How was your family chosen?" Beth asked.

He shrugged. "The MacKay's have always been closely linked to the Church, and the guardianship was decided well before I was born. I might have known more, if I hadn't been such a disappointment to my da. He would have given me all the tools I needed to protect the stone." He sighed, so was tired of reliving the "if onlys". His past could not be changed, but his future must.

"But if it's lost," Laurel asked, "then isn't it safe? I mean if no one can find it…"

"That's just it. It would be safe if only I was the last to know of stone, but the MacKenzie Clan found out somehow. Their family has been searching for it since before my death."

"But since they've never found it, it's probably safe," Beth replied. "If they haven't found it in over two hundred years, I'm thinking they won't."

"You're wrong," Laurel interrupted, chewing her lower lip in worry. "Alex is searching for it. You're right, Simon, it was never about the gold. Alex is hunting the stone."

Simon nodded. He could tell something more was bothering her. "Lass, what is it? You've been working with MacKenzie, how close is he?"

"I'm not sure, especially since I've been looking for Jacobite gold this entire time," her reply didn't hide her frustration. "But there's something else you should know, something about Alex…"

He stared, waiting, as Laurel wouldn't meet his eyes. She didn't look up until Beth nudged her arm.

"What don't we know about Alex?" Beth asked.

She turned to face Beth, obviously avoiding him. "I was doing research, you know, those letters we found? They painted Simon in such bad light. They didn't make sense. And well, Simon warned me off of Alex, which didn't seem right either. So I decided to research Alex. It wasn't easy, but when I found the first article, it was like an egg cracked open."

"What do you mean? What did you find?" Beth frowned.

"He might be responsible for three deaths."

"What?" Shock was written across Beth's face. "Alex is a killer! You must be wrong. I know him. He's a great guy. He's not a murderer."

"I don't know, possibly, maybe?" Laurel shook her head. "It doesn't seem right either, but it's too weird for the deaths to be coincidences. Two different assistants and one friend died. They could just be accidents, but that's hard to believe. I mean, how many people have that many close acquaintances die? I don't think they were accidents."

"Aye, lass. I told you he was trouble," Simon replied. He had no trouble believing a MacKenzie was capable of killing. One was responsible for his own death, and his father's. Maybe now, Laurel would stay away from him.

"Oh my God, it's like finding out Ted Bundy is my next door neighbor," Beth exclaimed. "I set you up with a murderer. You could have been killed!"

Beth grabbed Laurel in a fierce hug. "I'm so sorry!"

Laurel untangled herself and squeezed her friend's hand. "You didn't know. And we still don't know. He's never been a suspect in any of the deaths except one, and he was cleared. It really could be just a coincidence."

"It's not, lass, and you know it," Simon injected. "You need to stay away from him."

"But what are we going to do?" Beth asked. "What are the chances of Alex finding the Orb? Especially when his family has been searching longer than you've been dead? Besides, you can't even find it."

"Oh, but I have," he replied, obviously surprising them. "I know exactly where it is. I've seen it and held it with my own hands."

"Then I'm missing the obvious. Why are you still

here? Are you a ghostly guard or something?" Beth asked.

"Not quite. It's taken me over a hundred agonizing trips to find it, but that's not the sole problem. It's in a locked room below the manor in the catacombs."

"We've got catacombs—"

"Catacombs? Oh no—"

Both woman spoke at the same time making him frown. He turned to Beth first. "Yes, there's a whole labyrinth below Cleitmuir." Then he turned to Laurel. "What is it? What's the problem?"

Laurel sank down onto the couch shaking her head. "I think we're in trouble. Alex has a map. A geographical map of the countryside. I only got a brief glance, but my eye was drawn to a circle traced on the map. It surrounded some underground caves near Cleitmuir. I think Alex knows about the catacombs."

"Then we have to move the Orb right away!" Beth exclaimed.

"We canna," he replied. "A key is needed to open the door."

"Just pick the lock," Laurel suggested. "Or shoot it, or maybe use carefully placed explosives. There's got to be a way."

"We can't just pick the lock, it's not that kind of lock, or that kind of door. Do you think after all this time, I wouldn't have tried that or even broken down the door?"

They sat in silence. Stunned, as the pressure of what they were up against was felt. Then he saw Laurel straighten, sitting taller on the couch, a hint of an idea gleamed in her hazel eyes.

"How'd you get in though? You said you've seen it

and held it?"

"Aye, I'm a ghost," he shook his head. He knew where she was headed, and sadly the easy solution didn't work. "I passed through the rock into the chamber."

"Wow, that's totally cool. But why didn't you bring it back out with you?" Beth asked the question that triggered the hope he read in Laurel's face.

The gleam in her eyes disappeared as she figured it out. "It's just a guess, Beth, but I'm betting he couldn't"

"You'd win. I can't bring anything with me when I'm incorporeal. Well, somehow my clothes come and go with me, but that gift still remains a mystery to me."

"But again, if you can't find the key, then neither can Alex. So the Orb is safe," Beth declared.

"I believe MacKenzie has the key, but didn't know where the chamber was. But that's all shot to hell. He's closer to the stone than any member of his clan so far. Damn, bloody, treasure hunting, bastard."

"We need to find the key, steal it away from Alex. Without the key, the treasure is safe," Laurel announced. "I'm assuming the lock isn't your ordinary keyhole, right?"

"Aye, it's a small depression that's surrounded by notches. I haven't a clue what could fit into it."

"Huh?" Beth looked thoughtful but drew a blank. Laurel on the other hand had a guess if the sparkle in her eyes were a clue.

"What we need," she said while smiling, "is more information. I'll go into town tomorrow and do some research, 'cause that's my specialty."

"It's a plan at least," Beth replied. "What about

Alex?"

"Both of you stay away from him. He's dangerous," he warned.

"I still have such a hard time believing that," Beth shook her head.

"He is. I know clan MacKenzie like no one else can. He'll stop at nothing to get what he wants."

A chill settled deep into Simon's bones as he stared at Laurel. She sat on the couch looking thoughtful, her mind already deep on the problem. MacKenzie was using her to find the relic. He wouldn't stop, even if she managed to stay clear of him. If Simon could, he'd ship her back to America, keeping her safe and out of MacKenzie's reach. But sadly, he needed her as well. Not just for finding the lost key, but also for the life she had returned to his soul. That was more important than any lost family legacy or religious obligation. God, his angels, and the rest of the heavenly host could screw themselves. He loved Laurel and would suffer a thousand more drowning deaths to protect her. If MacKenzie so much as touched her, he was a dead man.

Chapter Thirty-Six

Cleitmuir Manor
August 1800

Simon crept down the dark hallway. He hitched his pack higher up on his shoulder and paused when he reached the top of the grand stairs. It would have been smarter to use the more private servant stairs, but at this late hour everyone would be abed, so it wouldn't matter. Besides, it was closer to his destination—his father's study.

Silent as a cat, he reached the foot of the stairs and then paused again before crossing to his da's sanctuary. It was pitch black inside the room, but he couldn't risk a light. He'd have to find what he needed by memory and feel. He wasn't about to be caught and stopped now, not when his plans were set.

He slipped into the room, using his hand to trail against the bookshelves to guide him. A few months ago, he had learned the crazy Frenchman, Bonaparte, had taken troops and crossed the Alps to defeat the Austrians at Marengo. The English were worried about France's aggression and put a call out for men willing to go to the Continent, unofficially. Though only ten and six, Simon's recent growth spurt enabled him to pass for ten and eight. He'd enlisted.

His ship was leaving at dawn, so all he needed now

was money for his military commission, and he knew just where to get it. His groping hand reached a break in the bookcases and quickly found the gilt-edged framed painting. From memory, he knew it was a stormy seascape, and from observation he knew there was a depression in the wall behind the canvas—holding articles his da preferred to keep hidden.

Simon pushed the painting to one side and felt along the wall until he found the hole. He patted around the inside, feeling books, loose papers, and then smiled when his tactile fingers discovered the small wooden box. It held the money he needed. As a member of the upper class, even if the English looked down on his Scottish heritage, he had to enter as an officer, which meant purchasing a commission. His da would be more than happy to pay the price if it meant his troublesome son was out of his life—even if he dinnae know he was doing the paying. Snatching his prize from the hole, he let the painting slide back into position. He slipped his pack off his shoulder, untied the strings, and dropped the box inside. It was then he heard the noise.

At first he didn't know where the sound was coming from, but when a bookcase directly across the room from him started to swing outward, his instincts had him dropping behind the chair he was standing next to. His eyes widened as the glow from a candle grew brighter and from behind the case, Murdoc MacKay, Cleitmuir's Earl, his father, stepped forward.

Simon glanced behind to reassure himself the painting was back in position. He almost sighed out-loud with relief, but caught himself just in time. His father pushed the bookcase, which closed with an audible click and then walked to his desk, first putting the low burning candle down before seating himself beside it. The soft flickering light revealed his da's careworn and tired face.

What was behind the bookshelves? He never knew Cleitmuir had secret passages and wondered where it led. What secrets was his da hiding now? He watched his father study the sapphire signet ring adorning his hand and his curiosity deflated.

The ring was the symbol of everything wrong between Simon and the MacKay. Responsibility Simon didn't want, especially if it came at a price of such seriousness and a world devoid of life and fun. He would never be good enough for his father, so why try? He had realized that over five years ago while kneeling in the Church. And now with Napoleon invading other countries, he had a way out. He watched his da sigh and then blow out the candle snub. Darkness fell, so he didn't see his father stand and leave the study, but he heard his da's dragging footsteps.

Who cares what troubled the old man and all the secrets he hid? Simon was done with him. He was doing his da a favor by leaving. His father would be free to disinherit him and claim a new heir to his liking. Neither of them would be burdened with expectations.

Simon stood and clutched his pack. He walked to the study door and paused, listening hard, making sure his da was long gone before venturing out. Silently he opened the front door and slipped outside. He walked down the steps and crossed the gravel stones of the drive, leaving Cleitmuir and his family behind. He never looked back.

Chapter Thirty-Seven

Cleitmuir Manor
July, Present Day

Simon materialized in front of the same bookcase his father had emerged from so long ago. It held no secrets now. He pulled a battered copy of the King James Bible off the shelf, reached into the barren slot, and then felt for the odd flaw in the backing of the case. Finding it, he pressed the knot of wood, replaced the bible, and stepped to the side.

On well-oiled hinges, the bookcase swung silently into the study. He entered and shut the case behind him. His body vanished, becoming incorporeal, since he didn't want to expend more energy than necessary. What was to come would be hard enough without draining himself.

The area was cramped, not much larger than a small closet, but then it needn't be larger for its hidden purpose. In a few short strides, the ground opened up before him. He stepped over the hole, hovering above the opening until he willed himself downward, not needing the wooden ladder that showed its age. The shaft was long, leading deep beneath the manor's grounds.

It ended above a cold, damp chamber that had four corridors extending in different directions—the start of the catacombs. It had taken Simon nearly twenty agonizing deaths to remember this secret passage, then another one hundred to solve the maze of the catacombs and find the room holding Uriel's Orb. After two hundred years, he didn't need to even think of the path, he simply ghosted through the carved tunnels bolstered by rotting timbers and thick cobwebs to reach the chamber of his frustration.

Simon stopped before the stone door and took the time to re-study the lock in order to describe it better to Laurel. He didn't want her down here. The catacombs weren't safe. That's why using explosives to blow the door wouldn't work. With the slightest of nudges, let alone a blast, a support timber could collapse, causing the tunnel to cave in. That was his fallback if MacKenzie beat him to the key and to this door. He'd trigger a cave in, killing MacKenzie and sealing the Orb in safety. He'd gladly do so now, but he doubted without MacKenzie dead and the key in Simon's possession, the artifact would be truly safe. The bugger was just too crafty.

He thought about what lay behind the door and all the torture he continued to endure because of the Orb. At least God had given him Laurel when Simon had been close to his breaking point. It was hard to stay sane after all these years. There were times he thought of letting go, blissfully let his mind collapse as easily as these catacombs, so he couldn't suffer anymore, wouldn't be aware, just a walking madman. But the consequences seemed too large, the Orb in MacKenzie's hands, the damage he could do to humanity, Simon's sense of honor wouldn't let him take the easy way out.

And now he was grateful he hadn't. Without a clear mind, he'd never have Laurel, or the return to feeling human again. But was it truly a gift? When all was said and done, it would be taken away from him. Would he ever have justice for himself? Or was this some grand punishment for his childhood selfishness? In the end he was dead. Life had no relationship with the dead.

He supposed it didn't matter. Simon gathered his will and his courage then stepped forward. This was different than the wooden spikes that speared him as he passed through his locked bedroom door—as different as ice was to fire, though both could be painful in their own ways.

Instead of a sharp pain the smothering weight of the earth pressed on his soul, crushing him, the granite dust filling him until he felt like his body would explode. The wall was thick. It took time, endurance, and strength of will, to pass through the stone. More pain for him to catalog and simply accept, after all, he didn't have a choice if he wanted inside the chamber.

He emerged into an austere open space. The small room contained a strangely preserved rug that lined the floor, a plain wooden altar upon which the diamond was placed, and a simple silver Celtic cross hung on the stone behind it.

Simon materialized and in three long strides reached the altar and knelt before it. He bowed his head and crossed himself. Hesitating, he lifted his gaze and stared at the Orb. He could see it, even though the room had no windows, essentially an underground cave. The chamber wasn't pitch black. A soft yellow glow filled the space and it emanated from the diamond. The Fiery

Stone was lit from within.

The soft illumination revealed the diamond's flawless state, an item of unearthly beauty, and the cause of all his torment. He had come here every year of his monthly manifestation since he'd located the Orb. He'd knelt before it as he had done during the night's vigil before the Archangels' Shrine when he was but eleven. If only his da had spoken more plainly, told him, instead of hinted. It could have been possible his father and even himself wouldn't have been murdered. His family might have remained together, grown old together, seen his and Jean's children and then grandchildren. But that hadn't happen. After all these years, Simon was beginning to understand his father. How could the MacKay trust his selfish, irresponsible son? Because he was sure that was the only description that bore out when it came to his da's opinion of him. He had been exactly as his da depicted him. If only…

He closed his eyes and sighed. He was tired. The thought of drowning in that dark cave, alone, once again, was a nightmare he couldn't suffer. He had reached his limits. Even knowing his drowning death would allow him to return once more and perhaps spend another month with Laurel at his side, didn't ease the sour bile circling his stomach. Time was running out. There was only a fortnight left, just fourteen short days. He was at the end. So tired, so exhausted. He wanted to see his mother and sister, again. Beg their forgiveness. And the MacKay, his da? What could he ever possibly say to make amends to his father?

Simon opened his eyes and stared at the glowing stone. There was only one way to make reparation and redeem himself. Get the key, retrieve the Orb, and hide it somewhere it would be safe for eternity.

He took a deep breath and held it. If it meant drowning another hundred times, so be it. He'd find a way to survive, keep sane. He would not fail he vowed as he bolstered his inner strength once more.

"This I do so swear," Simon declared, as he did every time he knelt before the Orb.

He stood and dematerialized. Hopefully, Laurel's research held the answers so elusive to him. If it did, she just might save his soul and his family's honor. *Bi Tren.*

Chapter Thirty-Eight

Laurel stopped her rental car in front of Sinclair House and stared at the front door, trying to calm herself. Simon hadn't liked it, but in the end they had agreed to her playing double agent. It was really the only way for her to continue to go through Alex's research. And it afforded her the opportunity to find the key if it was actually in Alex's possession. All of Simon's wishes for her to stay clear of Alex were just impossible. She needed to brave the lion's den to find the key.

She knew she'd find it. Or at least discover what the key was. Simon had carefully described the indentation in the rock face which was the door to the Orb's location, as well as how to get there in great detail. However, she had to endure a long lecture and multiple warnings about the labyrinth, how dangerous it was, and that it was on the verge of collapse. Laurel finally vowed never to enter the catacombs. The promise was the only thing keeping Simon from dogging her every step. She would focus solely on identifying the key. Small, round, and with serrated edges. How hard could that be to find?

Her gaze fixed on the front door, looming large and ominous in her mind. She so wasn't a field guy. She longed for her basement office at the Field museum, her computers, her books. Sighing, she made herself get out of the car and walk to the door. It was just research, she reassured herself. Who cared if she was alone in the house with a supposed killer who was mentally unhinged? A nervous chuckle escaped her. Yeah, right.

Buck up, Saville, she admonished. He hasn't even threatened you—yet. Besides, Alex needs you even more than Simon. Simon at least knew where the treasure was. As long as she made herself useful in Alex's eyes, there would be no reason for threats or murder. Comforted, Laurel knocked, and waited for the duplicitous bastard to answer the door.

She had spent the last two days getting her hands on anything to do with Archangels, Uriel in particular and the MacKay's history. She had learned a lot, some of it, she was sure, would be the information that would help. It was a matter of seeing the tree through the forest. And she would.

Alex opened the door, and Laurel plastered a smile to her face.

"You made good time," he greeted her. "I wasn't expecting you for another hour yet."

Still smiling, she replied, "Inverness was a wash, so I decided to head back early. I hope you don't mind?"

"Of course not, it's always a pleasure to see you."

Alex stepped aside and let her into the foyer. They walked side-by-side until they reached the sitting room acting as their research center. She strode right in, but Alex stayed at the entrance.

"I hope you don't mind, but I have some things I need to finish."

"Oh, sure. Don't worry about me. I'll just lose myself in all these papers anyway. I won't even notice you're gone." Her cheeks were beginning to ache from her fake smiling. This was way worse than the millions of museum functions she had to pretend to enjoy. It'd be much easier without MacKenzie around.

Alex struck his hand to his heart. "Ah, I'm shattered, lass."

She managed a chuckle at his dramatics. "I'm sure you'll live. Now, go. Do whatever it is you need to do and don't worry about me."

"I'll be down the hall if you need me. Just give a shout."

She turned her back on him and waved him off as she headed to the stacks of files. "I'll be fine."

She didn't check to see if he left, but since Alex hadn't spoken, she assumed he had. It didn't matter. Her mind had an itch. A feeling she came to know over the years as her unconscious understanding something important. She knew she had an answer, it just hadn't popped to the forefront yet. Picking up some random files, she began to shuffle through them. It would come to her if she didn't directly think about it. Laurel settled on the couch and let herself get lost in history.

An hour passed, possibly two, and Alex hadn't returned. Thankful for small favors, Laurel's attention was glued to the file sitting open before her. There was something here. It was so obvious it bugged her she couldn't figure it out. The document was about the clan MacKenzie, not the MacKay's, and it taunted her. She frowned.

"That's a serious expression on your face. What's the matter?"

Startled, she looked up and saw Alex standing next to the couch. She hadn't heard him enter. That wasn't good.

"My Latin is a little rusty and don't get me started about Gaelic. Do you think you can translate?" Laurel handed the paper over to him.

"Och, aye, this will be easy." Alex pointed to the paper. "*Luceo Non Uro*, is our clan's Latin motto. It means, 'I Shine, Not Burn'." He moved his finger a little lower, highlighting another set of words. "Every clan has two mottos, one in Latin and the other in the Gaelic. *Cuidich 'N Righ* is the MacKenzie's Gaelic motto, 'Help The King'."

"So, the MacKay's would have two mottos as well, right?"

"Aye."

"Do you know what they are?"

"No. But if it's important, I can find out for you."

Alex didn't meet her eyes when he spoke. He was lying. Why would he lie? What the hell was she overlooking?

"Have you found something?" He asked.

She shook her head. "No. I'm on information overload." Laurel stood and stretched. "I'm calling it quits for today. I'm fried."

"I'm sorry I wasn't here earlier. My business took longer than expected."

She gave him a quick shrug. "We'll tackle it together next time. No worries." She grabbed her purse off the floor and walked out of the room with Alex at her side.

"Will you be by tomorrow?"

"I don't know," she shot him a sidewise glance. "Is that a problem?"

"Not really, I have an appointment in Edinburgh

tomorrow. I'll be gone all day. But you're welcome to come over. I can hide a key."

"Ah, sure. That'd be great. But I'm sure I'll probably be doing something with Beth."

"Good. You should be enjoying your holiday."

She gave him a smile, and ducked out the door, before he thought to kiss her. It was getting awkward avoiding his advances. She gave him a wave, then practically jogged to her car. She could feel his eyes on her. As she drove away, she prayed her time with MacKenzie would end swiftly. She wanted to be far away as possible when his urban mask slipped and his true evil self was revealed.

Chapter Thirty-Nine

The sun warmed her as much as Simon. Seated on the ground, with him resting against the limestone of the stable's outer wall, she sat curled between his legs using him as a backrest. It was lovely. With a contented sigh, Laurel closed her eyes and cuddled closer—enjoying the broadness of his chest. She felt his hand caress her cheek, trail down her neck then her arm until his palm rested lightly on her hip. It was late afternoon as they stared at the unending fields before them. Laurel felt like they were the only people on Earth.

"I could stay like this forever."

"Aye, lass. The thought crossed my mind as well." He shifted his large frame and settled them more comfortably. "Go on then, you were telling me about your research."

"Let's see," she paused and brushed a flyaway hair from her face. "Oh, so get this, besides being the angel of prophecy and his control over natural phenomena such as earthquakes, thunderstorms, and volcanoes, he's known as God's light. But here's the cool part, another title of Uriel's is the 'flame of God', and guess what your clan's name translates to?"

"Well, 'Mac' is 'son of' and 'Kay' means fire."

"Neat, huh? Uriel's the flame and you're the fire. Well the son of fire. I wonder how far back your clan's relationship with the Archangel goes? It's too coincidental. I wonder if he had a hand in naming your family?"

"I don't know. My da and I never really spoke about it or anything else that mattered."

Laurel heard the bitterness in his voice, and her heart swelled. She covered his hand with hers and gave him a squeeze.

"I'm sorry. It must have been hard for you to be estranged from him and never have the chance to reconcile."

His hand tensed, fingers gripping the denim of her jeans.

"Aye. The only link with my da I had was the damn signet ring. I hated the blasted sapphire symbol. He'd always brandished it in my face when I was a lad. It stood for everything I wasn't—the dutiful son, heir to an Earldom."

"I'm sure it wasn't that. It's always hard when you're young. Reading so much into things that aren't real." She raised his hand up to her lips and gave him a quick kiss before giving it a pat and placing his palm down upon her thigh. "Do you still have the ring? Can I see it?"

"Nay. It's lost. I wasn't wearing it the day I was murdered. I've searched for it since, but never found it. Never thought I'd miss the stupid thing."

"I'm sorry. That's awful. Your one tie to your father."

"Aye, well, nothing I can do now, except protect my family's honor. I'll get the Orb to safety."

He fell silent. She could tell he was brooding behind her. It was time for a distraction.

"Oh, I almost forgot. What are your clan's mottos?

You know, the Latin and Gaelic ones?"

"Why do you ask?"

"Just an itch. Go on."

She felt him sigh then he lifted his arm, his hand raised before her. He closed his fingers and formed a fist.

"*Manu forte*, 'With A Strong Hand'. And our Gaelic," his voice broke softly. She heard him take a deep breath. "Our Gaelic… *bi tren…* be true, be valiant."

Laurel spun in his arms and faced Simon. "What? What did you say?"

"*Bi Tren*. It roughly translates as 'be true'."

Holy shit, she thought. It couldn't be. "How's it spelt?"

"B-i, second word, T-r-e-n. Why?" He asked.

She shook her head. "What did your ring look like? The MacKay's signet ring?" She tried to suppress her growing excitement.

Simon tensed behind her. "You're full of questions today."

"I know, humor me. What did the ring look like?"

"A deep blue sapphire set on a gold band," he described. "Our clan's motto was etched inside, 'bi tren'."

A grin broke across her face. Was it really that simple? The family ring Simon's father always flaunted in front of his son was actually the key to the Orb's chamber. His description of the keyhole fit the rings dimensions. She knew what the key was. She'd even held it and knew where it was! Alex's ring was the key, he had the MacKay's signet ring. How many sapphire rings with *bi tren* etched inside could there be?

"Something I should know?" Simon's question broke through her jubilant thoughts.

This was so cool. She knew not only where Simon's lost ring was, which would make him feel closer to his father, but it was even, more importantly, the missing key. His suffering was at an end! She so wanted to surprise him with this gift. She wanted to hand it to him personally.

"Nope," she replied. "Just a small piece of the puzzle may have snapped into place. I'm not sharing until I have more proof."

Like the ring in her hands. She made a mental note to corral Beth to do a little treasure hunting. "I don't want to get your hopes up. Give me a little more time."

She couldn't wait. It'd be an amazing bombshell. Just like Simon entering her life. Dear God, what would she do when he was gone? The smile slipped from her face.

"*Mo aingeal*, what is it?" He brushed her hair behind her ears. "One moment aglow and now so serious? What's dancing around in that clever head of yours?"

"I should never play poker, huh? Face. Open book."

"Probably not. Talk to me," he cajoled.

"Well… It's… I don't know where to begin." She was lost. How could she explain what he'd come to mean to her, yet there was no hope for their relationship? He was a ghost. He'd pass on, go into the light, whatever, but there'd be no happily-ever-after for them and that broke her heart. But she couldn't *not* say it, she wanted him to know.

She swallowed hard, remembering the last time

she'd said these next words. How exposed and hurt she had become later, because of Derek. And also how these next words would lead nowhere. But Simon had branded her, burnt her deep into her soul. She'd never regret giving him these three little words that held such power. "I …I love you. Crazy, huh?"

Simon stared at her for a moment before bestowing her the most tender kiss of her life.

"*Aingeal*, my angel. You have no idea," he trailed off. His silver gaze pierced her straight to the heart. "If there was a raging inferno separating us, I'd gladly walk through fire to be at your side. I love you too, *mo aingeal*."

He gathered her close in his arms and she lost herself in his deep kiss.

****

Alex took a step back and tore his gaze from the lovers' embrace. He had been right to follow Laurel. He hadn't heard a word they spoke from where he hid, but that wasn't what was most important. Simon MacKay. There was no mistaking him. Alex would never have believed it if he hadn't witnessed it with his own eyes. MacKay had materialized out of thin air next to the barn. He would have the man as a look-a-like descendent if it hadn't been for his appearing act.

By all the Saints and the Holy Mary, mother of God. *Shite*! There were ghosts and Simon MacKay was very real and one of them. And he was conspiring with his American, that deceitful bitch. It was jolting and yet, it explained so much. Had MacKay been hindering the MacKenzie's all these years? Was that why he couldn't find the Orb? Ghosts. How much could they do? MacKay looked so solid sitting there with Laurel in his arms. He needed to think.

He stumbled past the stable, toward his car, unconsciously shaking his head the entire time.

He had phone calls to make. There was always a solution. There were ways to rid yourself of unwanted spirits and there were definitely ways to deal with conniving, duplicitous women as well.

Chapter Forty

"I can't believe we're doing this! It's so exciting! So cloak and dagger-ish," Beth exclaimed.

"Hush," Laurel admonished. "We don't know if Alex is out of town or not."

She reached the door and rang the bell to Sinclair House, waiting to see if he answered.

"But I thought you said he'd be gone?"

"I said, Alex *thought* he *might* be gone. There is a difference." She rang the bell again, still no answer. "I think it's safe. Let's look for the key. He said he'd leave one."

She and Beth didn't have to search long. It was in the first place they looked—under the doormat.

"Well, here we go," Laurel whispered as she unlocked the door.

"How do we know the ring's even here? I've seen Alex wearing it," Beth asked as they slipped inside and shut the door behind them.

She dragged her friend toward the front parlor where Alex and she had their impromptu research center.

"He wasn't wearing it yesterday and it was sitting on the mantel in the same place he had put it after it snagged in my hair a week ago."

"Oh good, then this should be easy," Beth replied as she followed closely behind. "Though it's hard to believe he'd leave an heirloom sapphire just laying about. I mean, it is valuable." She continued to babble. "How cool is this? We're treasure swiping from a treasure hunter. I can't believe Simon never noticed Alex wearing it. And wait until we give the ring back to Simon. He's gonna be speechless. And when he finds out it's the missing key, double rainbows all the way! Oh, and can you imagine what Alex will do if he ever finds out he had the key all along—oof!"

Beth slammed into her, since she suddenly stopped.

"Shit."

"What? A little warning about the stoppage next time, friend."

"The ring, it's not here."

"So much for simple."

"Damn."

"Maybe he's wearing it?" Beth suggested.

"Let's hope not. We need to search the house," Laurel looked around. "Crap, the place is huge. We've got to think about this logically." She closed her eyes and willed herself to think like Alex. "If he's not wearing it, where would you keep your jewelry?"

"Either a safe or my bedroom. That's what I'd do," Beth replied.

"Good, we'll try his bedroom. I don't even want to think about locating a hidden safe. Any idea where it might be? His bedroom, that is."

"Of course. I had a tour of Sinclair House eons ago. He never took you to his bedroom? Some seducer he is… Yeah, right, probably a good thing. Follow me."

Laurel did—up the grand stairs, down the hall to its end. Beth paused at the open door on her right.

"Here you go. Now what?"

"Get searching. We split up."

"Aye, aye, *mon Capitán*!"

Laurel went straight to the dressing table next to the mahogany wardrobe while Beth went to the nightstand next to the bed.

"Wow! *Black Code* by Armani. No wonder he smells so good. I wonder if he's a boxer or briefs guy? Oh, maybe commando!"

"Beth, focus," she called across the room. "We don't know how much time we have."

"Sorry."

She ignored Beth's contrite reply as she pushed the clutter on the dresser around continuing her search.

Beth let out a startled shriek just as something sparkly blue caught her attention. She reached out blindly, snatched and slipped it into her jean's pocket when MacKenzie spoke.

"And just what are you lasses doing here?"

Shit. Hopefully he hadn't seen her snag the ring. She turned and faced Alex, who was casually leaning against the doorframe with an arm behind his back.

Laurel shot a quick glance to Beth, willing her to keep her mouth shut. For once, it appeared Beth was speechless, thank God.

"Um, Beth dropped by while I was researching," Laurel lied. "We got to talking about the house and when she found out I hadn't toured the place, she offered to show me around."

She noticed the relief on her friend's face at the plausible explanation. Beth nodded in agreement, but remained silent.

Alex let out a low chuckle. "Is that the reason you're pawing through my personal belongings? Don't get me wrong. I've always wanted you in my bedroom and with a friend, I'm open for doubles," he glanced to Beth. "It's boxers by the way," he replied proving he had been there long enough to eavesdrop. Alex locked his blue gaze back to Laurel. "However, you seem to be on a mission. What are you searching for?"

"Nothing. Honest." Laurel held up two fingers in the Boy Scouts' pledge, and then dropped her hand. "Chalk it up to curiosity. I wanted to find out more about you. So I was snooping. I'm sorry and truthfully, quite embarrassed. I apologize."

Again, Alex gave a throaty laugh. "You're a horrible liar, Lori. Now, I'll ask again, what are you looking for?"

She kept her mouth shut.

Alex tsked. "I warn you, I'll only ask so many times. I'm not stupid. I know you figured something out yesterday. Where's the treasure, lass?"

"The gold? Surely you don't think I was going to find it in your bedroom. After all, I would have thought you'd have noticed a horde of Jacobite gold lying about, you being a treasure hunter and all."

He shook his head. "You and I both know it's not gold," anger leaked into his voice.

"I—"

"No!" He interrupted. "One and only one more time. What are you searching for?"

A chill chased down her spine, and she shot a worried glance at Beth, who stood mute, eyes wide, terrified.

"Alex," she attempted to diffuse the situation. "It's nothing, really."

"Wrong answer."

MacKenzie's hand came from behind his back. He held a sleek matte-black gun complete with silencer, pointed into the room. He straightened his stance, and an evil smile curled up his lips.

"You'll learn I mean what I say."

"Alex, no!" Laurel pleaded.

A muffled pop filled the sickening silence as Alex fired off the gun.

Chapter Forty-One

Laurel's scream reverberated through the room. Beth's eyes widened, and her face paled in surprise. A bloodstain quickly appeared and soaked through the lavender cotton of Beth's shirt.

"Beth!"

She bolted across the room just as Beth's knees gave out, and she collapsed to the floor. Laurel dropped to the ground and cradled her friend.

"Beth, Oh God, Beth. Hang in there. I'll get help."

Beth couldn't reply. Her breaths came in short, sharp gasps.

"No, Beth, please." She pressed her hand to her friend's chest and tried to staunch the flow, but the blood continued to ooze out from under her palm no matter how hard she applied pressure.

This can't be happening. Please God, it can't be. Her hand was enveloped in blood and she heard herself groan.

Beth gasped a final time, and Laurel stared into her best friend's sightless eyes. How could a life be taken so quickly? Reality wouldn't sink in. She studied the blood covering her hands and her friend, before dragging her gaze back to the empty blue eyes staring back at her.

"Beth!"

She collapsed over Beth as sobs wrenched out of

her. Beth was gone.

A vise grip encased her upper arm, and she was jerked away from her best friend.

"NO," she screamed. "Leave me alone." She struggled, but wasn't strong enough.

"Get up," Alex ordered, jerking her to her feet. "We haven't time for this nonsense." He wrenched her arm behind her back and placed the silenced barrel of the gun against her head.

His breath was a hot whisper next to her ear. "You're coming with me. One wrong move and I won't kill you, but you'll wish I had."

Another jerk on her arm caused a hiss to escape Laurel's lips, and Alex pushed Laurel forward as tears continued to stream down her face. *Beth was dead*! She struggled to get control of herself, trying to push aside her grief for later. She needed to deal with MacKenzie.

Alex oblivious to her emotional struggle guided her back down the hall and stairs, and into the parlor.

They arrived in time to see two men rolling the oriental carpet back into place. Before it settled, she caught a glimpse of a strange marking on the floor. It looked like a large circle with a pentagram in the middle.

Numb with shock, her mind didn't even wonder why there was a pagan symbol on the floor.

Alex dragged her across the room and dumped her into the chair where she once sipped tea. She tried to will herself to move, but before her muscles responded, Alex shoved her against the chair's back and started to restrain her, with duct tape no less. Soon she was securely taped and even if she wanted to, she couldn't move.

"Why… Why Alex? You didn't have to kill her."

MacKenzie held up a finger, silencing her. He turned his attention to the two men in the room.

"All's set, sir," the taller of the two replied.

"Great. Let's see if you earn your money today. I'm putting a great deal of faith in you."

"Not to worry, Mr. MacKenzie. We'll get it done." Though shorter than his partner whom he exchanged glances with, this guy was much broader and way more muscled.

"Very well, now make yourselves scarce. It shouldn't be much longer."

The men nodded and going in separate directions, hid themselves within the room. The tall one slipped behind the long damask curtains and the other behind an open door.

Alex turned back to her.

"Where was I? Oh yes, you wanted to know why I killed Beth. Well," Alex stepped to the chair and braced his hands on her arms, pressing them into the hard walnut of the chair and leaned in so he was close enough to kiss her.

"First," his voice was a low, caressing whisper. "I *always* do what I say. You were warned after all. Second, she was expendable. I couldn't kill you, at least not yet. And third, I wanted to hurt you where it would count the most. I saw you. At the stable…with your lover. Or should I say, ghostly lover? You would choose him over me?" Alex snarled.

He straightened, and his hand reached toward her face. She flinched and pulled away, but there was no place for her to go as her head hit the back of the chair. He chuckled and then tucked her hair behind both ears—a gesture Simon was fond of doing. She felt tears fill her eyes. She wouldn't cry, not again, she wouldn't give him the satisfaction. Laurel swallowed, hard.

"So now, you understand I'm serious and when I ask a question, you'll know to answer. Truthfully."

His finger feathered down her cheek causing her to cringe again, which made him smile.

"But before I start interrogating, you have another role to play."

Though her mouth went dry with fear, she managed to find her voice. "What's that? You won't kill me. You said so yourself. You need me. There's no one left you can threaten me with. So why don't you stop playing games? I won't tell you anything."

Alex shook his head. "Oh, you're wrong. You'll learn. But first, you're bait."

"Bait?" She choked out. Chills ran through her body, causing her to shiver. He couldn't hurt Simon, could he? Simon was already dead. There wasn't anything Alex could do him.

"See? I hold all the cards, Lori."

"No… No, you're wrong. There's nothing you can do to hurt him. He's dead. You can't harm him."

"Are you so sure?" When Alex chuckled, her worst fears were realized.

Her mind raced back to the circle painted on the floor beneath the carpet. Her blood turned to ice.

"There's *always* a solution, love," Alex smiled. "That's why I'm so successful. I never give up. MacKay will truly be dead and gone when I'm through." He yanked a final strip of duct tape and pressed it against her mouth, sealing it close. "No sense in you spoiling all the fun with a warning." He leaned in and kissed her forehead. "Now be a good lass and enjoy the show. You'll have my full attention again, soon."

Despair filled Laurel. No, this wasn't right. This wasn't happening. She couldn't live if she lost both Beth and Simon in a matter of minutes. She prayed Simon wouldn't show. After all, he had no idea where she was.

"Step away from her, MacKenzie."

Chapter Forty-Two

"At last." Alex slowly turned and faced Simon MacKay, who had materialized out of nowhere. He'd seen him before, with Laurel at the barn, but it was still unsettling to witness the man appearing in front of him looking not a day older than thirty. After all, Alastair murdered him over two hundred years ago. In fact, MacKay in his jeans and T-shirt, wouldn't have given Alex pause if he had passed him on the street. Well, except for those eyes. Those damn spooky gray, holier than thou, MacKay eyes. God, it was going to feel good to kill him once and for all.

"If only you'd been a little faster, Beth might still be alive," he jeered as he stroked Laurel's hair. He was doubly rewarded when she jerked her head away from his touch and at the same time, a horrified realization dawned on MacKay's face. "Just like your father, so I'm told. Completely ineffectual. And now you're in time to watch Ms. Saville die."

He watched in satisfaction as MacKay's gaze snapped to Laurel's and almost laughed. *Ah, true love.*

"Get away from her, MacKenzie," Simon growled.

"Or what? You're a ghost. Albeit extraordinarily solid, but you're still a ghost." He needed MacKay to step further into the room, more precisely, onto the center of the carpet where his little trap awaited. "Are you going to stick your hand through me? I'm quaking in my shoes."

"Bastard, you'll see what I'm capable of," Simon lunged faster than Alex had anticipated. Simon was across the circle before he or his men could react. MacKay plowed into him, crashing them to the ground. It felt like a boulder had landed on him. Christ, the wanker was heavy as he was solid, which was all the time for thought Alex had when MacKay reared up and his large fist connected with Alex's chin. He saw stars. *God. Damn It!*

Before MacKay could land another blow, Alex twisted enabling him to move his knee in a solid blow to MacKay's ghostly jewels. It had the expected results—MacKay fell back allowing him to slip free. He gained his feet just as MacKay did. The dirty blow barely slowed him, but Alex wasn't worried. He knew how to fight, and he wasn't about to lose this one.

Just as Alex was closing to engage, one of his hidden men, Cameron shouted.

"Down, MacKenzie!"

Alex ducked and the roar of a shotgun exploded in the room. The loaded ammo of rock salt hit MacKay solid in the chest, rocking him back, but not doing much more. Alex began to doubt his hired help. He had a hard time believing rock salt was better than bullets.

"Again!" Riley, Cameron's taller, supernatural hunting partner, yelled.

Twin blasts sounded as both men fired. The direct double hits made an impression. For a brief moment, Simon flashed out of existence and then popped back in, a few steps further away. They fired again. MacKay blinked out and reappeared a few more feet back.

Salt hurt ghosts, who knew? Seeing his chance,

Alex avoided the hunters' line of shot and reached Laurel's side. He grabbed the Sig P220 from the table and pressed the muzzle hard against her forehead. With his free hand, he tore the duct tape from her mouth.

"Simon!" Her cry was perfectly timed between shotgun blasts. Everyone froze.

Alex locked gazes with MacKay and smiled. "We can end this now, or, you can play the hero and do as I say."

"No, Simon, it's a trap. Don't listen to him!"

He placed his free hand on top of Laurel's head and leaned in, pressing the gun harder into skin. In a theatrical whisper, he replied, "well of course it's a trap, but he has little choice, love." He straightened, taking his hand away, but leaving the gun in place. "Right, MacKay?"

If looks could kill, Alex had no doubt MacKay's silver glare would have vaporized him on the spot. Guns could, even knives, but he wasn't afraid of an angry glare. "Well?"

"What do you want, MacKenzie."

"Ahh, what a question. Much too involved to answer completely now; however, at this moment, I want to you to stand under that chandelier and not move." He pointed at the light and then leaned his weight into the gun causing Laurel to whimper. "Understand?"

MacKay's reply was another glower before looking at Laurel.

"No, Simon, don't. He'll kill me anyway. Don't do this," she pleaded with him.

Oh how very touching.

MacKay shook his head, turned his back, and

walked to the center of the room. Directly below the chandelier, he stopped, turned, and faced them. He stood silently, like an immovable block of granite. *Perfect*.

"All right, lads. Time to earn your pay."

Riley lowered his shotgun, but Cameron kept his level on MacKay, covering his partner as he bent behind the couch. Riley rose back into view with a five-pound bag of salt. He tossed it through the air, where Cameron deftly caught it one-handed.

Cameron turned to Alex, who nodded. The men didn't waste time or effort as they ripped open the bags and laid a circle of salt around MacKay about two meters in diameter. These men were good. Better and more practical than the pansy ghost hunters Beth hired. Riley and Cameron were the real thing and they had the credentials to prove it. Better yet, they weren't squeamish and their morals were of dubious ethics—just his kind of people.

"It's done?" Alex asked.

"Should be secure," Riley replied.

Well there certainly was one way to test it. His hand snaked out and slapped Laurel across her mouth in a stinging blow, leaving behind a red handprint, bleeding lip and her echoing cry of pain

It was poetry in motion. MacKay lunged forward with a growl trying to reach her only to slam into an invisible wall at the perimeter of the circle.

Holy shit, it really worked. If there're ghosts, Alex supposed, there could be magic, too. He hadn't believed a circle could become a cage with just some ink and salt. *Glorious*.

He beamed as he watched MacKay test his cage.

Riley and Cameron closed in, rifles loaded with rock salt at the ready, covering the man in case he found a way out of the charmed prison. The boys were definitely earning a bonus.

Still smiling, he gave Laurel's head a couple of pats. This day was certainly shaping up.

"Simon!" She shouted.

"MacKenzie, I'll find a way out," MacKay threatened. He stopped throwing himself against the barrier and prowled his cage like a giant cat.

"I doubt it, but feel free to try," he encouraged. "But before you get yourself all hot and bothered, maybe you'll answer a question or two, that way, I won't have to torture poor Lori here." He gave her head another pat and watched as Simon stopped and glared at him.

"Where is the Orb?"

His question was met with stony silence. Alex shook his head. "I'll give you one more chance, then I'll kill you and move on to torturing the girl."

MacKay continued to glare at him.

"No? Hmmm? I'm a man of my word, just ask Laurel. She learned her lesson the hard way."

Simon continued his impression of a statue. *Oh, well.* He hadn't thought it would be that easy, but he had to at least try.

"Right, then." He nodded toward the hunters.

Riley lowered his rifle as he pulled out a battered leather book from the back pocket of his jeans. He flipped pages to a well-worn section that obviously had frequent use, it stayed easily open on his palm with no additional help.

"Ready, mate?" Riley asked his partner.

"Anytime," Cameron answered.

Alex stood transfixed. If all went well, this was the end of MacKay. He leaned down and whispered to Laurel. "Watch carefully, love. You're about to witness a one-of-a-kind show."

"Alex," her voice choked out. "What are you doing?"

"Finishing something my ancestor, Alistair started centuries ago."

"Stop. You can't. Please, Alex."

"Now you beg? Too late. Hush now, or I'll gag you again," he admonished and watched as she bit her swollen lip and struggled not to break down. Duplicitous bitch. He'd enjoy breaking her, taking his time. She'd learn she put her faith in the wrong man.

"*Exorcizamus te, immundus spiritus*," Riley intoned in perfect Latin.

It began, Alex relished. He hoped MacKay ended in hell where he belonged.

"We exorcise you, impure spirit," Cameron translated.

"*Satanica potestas, incursio infernalis adversarii*."

"Satanic power, incursion of infernal adversary."

"No! Alex, stop!" Laurel screamed.

Would she not shut up? His hand whipped out again, landing a second slap to her face.

"Laurel!" Simon threw himself at her, but slammed into the barrier with such force he was flung back and nearly fell. "I'll kill ye, Mackenzie."

Riley and Cameron continued without a pause, the incantation. "*Ergo, spiritus maledicte, exorcizamus te*."

"Therefore, cursed spirit, we exorcize you."

MacKay froze, his pacing stopped, and his body

stiffened as a grimace crossed his face. It was working! He heard Laurel whimper, but ignored her, too fascinated with the ceremony. He could swear MacKay was becoming translucent.

"*Votum nostrum Deus audit*."

"God, hear our prayer."

"You're invoking God? How dare ye, MacKenzie. God doesn't hear Satan's servant," MacKay shouted.

"Ironic, isn't it? Kettle, black. I'm not the haunted soul, cursed to walk the earth. But don't worry, your time's at an end."

"*Ecclesiam tuam securi tibi facias libertate servire, te rogamus, audi nos*." Riley picked up the pace as the Latin spun out.

"We'll see who God protects," MacKay threw back.

"You make your Church safe to serve you freely, we ask you, hear us."

He watched Simon struggle, fighting the effects of the prayer. It was to no avail as MacKay became transparent then flickered back to solid, as the time between transitions grew. MacKay was definitely losing the battle.

"*Exorcizamus te, spiritus immunde, in nomine Dei Patris omnipotentis, et in noimine Jesu Christi Filii ejus, Domini et Judicis nostri, et in virtute Spiritus Sancti, ut descedas ab hoc.*"

"We exorcise thee, unclean spirit, in the name of God the Father Almighty, Jesus Christ, His only begotten Son, and in the power of the Holy Spirit, that thou depart."

"Per eumdem Christum Dominum nostrum, qui venturus est judicare vivos et mortuos, et saeculum per

ignem."

"We cast you out, spirit, through the same Christ our Lord, who shall come to judge the living and the dead, and the world by fire."

Alex watched Simon's futile battle. Now, the bastard actually disappeared. Each time he returned, MacKay's lips were a thin-lined grimace, his hands fisted at his side, while his body thrummed with tension. He appeared in agony as he fought against the exorcism. Alex grinned.

"No, Lord! You canna let this happen!" MacKay shouted.

"Simon!" Laurel screamed.

MacKay's pain-filled gaze locked onto Laurel. "*Mo anigeal*," his voice cut off with a gasp of pain.

"No, please no," her voice broke.

"Stay alive," Simon's whisper matched his translucent outline.

"Simon!"

"*Nomine Patris, Filii, et Spiritus Sancti.*"

MacKay disappeared. Everyone in the room held their breath, waiting to see if he'd manage to return. The only sound came from the ticking clock sitting on the mantel. He didn't reappear.

Riley slammed the book closed.

"A-fucking-men!" Cameron concluded while giving his partner a high-five.

Alex turned to Laurel, who was sobbing once more. Damn, he was tired of her crying.

"Well done, lads. You've earned your money. I've even left you a wee bonus," he faced Riley and Cameron, who stood there grinning. "Pardon me for not showing you out. Your pay is on the table beside the door."

"Thanks, Mr. MacKenzie," Cameron nodded in acknowledgment of the payment and the bonus.

"Yeah, and if you need anything else, anything at all, be sure to contact us," Riley added. The men took the hint and swiftly departed, asking no questions or giving second thoughts to what had just happened. They had been discreet. They had even bought his explanation he was trying to free Laurel from an evil spirit. Granted they had heard him mention Beth's death, but they hadn't batted an eye, even at the sight of Laurel's blood covered hands and clothes. Good help was hard to come by and Alex would use them again if he needed to.

It wasn't until he heard the front door close, that he turned his attention back to the empty circle. He walked to the edge and stared down at the thick line of salt. He raised his foot to smudge the line, but stop himself with second thoughts. It appeared the exorcism worked, but just in case, he'd leave the cage intact. If MacKay managed to return, he'd still be trapped.

Laurel. He stared at her with disgust. Her hair, mostly escaped from the single tie that had held it back, was a stringy mess around her bowed head. But it couldn't hide the tears streaming down her face, past the red welts and swollen lip. Blood dripped erratically, but enough that it stained the shoulder of her white T-shirt bright red.

It could have been so different. She was pretty enough and certainly smart enough, he might have let her live. Oh well, with MacKay gone for good, Alex had plenty of time to play. No time like the present.

"Enough!" He walked back to her and hauled off,

smacking her. Laurel's head was thrown against the chair with a satisfying thud. It had the desired effect, her tears dried up while she glared at him. New blood trickled from her mouth.

"You, son-of-a-bitch. I won't talk. If you thought killing Beth and Simon would motivate me, you're an ass."

Nice to see she still had some fight left, it would make the game all that more interesting. He stepped in front of her and rested his hands on top of her arms again, grinding them into the chair and leaned in. Before she could think to spit or bite him, he took her mouth with his, invading her forcibly, as a prelude to what he had planned for later.

His hands gripped her tighter, forcing a groan from her. Ah, he was so going to enjoy this. He broke the kiss, biting hard on her lip as he withdrew causing her to cry out. Straightening, he took a look at his handy work. Her lips were a mess and the lower one had blood flowing freely now. She was gasping for breath, and if he wasn't mistaken as he held her gaze, a hint of fear now showed in their hazel depths. Good. She'd learn the meaning of terror before he was done.

He walked to the hearth, out of her view and picked up a dagger from the mantel. Taking his time, he crossed back and stood behind her. He let the sharp blade dangle over her shoulder and into her view. She stiffened and held still.

"Now, love, we're going to play a game. I'm sure you recognize this weapon. After all you work for a museum." He twisted it so it lay across her bare throat. He watched as sweat broke across her brow. "Tell me what this is."

She closed her mouth in a tight line as air continued to hiss in and out of her nose. The poor girl was close to hyperventilating. "You know the ground rules. I'm a man of my word, remember? Answer my question. What is this lovely blade across your throat?"

He tightened his grip and felt her skin give ever so slightly. A drop of blood gathered on the bright edge. He eased off, so she'd be able to speak.

She swallowed, then whispered, "*Sgian dubh*."

"Correct. Now that wasn't so hard was it?" He removed the short Scottish blade and walked around the chair to stand in front of her once more. "I'm going to cut you free. If I were you, I wouldn't move. The blade is sharp, as you already know." He glanced at her throat then down her body, noticing her slight tremble. Life was good. He'd give her some hope before showing her hope was impossible. Let her think she might escape. It would be so much fun proving he held all the cards. She'd never get away from him.

Alex knelt before her and placed the blade between the chair and tape. Duct tape, ever so versatile. He made quick work of it and when the tape separated from the chair, he casually reached over and ripped the tape off Laurel's bare arm, leaving a red hairless mark in its wake. Her cry was almost a scream, but smart lass, she didn't move.

He quickly cut the other arm free. Laurel, prepared for the pain, barely whimpered when he tore the tape off. Keeping an eye on her, he seared through the tape holding her legs to the chair. Ripping off the tape held no satisfaction because of her jeans, but he knew what was coming and he waited in anticipation.

She didn't disappoint. The moment she was free,

she bolted from the chair. Expecting it, Alex was up in a flash. His arm snaked out and encircled her waist. He pulled her flush against himself.

"No!" She shouted and struggled. She was no match for him and in moments he had the dagger back up against her throat. She froze, breathing hard.

"Yes," he murmured in her ear. "We can't have you leaving. The fun has just begun, love."

Her whole body trembled the length of his. He was sure she felt how much he was enjoying himself. Let her worry, because in time that would come too, right after he had some answers. He spun her around and let her go.

"There's no escaping," he warned. "To trot out the old cliché, we can do this the hard way or the easy way. Either is fine with me."

"Screw you." She glared back at him.

He laughed. "In time. But first a wee chat, apparently the hard way." He flipped the knife to his left, formed a fist with his right, and landed a solid blow to her stomach. She doubled over and fell to her knees. He grabbed her hair and hauled her back to her feet. He let go and slapped her hard and watched as her cheek turned dull red.

"Bastard!"

He didn't see her right hook until it landed solidly on his chin. His head snapped back, but he kept his feet. He reached out blindly, but she managed to land a glancing blow to his shoulder. His temper snapped.

He dropped the *sgian dubh* and grabbed her from behind as she spun to escape. Momentum and his own strength had him flinging her past the chair she'd been bound to and directly into the stone hearth.

There was an audible crack as she hit and crumpled to the ground. He watched as her eyes rolled up and blackness claimed her. *Damn.*

Chapter Forty-Three

Awareness crept upon Laurel. It snuck into her consciousness like a patient hunter, a stealthy step at a time. Her head pounded in her skull, while her face matched throb for throb.

This was one hell of a hangover.

She was afraid to open her eyes, wondering if light would pierce straight into her cranium causing her brain to explode. She had told Beth she'd been drinking way too much since arriving in Scotland.

Beth, there was something about Beth.

She couldn't concentrate. New pain and aches kept infiltrating, all clamoring for attention. She felt bruised and battered. This was more than a hangover. Had she been in an accident? She didn't remember an accident. Why was everything so mushy?

She shivered and then couldn't stop. Cold swept through her, chilling her to the bone. What the hell was wrong with her? She forced her eyelids open, and the room swam into view. It was Grant's study at Cleitmuir and she was lying on his couch. She couldn't remember getting here.

Bracing her arms, she pushed herself upright. Pain lanced through her skull, and her vision pinpricked, all but going black. Nauseous bile climbed her throat. With a groan, she collapsed back onto the couch, eyes clenched tight, willing herself not to hurl.

"Damn it, MacKenzie! Where is Beth? And you didn't need to beat the shit out of Laurel." Grant's raised voice reached her from outside the closed study's door.

Reality came crashing in. Everything swirled and collided inside her head. Beth was dead. The exorcism from hell, Simon gone. Where had he been sent? Heaven, hell, oblivion? She was alone. What was she going to do? Grant. He could help her. He had too. Once she told him all about Alex and how he killed Beth, she'd have an ally. The next voice behind the door froze her in place.

"Your concern for the lasses is touching, Murray, however a bit late. You knew what you signed up for. I told you if you stepped out of line there would be consequences. Beth was one of those. She's dead. Maybe now you'll understand just how serious I am," Alex's oily response sent new shudders racking her body.

To think once she had loved the sound and cadence of his voice. She choked down more rising bile. Grant Murray, Beth's husband. He was a part of this, involved. He's helping MacKenzie.

She really was on her own against a monster. She crammed her hand against her mouth stifling the moans she had no control over. Curling up into a ball, her shaking started anew, she was both sick and terrified. Shock. She was in shock.

They were just outside. Only a door separated them.

Oh God, oh God, don't let them come in. Don't let MacKenzie come in. Laurel prayed as she broke out in a cold sweat. She had to get herself together. She had to do something. She wouldn't be a victim anymore.

"Bastard! You fucking killed my wife!"

"You couldn't control her, so I did."

"What? I didn't know about the séance, ghost-hunting thing. Beth arranged it behind my back. I wasn't hiding anything from you. It was harmless. I warned you MacKay was here. You didn't need to kill my wife."

"Watch your tone. Don't tell me what I should or shouldn't do, Murray," Alex's voice dropped to a lethal whisper. "If I wanted to kill her, or in fact you, just because you annoy me, that would be reason enough. You don't give orders."

"I guess I'm useless to you. Might as well kill me."

"Now you're getting it," Alex retorted as they continued to argue outside the room.

Laurel was stunned. Why wasn't Grant doing more than verbally sparring with Alex? Beth was dead. He should be strangling MacKenzie, beating the shit out of him, or at least taking him to the authorities. Did Grant care nothing for Beth? Both men were assholes, and she couldn't let them win. Beth and Simon's lives had to mean something. Their deaths couldn't be for nothing. She gathered her will and managed to sit up. The room swayed, and her stomach turned, but she managed to remain upright and not throw up. Good for her.

"You were too unfocused. I did you a favor, Grant. The world is within our grasp. Quit your belly aching, find your backbone, and become useful."

"Well, our one lead you beat senseless. We'll be lucky if she's conscious by tomorrow."

"It was an accident. The bitch landed a lucky hit. I was a bit over-zealous in my response. She'll wake. But

I'd like to know what she figured out before she comes to. I need an upper hand with that stubborn bitch."

The ring! She patted her jeans and found the sapphire miraculously still in her pocket. He never searched her. She still had the key. In fact, as adrenalin kicked in, she had a plan. The idiots had left her alone in the room leading to the catacombs. They'd never find her down there. Simon had told her the secret to the maze—how to gain entrance from this very room and the twisting path to the Orb's lair. He warned her off the catacombs, telling her she must never enter, made her vow in fact. The tunnels weren't safe. Too late now, she'd break her promise. There was nowhere else to go. She would rather chance death by cave-in than by MacKenzie's hands. She couldn't let him win. She would go into the labyrinth. Once safe, she'd find the Orb and take it to safety. Simon's honor would be upheld and Beth's death would mean something.

Laurel stood on wobbly legs and silently went to the bookcase hiding the secret passage. She hesitated. Alex and Grant continued to argue. They could enter at any moment. She had to escape, but couldn't just disappear out of a locked room. Scanning the room, her gaze fixed on a window. As swiftly as her battered body would allow, she crossed the room and opened the far window. With any luck, they'd think she fled that way.

Light. It'd be dark in the catacombs. She went to the desk. Sliding drawers open as quietly as possible, she searched for a flashlight, a lighter, anything that would help her see in the pitch-black labyrinth. She hit the jackpot when she found a small but powerful LED penlight.

She stuffed the light in her back pocket and went to the bookcase. The battered copy of St. James' Bible was right where Simon said it would be, third shelf up, first in the row. She pulled it out and reached in. Finding the irregular knob in the wood, she pressed and the bookcase clicked then swung out toward her. She stepped out of the way and peered into the revealed space. It was a tight area, barely room enough for two adults. She could make out the hole in the ground. Satisfied, she put the Bible back in its slot and stepped into the secret passage. The bookcase had a handle on the inside. She grabbed it and heard the case click home just as the door to the study opened.

Chapter Forty-Four

Alex was one step behind Grant as they entered the study.

"Shite," Grant cursed.

He saw in an instant what bothered Murray. Laurel was gone.

"She must not have been as hurt as she looked. The window," Grant crossed the room to the open window. He joined him.

"If we hurry, I'm sure we could catch her. "

"Don't bother."

"Why," Murray turned to face him. "She couldn't have gone far, not in her condition."

"Because she didn't leave by the window."

"What? Of course she did. We were right outside the door. There's nowhere else to go."

"Use your eyes," Alex pointed at the ground below the window. The earth was pristine, not a mark, or footprint marred the soft, wet, well-tilled soil. "Search the room. She's here."

Alex took the most obvious choice, the study's large desk. He crossed the room and checked inside the leg space, but it was empty. He examined the room. There were no additional places to hide. They had already seen behind the couch. The chairs weren't large enough to use as a shield. Crafty bitch, how did she disappear? A slight smile curled up his lips as he contemplated the puzzle.

"She's not here, MacKenzie. She had to go out the window. Maybe she pushed herself far enough out to land on hard ground."

"No. Not in her shape. It's just a decoy. It's too obvious."

"Then how'd she escape the room?"

"Obviously there's another way out. A secret passage. These old estates are riddle with them."

Grant stared at him as if he were crazy. "I've lived here for years. There are no passages. I've done remodeling. No one has stumbled across anything like that."

"Murray, don't be an idiot. Start searching. There's a passage. I know it. I haven't made money treasure hunting all these years by not listening to my gut. There's always a secret passage."

Grant just stared at him. Alex shook his head. Grant's usefulness was quickly coming to an end. "I gave Laurel the option of the easy or hard way. I'll do the same for you. You can be helpful and remain my partner in the most priceless treasure the world has ever known," he paused, knowing the easy option would never reach its conclusion, because he'd kill Grant first, but there was no reason to point that out to him. "Or, I can kill you now."

Grant still hesitated, but then shook his head. "You know I need the money."

He shrugged. "Well then, you know what to do. Get searching."

Grant went to work. By his thin pressed lips and furrowed brow, he wasn't happy with the situation. Well, too bad. He had warned him from the start. Alex started with the most obvious, again—the bookshelves. There were shelves covering two of the four walls. He began with the far corner, the wall next to the open window.

Methodically, he examined each shelf, looking for anything that might be out of place. He even rapped his knuckles against the wood listening for differences in sound. Pulling books, he tossed them to the floor in careless heaps in order to get to the inside of the cases. Grant kept his grumbling low since it was his job to search for trap doors in the floor and occasionally got nailed by an errant throw from Alex. At least he knew better than to complain outright.

It was a slow and tedious process. Minutes ticked by, becoming close to an hour, when Alex's meticulous search bore fruit.

He had reached the shelves that were across from the open window. He should have started there first. It seemed obvious now. She would have felt rushed, even panicked, the direct path would have been easiest. However, he never would have become rich if he had skipped over other possibilities and hadn't searched thoroughly.

Alex studied the third shelf from the floor, his gaze locked on an old bible that didn't quite line up with the rest of the books. He would have missed it if he'd been glancing casually. Pulling the book out, he examined the battered leather cover. Nothing made it remarkable. Discarding it, he bent and peered into the empty slot. There looked to be something in the back, something irregular. Reaching in, he felt the worn, smooth knob and pressed.

The click was almost inaudible. He stepped back as

the bookcase swung outward into the room. *Found you, bitch*.

He heard Grant's gasp and Murray was at his side when he pulled the bookcase all the way open. They stared into the small alcove that was little more than a space for a hole in the floor.

"I had no idea this was here," Grant murmured.

"Don't ever doubt me, Grant," Alex said. "You're becoming a loose end to me. I don't like loose ends."

Grant had the foresight not to reply.

"We'll need torches. I doubt there's electrical."

"There're a few in the pantry," without waiting for a reply, Grant jogged out of the room.

Adrenalin rushed through his veins, pumping him up. He itched to get down there. This had to be where Uriel's Orb had been hidden all these years. Excitement caused him to pace. Where the hell was Grant?

The Orb was almost in his hands. He was finally going to end his family's search for the relic. Out of everyone, he'd won. Soon he'd have prophetic powers that would have the world coming to him for answers, begging on their knees. They would exalt him. And of course, they would pay him. He'd have it all, money, power, influence. He'd be a god on earth.

Grant ran into the study with two torches and tossed one. Alex snatched it out of the air. Turning it on, he pointed its light at the hole in the hidden alcove. It was rough, but solid looking enough, but more importantly, in the centuries of dirt and dust covering the floor, obvious footprints were revealed.

It should be a simple matter of following Laurel straight to the Orb. There was no way for her to conceal her passage. Smiling, he looked forward to the hunt.

She would believe she was safe. He couldn't wait to see her surprise and fear when she realized they had found the passage and followed her.

"Grant, you get the pleasure of going first."

Murray shot him a frightened glance, but didn't say a word as he entered the secret passage. Alex almost laughed. Smart man to be wary. Any faulty construction or traps and Grant would meet them first. That was about as useful as Grant could be now.

He waited, giving Murray some distance. When no shouts or cries of pain reached him, Alex entered. He reached the hole and looked down. Grant's torch was bobbing below as he climbed down the wooden rungs fixed into the hardened earth. Pocketing his light, but leaving it on, he eased himself down into the hole and began the long climb down.

Chapter Forty-Five

I hate this. Laurel was in a horror film. Too bad the credits wouldn't roll and the lights wouldn't come up to reveal it was just make believe. Sadly, her situation was all too real as she crept through the labyrinth of tunnels—a dark place filled with cobwebs and the unseen skittering of bugs. She shivered. Her progress was slow, hindered by the absolute darkness, and fallen support beams she had to squeeze, climb, and shimmy past, and all the while getting coated by the endless webs. Simon hadn't been kidding when he warned her off the catacombs. Part of her was grateful she couldn't see more than the few feet in front of her, or she might have been too scared to continue. She had no idea what she'd do if she found a skeleton.

It was obvious she was the first warm body down here in years, she thought as she broke through yet another web barricading her path. Using the flashlight, instead of her hands, the sticky strands smothered the metal casing as if to strangle the beam. She didn't want to think about the creature that could have spun a web this big and thick. No matter how careful she was, they covered her in their clingy grasp. She could feel strands on all parts of exposed flesh. It'd take a million hot showers to make her feel clean again.

She reached the next intersection. This time she should take a left, Simon's directions were imprinted on her brain. Shining her light down the tunnel, it pierced the darkness revealing more of the same—wood debris, rocks, and webs. The tunnels went on for miles. They were all the same, long and no openings until she'd reach an intersection. An underground maze. She was beginning to feel trapped and claustrophobic.

The passageways were narrow, wide enough for two people walking abreast if they didn't mind getting cozy with each other. The height wasn't much better, maybe a little over a foot above her head, not much clearance. Simon would have had to worry about smacking his head on something. The weight of the earth, tons of dirt and rock above her, pressed down on her. It was too tight, too dark down here.

She tried to ignore the dark and the niggling feeling she might be lost. No, she wasn't lost. Absolutely not. She'd worry when she reached the end of Simon's directions and there wasn't a door. She turned left and entered the next tunnel.

Laurel felt so alone. Her grief continually slammed at her, draining her of hope and determination. It cost her everything to dig deep and continue through the catacombs. She was a bookworm, a researcher. Adventure, near death experiences, and fatalities weren't in her repertoire. She longed for her best friend, who always managed to make her laugh. She longed for Simon, wishing for his strength and fortitude.

Her battered body screamed at her to sit down and rest, but she couldn't. She knew she had to press on for Simon and Beth. She wouldn't give in. She'd drive herself until she collapsed if necessary. Her head throbbed, and she pressed fingers from her free hand to her temple. She wished her head would stop pounding, but the more she walked, the worse it got. She thought she might be hallucinating. Movement appeared to flicker just out of range of her light and sounds dimly echoed in the tunnels. There was no telling where the sounds came from as they bounced off the granite walls. Concussion. It was playing with her mind. The only thing down here was her and some creepy crawlies. She squeezed past another beam. Her only course was to go forward.

Sighing and brushing another cobweb off her face, she forced herself to walk. She could do this. From her calculations only one more tunnel to go.

Chapter Forty-Six

Alex was pleased. They were making excellent time. He could feel the gap closing. He'd catch Laurel. It could be just around the next corner. In his excitement and anticipation, he took the lead over from Grant since it was obvious by now the catacombs held no booby traps except its own decaying dangers, but it behooved him to keep an eye on Grant, he didn't trust him at his back.

He'd been worried Grant would make an incompetent tracker, but Laurel's passage was clear in the disturbed dirt, any idiot could have followed her path. Good of MacKay to have shared the directions with her, or at least that's what he assumed. After all, that's how the trail read—at every intersection a choice was made with no back tracking, relieved doubts, or misleads. Her path appeared to lead true and following her to the Orb was child's play.

A low rumble and Grant's cry of pain halted Alex. He shined his torch behind him, discovering dust filled the air like a filthy fog bank. He heard a groan and took a careful step into the cloud using the crook of his arm to shield his nose and mouth from the swirling thick particles.

"MacKenzie."

His name drifted to him followed by another groan of pain. The air was clearing, and his torch pierced through revealing the partially collapsed tunnel. Half of the wall and some of the ceiling had caved in, the tunnel was almost completely blocked. He studied the rock pile and thick support beam. With a little effort, he'd be able to get through. It wouldn't be comfortable, but more importantly he wouldn't be trapped on the return trip out, unlike Grant Murray.

"MacKenzie. Help me."

He stared down at Grant. Murray was crushed flat, the rubble piled thick and high on his back and legs, only his head and one arm flung out before him were visible. He squatted down next to his former partner.

"Help you?" He whispered.

With agonizing effort, Grant turned his head and managed to glare at him. "Dig me out."

He shook his head and treasured the look of anger that was quickly followed by fear as Grant realized there was no help coming to him.

"Look, Grant. We had a great run, but the clock is ticking. I can't spare the time or effort. You're on your own." Alex stood and followed Laurel's trail without a single look back.

"Ye arse," Grant's pain-filled voice choked out. "Don't leave me like this. You owe me—" his plea was interrupted by a coughing fit. "MacKenzie!"

He halted. There was no telling how far ahead Laurel was. The advantage of surprise might have been lost with the noise and Grant's shouting. There was no telling what lay ahead of him now. He weighed his options. It always paid to have multiple plans. It had saved his life more than once.

He turned and walked back to Grant. Murray's eyes were glazed in pain, and he now had blood on his chin from his earlier coughing fit—internal bleeding. Well, that narrowed his choices.

"Thank you, Alex," Grant gasped out.

"Aye, well, couldn't just leave you here, mate."

He crouched down and placed his torch on the ground beside him. With one hand he covered Grant's mouth and with the other, drew his *sgian dubh* strapped to his leg and slit Grant's throat.

He wiped the dagger on Murray's exposed sleeve and stepped away from the spreading pool of blood. He snatched up his torch and slipped the knife back into its sheath.

Back on Laurel's trail, he began to jog, his footfalls light and silent as he dodged debris. The time for caution was over.

Chapter Forty-Seven

The deep rumbling boom froze Laurel in her tracks. She swung her light back down the tunnel and it broke through the airborne dust of her passage to reveal nothing unusual. She shivered with foreboding. The catacombs had collapsed somewhere. Dear God, was she trapped down here? Not after everything she'd been through. A cold sweat drenched her skin, and she started to tremble. Her knees buckled crashing her to the floor. Her breath came in ragged gasps. She was going to pass out. Quickly, she forced her head between her legs and tried to slow her breathing.

She wrapped her arms around her legs, hugging herself, and willed herself not to give into the panic. Long breath in, hold, measured exhale, repeat…repeat…repeat. Her breathing quieted, and her eyelids slid close. God, she was tired. She hurt, mentally and physically. She wanted nothing more than to lie down and give up. She couldn't do this anymore. Lara Croft, she was not.

A choked laugh turned into a sob and she started trembling anew. Beth and Simon were dead. She was alone. She wasn't strong enough. *God, please help me.* Tears streamed down her face as she slowly rocked in place. She was at the end of her rope as shock took a strangle hold and squeezed. Why hadn't she died? It should have been her. This was a nightmare.

Her tears dried up leaving her drained. Resting her cheek on her knees, she stared blindly down the tunnel. Her mind drifted. She remembered Beth's smile and easy laughter, her sense of adventure and caring heart. Beth's sixth sense when it came to Laurel and the straight advice freely given made her the sister she'd never had. And Simon…

Laurel blinked rapidly, forcing the tears away. She wished he were here. His strong arms wrapped around her, his deep brogue caressing her in Gaelic. She closed her eyes, summoning his image. He stood before her, barefoot, bare-chested and wearing low-slung jeans—her favorite vision. His black hair, loose, brushing his broad shoulders and framing his face, wearing a slight, mischievous smile. And his crystalline gray eyes staring back at her, eyes that saw straight through her, to inside. Eyes filled with love. *Mo aingeal.* His angel.

The image blurred and changed to Simon's pain-filled expression as he stood trapped in the circle.

"*Mo aingeal. Stay alive...*" and then he disappeared. Left her. Abandoned her. Grief raked her. How? How was she supposed to go on? She needed him, needed his strength and he'd left her.

No. It wasn't his choice, he had fought so hard, struggled valiantly, and the bastards killed him.

Stay alive.

Laurel needed to live. She needed to fight. Giving up wasn't an option, not with everything she had been through. She could be strong. Simon expected that of her. Why was she just sitting here on her ass?

She picked up the flashlight and struggled back to her feet.

Stay alive.

Laurel dug out the signet ring from her jean's pocket, and the sapphire sparkled in the reflected LED light. The etched Gaelic leapt out at her—*Bi Tren*. Be true. She'd made a promise. She'd told Simon she'd help him protect the Orb. She wouldn't let him down.

This was the last tunnel. She had to be near the chamber. Get a move on, girl, she admonished herself. In this dark, you could be a few feet from the door and not even know it. Give up when you're that close? Never.

Her hand closed around the ring, forming a fist, in her new determination. She'd do this. She'd get it done. Her pace quickened. It was close, she could feel it in her bones.

Shortly, her light revealed not another intersection, but a dead end. She slowed and then stopped before the granite wall. Had she taken a wrong turn? Mentally, she went through Simon's directions. She was positive she hadn't misstepped. This had to be the door.

Shoving away any negative thoughts, she slipped the ring back into her pocket and started to meticulously study the wall with her hand and light. After a minute, she found the small depression. It was low, just a few inches from the floor on the right corner of the wall. She squatted and shone her light directly on it. Reaching out her hand, her fingers brushed the impression, revealing a clear spot on the rock. Simon's hand over the years had kept it clean as he studied the lock to the door. It was a concaved circle with grooves lining its diameter, just as he described.

Laurel pulled the ring back out of her pocket. She pressed the ring into the hole and felt it lock into place. Excitement tingled down her spine. This was it. She had found the Orb's resting place and was about to gaze upon the treasure with her own eyes. She waited, almost shaking with the anticipation.

Nothing happened. Really? It was way too anticlimactic. Of course, it couldn't have been easy. Nothing had been so far.

Sighing, she released her hold on the ring. She stood and placed her hands flat on the wall and pushed, then shoved. Still nothing. It'd been ages since the vault was opened. Simon's father the last to do so. Was it possible it was stuck, like a painted window frame? She took a step back, thinking. Maybe she needed to turn it? She crouched down and twisted the ring to the right. Nothing again. Oh right, lefty loosey, righty tighty. She turned the ring all the way to the left. She heard a click, snatched out the ring, and quickly stood, backing away.

Seams appeared in the stone. Slowly, the chamber door silently swung inwards.

Chapter Forty-Eight

Light spilled from the chamber. The glow, like the sun on a late summer day, embraced Laurel then surrounded her. The golden yellow light filled the tunnel behind her and flooded the room before her. Blinking rapidly, her eyes adjusted to the sudden illumination. She stood, stunned and mesmerized by the sight.

St. Uriel's Orb rested on a simple linen and lace cloth covering a small wooden table. It was exactly as Simon described, but for one thing. He'd never mentioned the way the teardrop diamond shone. The light within proved the diamond's flawless perfection—smooth and crystalline clear. She had never seen anything like it. The Orb seemed to call to her, its warm golden radiance, a lure to her soul.

She stepped into the rough hewed chamber and paused when she crossed the threshold. A quiet peace enveloped her, and she slowly exhaled the unconscious breath she had been holding. By the grace of God, indeed. Hesitantly she stepped forward, her footfalls silent as she crossed the woven rug beneath her feet. She stopped in front of the altar.

She'd done it. She'd actually had both the key and the Orb. Grief swamped her. If only Simon could be here. If only Beth could be alive. She sniffed hard and blinked, determined not to break down again. She reached a shaky hand toward the diamond.

Her fingers brushed the shining surface and then caressed the Orb. It was warm to the touch. A feeling of peace descended on her again.

The Orb was beautiful, stunning. It stood about ten inches tall, wide at the rounded base about half its height, tapering to one inch at the top. It was completely smooth, like polished glass. The relic's interior matched its exterior. You could see straight through it, no roughness, or fracture lines marred its perfection. She had never seen an uncut gem like this one, she doubted the world had ever seen its like. Truly holy, as if God had shed a single teardrop and upon reaching Earth, transformed it into the tangible diamond she dared to touch.

Quickly, before she changed her mind, Laurel scooped up the relic with both hands, juggling her hold on the flashlight, trying not to drop either. She wished for a backpack or satchel, but there hadn't been time before her descent into the labyrinth. Settling the Orb in the crook of her arm, she was able to free her other hand for the penlight, though she probably wouldn't need the light with the glow of the artifact. She had to get out of the catacombs. Hopefully by the time she returned to Cleitmuir's study it would be empty. Where'd she go from there, she hadn't a clue, but escape she would. She'd find a place of safety for the diamond, where no one would be able to use it for harm ever again.

Laurel turned and froze.

"Hello, luv. Surprised to see me?"

No! Alex stood with the sharp *sgian dubh* casually held in his hand, blocking the exit from the chamber.

How had he known? Dear God, she had led him straight to the Orb and now she was trapped.

"Did you think I'd be so stupid to fall for the open window? Honestly, it was simple to find the secret entrance, it's how I make my living." He took one menacing step forward. "Now, be a good lass and hand over the Orb. Make this easy and I just might let you live, after all, it might have taken me months searching these tunnels, but," he gestured to the floor with the clearly disturbed dust and dirt. "You so helpfully showed me the way."

Her heart sank. It was her fault. She should have really left by the window, or found her spine and kept her mouth shut, even if he had tortured her. Anything would have been better than leading him to the Orb. How had she failed so miserably? She had to do something, but didn't know what. She couldn't think through the panic flooding her system.

She had to escape. Though she never got around to taking those self-defense classes, she had grown up with brothers. She knew how to fight, as her right hook proved earlier. Laurel hadn't come this far to give up without a fight. If the diamond wasn't indestructible, she would have tried shattering it on the stone floor in hopes of keeping it away from MacKenzie.

Alex lunged, grabbing at her. With a shout of alarm, she darted behind the table. His hand tugged at her T-shirt, but she managed to slip free. Turning, she kicked over the altar. It caught and tangled in his legs. And as he started to go down, she made her bid for freedom. Dodging past him, she leapt the table and headed for the chamber's opening.

Her jeans snagged and she fell, dropping both the

Orb and flashlight. She kicked her leg, trying to free herself, only to realize Alex had a hold of her.

"I don't think so, bitch," he growled.

He plunged his dagger into her thigh, and she screamed. Pain flashed through her. With her free, uninjured leg, she kicked him in the face. He fell back, tearing the knife from her leg as he went. She scrambled on knees and hands away from him and staggered up. As she stood, her wounded leg almost gave out, but the entrance was before her as well as the Orb, so she gritted her teeth and took a wobbly step forward. He snagged hair, and she was yanked backward.

Laurel slammed up against Alex and turned, trying to claw his face. He cursed, letting go of her as he pushed her behind him and away from the door. Her leg crumpled, and she started to collapse. Twisting, she grabbed for Alex's waist trying to catch herself. Her hand landed on the gun at the small of his back, and she snatched it. The gun slipped free from his pants as she crashed to the ground. Instantly rolling onto her back, she flipped the safety off and fired blindly.

The gun's report was deafening in the small chamber, swallowing Alex's cry of pain. She'd hit him in the shoulder

"Bitch!"

Before she could move, his foot connected with her hand and sent the gun flying. Next, he closed the gap between them, then pressed the heel of his boot into her thigh, grinding it into her open wound.

She screamed again, her vision tunneling as she curled in half on the cavern floor, clutching the knee of her wounded leg to her chest. Her breath came in gasps as she willed herself not to pass out. *The Orb*. Laurel had to protect the Orb.

Too late. She saw Alex holding the diamond as he reached for his gun. He turned and met her gaze. Her blood chilled as she stared back. She saw her death in his eyes.

"MacKenzie!"

Laurel tore her gaze from Alex to dart to the entrance.

"Simon!" She shouted. There he stood, no fanfare of trumpets or glowing holy light, nor in smoke and the smell of brimstone. Somehow he had returned. From where, she didn't care. All that mattered was he was here now. It was a miracle.

Simon stood in the opening to the chamber, blocking Alex's escape. Hope flooded her as she stared at him in disbelief.

It was quickly dashed, when in one long stride, Alex reached her side, squatted down and pressed the barrel of his gun against her temple.

Chapter Forty-Nine

Rage flooded Simon, giving him the energy he sorely needed after the exorcism and manifesting. Hate filled him, against MacKenzie, God, and his situation. He was too late. Laurel was hurt, the cur had the Orb, and he barely had the energy to remain solid. Only pure strength of will kept him here. But MacKenzie didn't know that significant fact.

"Drop the gun, MacKenzie."

"Or what?" His flippant reply came. "I have the advantage."

His mind raced. Laurel would not die for him or that blasted relic. He'd willingly damn himself to save her.

MacKenzie stood, keeping the gun aimed squarely at the top of her head. By God, he wanted MacKenzie dead. The smug devil smiled at him before issuing orders.

"MacKay, I don't know how you managed to return, but if you want your precious girlfriend to live, you'll enter. Carefully. I want you to hug the walls and make your way to that cross." He nodded in the direction of the Celtic cross hanging opposite the entrance. "Do it! Or she dies now."

Blood boiling, Simon stalked into the room and started to edge around. He went slowly, stalling. There had to be an opening, a weakness somewhere. Laurel wouldn't die.

"Simon."

His gaze snapped down to her pain-filled eyes. His gut twisted. If only he had managed to get here earlier, but his energy had been all but drained from the exorcism. He had returned to that cursed circle as soon as he felt himself recharging, but he was weak, too weak, so nearly empty. His heart had plummeted when he saw the evidence of a struggle, the knocked over chair, the damning blood on the fireplace, but the fight had at least one benefit. The circle had been broken, and he was no longer trapped. He instantly started his search for Laurel. Dread filled him, knowing she was hurt and with the enemy.

He stared first at the large bloody bruise marring her forehead before allowing himself to inspect her open bleeding thigh. Accessing it in a blink, he knew it was bad. He'd seen enough battlefield wounds to know if he didn't do something soon, she'd die. He met her wide-eyed gaze. *Stay alive, mo anigeal.*

"Keep moving, MacKay. I don't mind shooting her."

Simon jerked himself back to awareness, never realizing he had stopped walking.

"This isn't over, MacKenzie. I'll hunt you down."

"We'll see," Alex replied as he stepped away from Laurel and one step closer to the cave's entrance, always keeping the gun trained on her as she laid curled on the floor. "Though I admit, you're a hard ghost to get rid of. I thought the exorcism had worked."

"Exorcisms are for evil—demons and spirits. Which I'm neither."

"What *are* you?" MacKenzie asked with a curious

tilt of his head, keeping the gun pointed at Laurel's temple."

Good question, he thought, but only replied with a half smile.

"Simon," Laurel drew his attention as he passed her on the way to the cross. "The Orb, it has another name. Remember? The link," she pushed herself up, grimacing in pain as she managed to sit upright. "Remember who you are. Have faith."

What was she telling him? He looked at Alex, holding the glowing Orb—St. Uriel's Orb, the fiery stone. The fiery…. The stone was just an instrument for prophecy. It didn't do anything else.

He cursed himself once again, for failing his father. If he had he might have the answer he needed now to save Laurel. Now he was failing her. Grief and helplessness flooded him. He couldn't save her.

Simon stared at her hopeful face. Had she discovered something else about the Orb? Was there a built in defense? There was too much he didn't know. The Orb was known as the fiery stone, and he was the son of fire. He was dithering while Laurel slowly bled out. He had to do something. Have faith. Something he sorely lacked. He'd never trusted his father, himself, or anyone, he realized. It was time to let go his anger, his distrust. It was time to believe in something…someone.

He believed in Laurel, his angel. He could have faith in her. Walk through fire, brave death for her. She would not die. In a blink, he made his decision. *Uriel, help us, if not for me, but for her*.

Simon attacked, praying he'd catch MacKenzie by surprise before he could shoot. He leapt over Laurel who had collapsed back to the ground and barreled right into MacKenzie. The gun went off. Another deafening boom in the chamber, but he ignored the shot. With both hands he grabbed the Orb and glared MacKenzie in the eyes.

"Your family motto, *luceo non uro*, is wrong, *neach-dìolain*. You burn not shine," Simon growled.

Alex grappled with him for the stone, but he didn't let go.

"Hear me, Uriel. *Manu forte!*" With the last of his energy, he willed it into the Orb.

The results were immediate. Simon vanished as the relic gave a blast of energy then burst into flame, engulfing Alex.

MacKenzie screamed in agony, his cries echoing through the chamber. He fell to the ground, still clutching the blazing stone. Yellow flames crawled over his body, creating a human torch. The Orb flared and a pulse of light flashed outward, piercing Simon's ghostly self, thrusting him back into solid form. His body thrummed with energy, his skin tingled like a million spiders were crawling all over him. He vibrated with energy. He felt powerful as he watched his enemy dying at his feet.

A low rumble joined MacKenzie's death cries. He tore his gaze from the burning man to the chamber's entrance and saw rocks fall from the ceiling. He acted without thought. He spun and dropped, throwing himself over Laurel.

Rumbles became crashing thunder as the tunnel collapsed.

Chapter Fifty

An eerie silence descended though Laurel's ears rang with the aftermath of the cave in and Alex's horrible screams. She shivered beneath Simon's hard weight, willing the phantom death cries away. And the smell, the musty scent of dust didn't hide the hideous cloying odor of cooked, burnt, meat. She swallowed hard as her stomach churned.

Simon shifted, lifting his body away and taking his warm sheltering presence away from her.

"*Mo anigeal?* Laurel, are you all right?" His hand caressed her cheek then tucked a trailing strand of hair behind her ear. "Open your eyes, lass."

She did as he asked and saw him gazing down at her, his pale eyes filled with concern and a hesitant smile on his lips. She coughed as the dust swirling in the air continued to settle.

"He's dead?" She murmured, afraid to look around.

"Aye, lass."

Her stomach twisted and roiled. She sat up with Simon's help. Clutching his arms with her hands, she peered past his shoulder. The Orb still glowed, resting in Alex's charred skeletal hand. She followed his bony hand to a blackened wrist, to his arm and saw no more. The collapsed tunnel covered the rest of his body as well as the entire entrance to the chamber.

Laurel slapped her hand over her mouth to stifle

the scream desperately wanting to escape. There was no way through the rubble. They were trapped.

Simon wrapped his arms around her, and she tucked her head into his chest, shaking in her fear.

"Hush, *anigeal*. It will be all right. I'm here."

Oh, God, she was going to die. Her breaths hitched before exploding in short exhalations, the pain in her leg ignored as terror clenched both mind and body.

She didn't know how long she stayed that way. Simon continued to murmur to her in English, sometimes in Gaelic, but she never truly heard or understood the words. Eventually she quieted as exhaustion replaced fear. She didn't want to move. She wanted to stay sheltered within his arms forever.

"Laurel, sweetheart. We need to look at your leg."

She moaned her protest when Simon gently pushed her upright.

"It doesn't matter."

"Yes. It does."

She bit her lip when he straightened her wounded leg. The piercing pain that had been her constant companion since Alex stabbed her was down to a dull throbbing ache. Even she knew that wasn't a good sign, especially since it was still bleeding.

Simon reached past her and pulled the linen altar cloth over to them. He tore a strip off and then folded the remaining large piece into a tight square. He pressed it down on her open wound and a groan escaped her.

"I know, lass, it hurts." He took her hand and placed it down on top of the cloth. "Keep the pressure on the gash."

"Simon, stop. It doesn't—"

"No!" His shout of denial jerked her head up to

gaze at him. His expression was fierce, lips pressed thin, his silver eyes filled with anger, glowing almost in his need. She was caught by his strength of will.

Did it really matter? She nodded once, giving in to his demand. She watched as he tenderly raised her leg to slip the strip of linen beneath her. He twisted the fabric and started to pull, she slipped her hand out of the way. Quickly, he jerked it tight, causing her to grunt. He made a knot and then tucked the edges under the fabric. Her leg was back on fire with pain.

He knelt beside her, head bowed with hands fisted at his sides, unmoving. She reached out and placed her hand on top of his head. Her fingers gently stroked the silken black threads before trailing down his face to grip his chin and tilt his face up. Her breath caught.

He was silently crying. Tears dripped down his cheeks, to fall wetly on her palm.

"I won't..." his voice broke. He swallowed and cleared his throat. "You can't die. I won't let you."

"Oh, Simon," she moved her hand to cup his cheek. "It doesn't matter."

"Yes. Yes, it does." His voice filled with determination. "Everyone I've ever loved has been stolen away. I'll find a way to save you."

"How, Simon? Don't you see—"

"No. There's something I can do." He pulled away from her and raked a hand through his hair, shoving it off his face. He glanced at the rubble filled entrance, then down to the Orb before meeting her gaze. "I have energy, more than I ever had. The stone did something. I can get outside. Get help."

"Where? The church is miles from here. The nearest neighbor is buried next to us. There isn't enough time."

"There is. We've stopped the bleeding."

"No, Simon. We just delayed the inevitable. Now I'll just slowly die when I run out of air, or starve. Even if there was enough air and you miraculously found someone immediately, it would take days to clear the passage."

He shook his head. Grief etched on his face.

"Simon. Please," she held her hands out to him. "Hold me." He gathered her into his arms once more, tucking her in close. She sighed and closed her eyes reveling in his strength. It comforted her, made it easier. "It's all right, you know? Forever is overrated." She opened her eyes and looked up at him, smiling gently. "I love you, Simon."

"I love you, too, *anigeal*." His hand stroked her hair.

She shifted and pain lanced up her leg. This had to stop. She didn't want this drawn out, before her courage gave. Laurel reached down and tugged at the knot of the tourniquet. "Help me?"

His swallowed curse cut right through her, but soon his arms unfurled around her. His hands engulfed hers, taking over and released the knot. Blood instantly bloomed, seeping up through the linen.

She leaned back against his chest, and Simon wrapped his arms around her.

"I'm okay. It's okay. Just hold me," she whispered.

His lips pressed a kiss to her head. "I'll stay with you, lass. I won't leave you."

"We'll meet again. In heaven, you know?"

She felt more than heard Simon's grunt. "What? Your duty's finished. The Orb is safe, buried here with us. Alex is dead. No one else knows. You've earned your peace."

"Aye, I wish that was true. You have more faith than I."

"Simon, how can you say that when you know God actually exists as does his angels? You called out to one of his Servants and were answered. Faith? You have plenty. You don't realize it yet."

"Aye, I do believe. That's the problem. I have nae been a good man," Simon's accent thickened as his voice became emotional. "I couldna protect my family, betrayed my da. I was selfish. And now, I canna save you."

"Oh, Simon," her voice broke. "You don't need to save me. You are a good man. The best man I've ever met."

"Ah, lass…" his voice trailed away. He pulled her closer and rested his head a top hers.

Exhaustion claimed her, and her eyelids fluttered closed. She shivered, as a chill chased through her. It grabbed her, sinking deep. "I'm cold," she murmured.

"I'm here, *mo anigeal*," he whispered. His arms tightened around her as her mind began to drift.

"Laurel?"

She was too tired and cold to answer, causing him to swear and then pray.

"God, don't let her die," he pleaded. "I've not asked for much. I'll happily suffer a thousand more deaths to save her. Punish me. Let her live. Please."

A bright light flashed, causing stars to appear behind her closed lids. Her eyes snapped open. She couldn't see. Light filled the chamber, blinding her.

Chapter Fifty-One

Laurel cried out against the searing pain of the bright blaze. Simon's arms closed tighter around her, sheltering her from the unknown intrusion. As fast as the blinding light had appeared, it disappeared. The room was once again reduced to the simple warm yellow glow cast by the Orb, but now, they were not alone.

She stared as her eyes adjusted. For a brief moment, two figures had been overlaid in an after-burn image from the white-hot radiance. A giant figure, standing over seven feet tall, glowing with impossible wide wings unfurled from its back to caress the chamber's walls and ceiling superimposed then resolved into a man. He was tall as well, but on a more human scale. There was a presence about him, belied by his casual dress of jeans and a plain T-shirt with the words 'Jesus Rocks' plastered across his chest.

Power exuded from his darkly bronzed skin and intelligence gleamed from the depths of his dark amber eyes. His face was chiseled, all hard angles, like a knife slicing through clay, giving him a harsh but stunning beauty. The only wildness about him was his long pure white hair falling to his waist. Everything else radiated calm.

Laurel, trapped by his golden gaze, was mesmerized, all her pain and fear forgotten, while looking at this impossible stranger. Simon exhaled softly and released her in order to edge himself slightly before her, a not so subtle signal he protected her. She reached for his hand. Their fingers clasped, twining together. Who was this man to appear out of thin air? Another ghost? Had she really seen wings?

The silent man released his strange hold over her when he dropped his gaze to the glowing Orb. A smile curled his lips before he glanced up and pierced them once more with his gaze.

"Retribution delivered and balance restored," his deep voice intoned. "Well done and well met, MacKay, son of Murdoc, heir of the covenant and child of my heart."

"Uriel?" The gravelly one word from Simon conveyed his mixed emotions. Disbelief warred with awe, yet underneath it all a hint of anger, causing her to worry.

The stranger dipped his head in acknowledgement.

Simon stiffened beside her, and she squeezed his hand in caution. After all Uriel was also known as God's Angel of Retribution. But Simon didn't heed her unspoken warning.

"You come now?" He taunted. "After all these years?"

"Simon, please." She wrapped an arm around him and rested her head on his shoulder, anything to break his angry fixation on the angel. "You can't…stop…" She didn't know what to say.

It might have been to reassure her, or maybe keep her close to protect her, but Simon tugged her from behind him and wrapped his arm around her waist, tucking her head against his chest. However his attention never wavered from the human manifestation of the Archangel.

The Archangel Uriel. Laurel studied him from the shelter of Simon's body. She'd never dreamed or even imagined she'd meet an angel. Oh, she believed in them, just as her belief in God, but it was another thing to be confronted by reality. Uriel was strikingly handsome and not at all how she would have envisioned him through her fact-finding trip. She had expected wings, but jeans and a holy-T-shirt. Really? She had always envisioned shiny armor or maybe a gown-like thing or even a robe.

"No, lass," Simon responded, drawing her attention back to him. "I want answers, but more, I want Uriel to heal and save you." His grip tightened at her waist. His tension radiated throughout his hold. If this kept up, he was bound to do physical violence. She didn't want him hurt, there been enough of that in his life already.

"While here in this chamber," Uriel replied, ignoring the heated tone of Simon's words. "Time stands still. Ask your questions."

"I have no questions. Only a demand. Heal her. Now!"

Laurel realized blood no longer seeped out of her thigh, and all her various body aches were gone. "Simon." She placed her hand on his arm and shot Uriel a grateful look. "Simon, look at my leg. It's not bleeding."

He tore his gaze away from the angel and carefully assessed her wound. He gave a slight shake to his head then muttered under his breath, "Nae, not good enough." His worry and fear were etched in his face before he looked challengingly back to Uriel. "Heal her!”

“I cannot.” Uriel’s compassionate gaze stared down at them. “Her fate is not in my hands, but while I’m here, she’ll neither die nor heal.”

“Damn it, save her! She’s an innocent. She helped keep your bloody stone safe. You owe her that much.”

Uriel shook his head. “She has been granted this time, earned it by her steadfast actions, to hear your story. Given time to say farewell and leave no words unspoken. It is not up to me, whether she lives or dies.”

“I canna except that,” Simon’s grief made his voice harsh.

Laurel didn’t get happy rosy feelings as the men talked about her fate. She had already accepted and made peace with herself before the Archangel had appeared. If Uriel couldn’t heal her than her fate remained the same. At least she’d be with Simon. And right now, there wasn’t even any pain, a blessing in itself.

“Please, stop arguing,” she pleaded, wrapping both her arms around Simon, trying to comfort and give him something else to focus on. “You knew my choice before he arrived. Nothing’s changed. We’ve been given some more time.”

He stopped glaring at the Archangel, to press a kiss on top her head then with his free hand reached up and fingered a strand of her hair. “I will not let you die.” His reply was soft-spoken, intimate. Her heart melted a bit more.

“Please, Simon, I want to hear why everything has happened. Give me that, at least.”

She loved him with all her heart, and she wanted to know everything about Simon, besides it distracted her from her immediate future. If time was really standing still in this chamber, then Uriel could speak forever while she stayed entwined in Simon's arms.

"I canna deny you anything," he looked up and held the angel's gaze. "Speak. Go ahead and tell your damn tale."

"Simon. He's an Archangel…"

He shook his head. "I've been tortured for two hundred years, left alone, and aided by no one, until you." He picked up her hand and placed a tender kiss on her palm. "He hasn't earned my respect. He has denied you of healing. I owe him nothing."

"But—"

"Hush, lass," Simon interrupted. "What more can he do to me that hasn't been done already? Kill me? I'm dead already." He looked up and glared at Uriel. "Go on, tell your story."

If Uriel was angered by a mere human's order, he showed none of it. Instead, he stepped away from the Orb and leaned against the chamber's carved wall. Austere and haughty, Uriel was regal making his jeans and shirt somehow appear like formal wear.

"Damned, you never were," a smile danced across Uriel's face making him seem more human. "As you figured out, your branch of the clan MacKay was given the Orb for protection. A covenant was signed by your ancestors, during the time of the Picts."

"I knew it! You gave them the name MacKay, didn't you?" It was rare for a researcher to confirm guesses when dealing with ancient history. But here and now, she had an actual eyewitness.

"Indeed," replied the Archangel, giving her another humanizing smile before continuing. "The covenant was struck when it became clear the Orb was too dangerous left in humanity's hands. With the growing population, evil spread as well as good, and the Orb in the wrong hands became a powerful tool of destruction. That couldn't be allowed.

"All was fine, up until your father's time. Alistair MacKenzie discovered the compact and hence, learned about the Orb and who protected it. MacKenzie killed your father, thinking that you would hand over the relic due to your estrangement with the MacKay."

"But he didn't," Laurel inserted, giving Simon's arm a squeeze, she was so proud of him.

"Aye, because I didn't even know it existed." As if the saying of his words had helped release some of his anger, Simon seemed to relax just a bit.

"True," Uriel replied. "Alistair hadn't planned on that. Impatient, he decided to kill you and get his answers from your mother and sister. That did not work either."

Laurel jumped to the question she wanted most answered. "Why? Why did Simon have to suffer, be tortured year after year? Is God that cruel? Couldn't Simon have stayed a ghost the whole time? It would have given him more time to look. Why did he have to drown for two hundred years?"

"Hush, *mo leannan*."

"Simon wasn't dead," Uriel replied, stunning her.

"He drowned in a cave. Over and over again. How's that not dead?" She demanded.

"The MacKays swore a sacred oath. When Alistair tried to kill him, the clan's vow tied him to the earth, because you," Uriel studied Simon, "were the absolute last male of your line. There was *no one* else left to protect the relic."

Laurel tensed, remembering Simon's agony just telling her of his drownings. There had to be a reason for all of his suffering. Her distress registered to him and his hand went to her thigh and made small, soothing strokes.

"Because of the vow and the Orb still in danger, Simon was held to his family's oath. When Alistair tied him in the cave, he drowned, but didn't die. He is neither living nor dead. Think of it as being in bodily limbo.

"In order for him to interact with your world, great power was needed. His drowning was the catalyst of energy needed to fill the battery. And as with all batteries, the charge depletes. His energy would last for little over a month and then needed to recharge. This was repeated until your family vow was fulfilled."

"But why have you nae intervened?" Simon asked, bitterly.

The angel sighed. "Free will. This battle between good and evil is waged between men and women. I wasn't allowed to interfere. But no longer. You have stayed true to your clan's motto and remained steadfast. Your father, your clan and myself, are proud of you."

Uriel pulled himself from his lazy stance against the wall, standing straight. "And now, Simon MacKay, it is time."

"No! I willna desert her." Any relaxation either she or Simon had achieved, vanished in a split second. Her pulse raced. She didn't want him to leave.

The angel sadly shook his head once more. "It isn't your choice. You are here solely because I stand within this chamber. Say your farewell and embrace your well-earned reward."

Simon literally growled as he turned from Uriel and clutched her fiercely to him. She already missed him, her heart shattering into a million tiny pieces. She lifted her head from his chest and stared into his familiar silver eyes and gave him a teary-eyed smile.

"I love you, Simon. With all my heart and soul. I always will."

"As will I, my love, *mo leannan*. I don't want to leave you."

"Just for a moment. I'll be—" Her voice cracked, before she could control it. "I'll be right behind you. We'll be together, soon."

"Aye, lass," a single tear rolled down his face as he cupped her chin with his hand. "I'll greet you like a queen. I love you, Laurel." He leaned in and kissed her.

It wasn't gentle. It wasn't soothing. It was raw, hungry and filled with claiming. She was his and he was hers. Why hadn't she found him sooner?

He broke the kiss and stared at her, looking for the entire world as if he was trying to permanently etch her onto his soul. It was a look of desire, a willing fierceness that would not be denied.

"I love you," he whispered. "Never doubt that."

He began to glow and a sob caught in her throat. He grew brighter and brighter, yet she forced herself to watch, sitting on the ground as tears streamed down her face. He shimmered, then in a blink, he was gone.

"Simon!"

She collapsed, lying on the floor, sobbing, when time began to march once more. First she felt the chill that turned into a bitter cold. Her wounded thigh pulsed in time with her heart, which began to beat slower and stutter. Her tears dried with the realization she'd be with Simon sooner than she thought. Good. She couldn't bare the separation. She wanted to be with him, she needed to be with him.

Laurel opened her eyes and watched as Uriel walked toward her. Would he aid her crossing over? Make it painless? His amber gaze glowed with empathy when he stopped and knelt beside her. He gave a gentle smile, then, magically, bronze-colored wings unfurled from his back spreading wide. They filled the chamber, curving around the walls. He gently gathered her into his arms.

"Have faith," his whispered words slipped into her ears as his wings folded around her. "You are stronger than you realize." Feathers softer than anything on earth covered and sheltered her. As his strong body held her and his wings embraced her, peace seeped into her soul. She gave in and closed her eyes.

Chapter Fifty-Two

The scent of freshly cut grass crept in and filled her nose. A comforting smell, reminding her of summer backyard barbeques and times with her family, when she had little to worry over except friends' opinions and what boy might like her. Laurel reveled in the scent.

Lying on her side, her back was warm, but not hot, a perfect balance between sunshine and breeze. She felt embraced. Was she in Heaven? She was afraid to open her eyes. She'd been through so much and wanted Simon more than she could bear, but was worried Heaven shouldn't smell and feel like a summer's day.

Taking a deep breath, she forced herself to open her eyes. Midges circled her head. This wasn't Heaven. She was pretty sure Heaven didn't have bugs. Crestfallen, she bit her lower lip and her hands clenched into fists. Drained of everything, including tears, she went numb. Midges meant Scotland. She was still in Scotland, but at least above ground and not in that godforsaken cavern.

Why had Uriel lied to her and Simon? He had led them to believe she would die. It didn't make any sense.

Laurel pushed herself upright and sat on the grass, light-headed and weak. She closed her eyes and took a few deep breaths, trying to gain some strength back. She felt weak as a newborn kitten. With a sigh, she opened her eyes and glanced down at herself, where she finally noticed for the first time she had been curled around the Orb. The large yellow diamond still radiated its impossible internal light. Was that why she was still alive? Uriel needed a new protector for his relic? She didn't want the job.

She picked up the glowing Orb, and something clinked against the diamond and fell to the ground. Cradling the Orb in one arm, she searched with her free hand and found the MacKay signet ring. Holding it up, she stared at the sapphire, stomach twisting in grief. What was she supposed to do now? How was she going to go on living without Simon or Beth? She felt lost, alone. How does one heal a missing part of her soul?

She choked back the sob threatening to escape. Her first priority was getting the Orb to safety. There was no way she could protect it herself, so she needed a plan, but first, she needed to figure out exactly where she was. Laurel forced herself to look around. Surprised, she found herself in the little graveyard connected to St. Brendan, the church associated with the MacKay's. From where she sat, she could see Murdoc MacKay's angelic tombstone, more appropriate now when she knew of Uriel's connection to the family.

Glancing down at the Orb, she thought about what to do. Uriel must have had a plan when he transported her here. She highly doubted she was meant to be the keeper of the relic. So the obvious path was probably the correct one. He meant the Orb for St. Brendan's. Fine, she'd give it into Father Campbell's keeping. At least she was clear on that single thought. Everything else in her head was blank, numb. She couldn't seem to connect the dots and manage to think anything through. It was probably for the best or she might just lose it, since she rode the razor edge of sanity.

She should get up, before she decided never to move again. But would she be able to stand? She checked her thigh. Her jeans were still torn and blood drenched, but the skin beneath, however, was unmarred except for a thin white scar. Laurel felt her face. No tenderness and her lips felt smooth and not swollen. Uriel had both healed and saved her from the catacombs. Why? And why hadn't he told Simon that's what he planned on doing?

Shaking her head, she leveraged herself up, and stood. She swayed a bit with lightheadedness, but soon settled, and then she took a tentative step toward the church. When her leg still held, her stride increased until she was walking confidently through the cemetery and to the church's side door. She reached for the handle, when the door suddenly opened.

Father Campbell gasped at the sight of her, taking in her dirty and blood stained appearance. "Lass! My God, what's happened to you?"

"Long story, Father," she replied when she noticed the priest had fixated on the glowing ten-inch yellow diamond in her arms. "May I come in?"

"What? Of course! Please," Father Campbell replied in belated courtesy and gestured for her to enter as he held the door open for her.

"Follow me." He let the door close behind them as he led her to the back room where the leather journals were kept. It felt like years since she had come here to do research. Everything remained the same, the small room with its shelved lined walls, a simple wooden table with four chairs, and a faded blue woolen carpet on the floor. It didn't seem right. Everything had changed for her, it wasn't fair, her life had changed so drastically and nothing else had. The world was different for her.

With a great deal of stiffness, Laurel sat in the chair Father Campbell held out for her. She placed the Orb in her lap, but kept the ring clenched in her hand.

"Laurel, what's happened? Are you all right?" Deep concern colored the priest's question as Father Campbell's gaze swept over her, but kept landing back to stare at the Orb in her lap.

She nodded, not quite able to speak. She felt lightheaded again, and her early numbness was disappearing to be replaced with body aches and pains and her shattered heart. She knew she looked like shit, because that's how she felt. Her hair was covered in dirt and dust from the cave in, cobwebs were entangled around her body from her trek through the tunnels, and of course she was covered in drying blood, both hers and Beth's. Though her outward appearance was dramatic, it didn't hold a candle to the wound in her soul.

The Priest continued to stare at the Orb. "Lass, is that what I think it is?"

She met his gaze. "If you think it's the Orb of St. Uriel, you'd be right."

Father Campbell pressed his hands to his heart, a look of awe written across his face. "I never thought I'd ever see it…"

"So you know," exhaustion laced her voice. "You knew. This Church was a part of the whole thing." She was so tired of all the deceptions and conspiracies. She knew the Priest was involved when she had met him at the door with a glowing ten-inch diamond and hadn't said so much as a word about it. It was kind of a hard thing to miss and he hadn't made a single comment until now.

"Yes," was his simple reply.

"Yeah, that's what I figured."

"Lass, having the Orb puts you in great danger. MacKenzie is looking for it. If he finds you with it…"

An unladylike snort escaped, Laurel. "Not really a problem. MacKenzie's dead, Father."

"Oh my…are you sure? MacKenzie would kill for the Orb.

"Ironic, considering the Orb killed him." She sighed before continuing. "I witnessed his death. The relic caught fire and burned Alex alive, and then…" She swallowed hard. "He was crushed under a pile of rocks when the catacombs collapsed."

Father Campbell crossed himself and then studied her intently, obviously taking in her disheveled and bloody appearance. "How is it you're here?"

Laurel let the question hang. It was a good question. One she's pondered since she first opened her eyes and found herself still living. The ache ran deep, would it ever disappear? She'd settle for numb again, if it would get her through her remaining days. When Uriel had wrapped his soft wings around her, she hadn't thought she'd be returning to the land of the living. She had been okay with that, she'd miss her family, but her heart belonged to Simon. She should have guessed by Uriel's parting words: *You are stronger than you realize.* What now? Everything was still so raw she really didn't want to get into it with the Priest.

"Let's just say a minor miracle," she tried a small smile, but failed miserably. She picked up the Orb and held it out. "Here, Father. I believe he wanted you to have it."

With trembling hands, he took the Orb from her. "He?"

This time she managed the weak smile. "Uriel."

"My God," the Priest whispered.

"Actually, an Archangel, Father."

"Of course, you're right," he acknowledged. "Obviously you've been through an ordeal. A story, I wish you'll share with me one day." He stood. "But for now, I'd like to share something with you. I believe," the Priest gestured to her. "You've earned it. Plus, since you were entrusted with this holy relic, I believe I can trust you with St. Brendan's greatest secret." He motioned for her to follow.

With slow tired steps, she left the room and trailed behind the Priest, who led her to the Archangels' shrine. Upon entering, she froze. The shrine held seven statues standing in a half-circle. St. Michael with his sword stood in the center. On his left was St. Gabriel the messenger and on his right, St. Raphael the healer. But it was the angel on Raphael's other side that caught and held her attention.

The sharp angled cheeks and nose, the square chin, the wide set eyes, without looking at the name on the placard on the statue's base, she knew she was staring at the Archangel Uriel. He looked exactly the same, except here he was dressed in armor and carrying a crossbow. Definitely the image she would have guessed, unlike the handsome man in jeans that had appeared.

"Laurel, for form's sake, I need your promise, a vow, that you won't tell anyone about what has happened to you or what you're about to see," Father Campbell requested.

She pried her eyes away from the stone Uriel and met Campbell's honest gaze. "Of course, you have my word." An easy vow because she doubted anyone would believe her, anyhow.

"Indeed. However, you never know where your words might land and we don't need another MacKenzie on our hands."

She cringed. The world definitely didn't need that kind of sociopath walking the earth.

"And now lass, be witness to the secret only the attending Priests of St. Brendan's know." He walked over to Uriel's statue and knelt before it. She didn't see exactly what he did, but in short order, a hidden panel opened and a chamber was revealed inside the statue's base. Reverently, the Priest placed the Orb inside and just started to close it when Laurel remembered the ring still clutched tightly in her hand.

"Father, wait." She stepped to his side and held out the signet ring. "I suppose you should have this as well." She realized her hand was trembling.

Campbell reached out and curled her fingers back around the ring and held onto her closed fist. "I believe it would be acceptable for you to keep it."

"Really?"

"Yes, I do." He released her hand and closed the panel, making the base appear solid once more. He stood and gathered both her hands into his. Their warmth was comforting and her trembling stilled.

"Laurel," his blue gaze filled with concern. "Do you need to talk?" He deliberately took in her ragged appearance before meeting her eyes again. "I'm here to listen. No judgments. It might help ease your burden. You've been though so much."

She shook her head, trying not to cry. How could there be more tears left in her? When would the pain go away? "No, Father. Thank you, maybe in the future, but I can't right now. I…I'm barely holding it together. I need some time." She sighed. "In the meantime, I could use some help. I suppose the police need to be notified. MacKenzie shot and killed Beth." Laurel swallowed a sob. "His body is crushed and buried in the catacombs below Cleitmuir. I'm not sure what's happened to Grant…"

"Hush, lass. I'll help. We'll see this through together."

He started to lead her out of the shrine when in afterthought; she stopped, and looked back. Each angel stood on a base identical to Uriel's. Uriel's statue now hid a priceless relic.

"Father?"

"Lass?"

She gestured to the statues. "Does each angel keep a secret?"

Father Campbell's answer was a simple smile.

Chapter Fifty-Three

Chicago Field Museum
October, Present Day

Laurel blinked, realizing she had been staring blindly off into space. It was a habit she'd caught herself doing these past few months. She leaned back in her office chair and lifted the necklace tucked away beneath her blouse. The sapphire ring at the end of the heavy silver chain sparkled in the fluorescent lighting of her windowless office. Fingering the ring, she studied her sleeping computer screen. She'd been out of it for at least thirty minutes. On a sigh, she tapped the keyboard, bringing her computer back to life. If only it was as easy to wake herself.

Since returning from Scotland, she had moved in slow motion as the rest of life passed her by. The colors surrounding her seemed leeched of brightness, conversations seemed pointless, and now her family was planning an intervention. She certainly had given them cause for concern since July.

Upon returning early from her long awaited and long anticipated vacation, Laurel had the pleasure of telling Beth's parents and her own family of Beth's death. Everyone was shocked of course and grieved as well. Everyone had loved Beth. That had gained her some time and an excuse for her anti-social behavior, but that pretext was quickly coming to an end.

Laurel kept mostly to herself in the basement of the Chicago Field Museum, and now even her colleagues were beginning to wonder about her. Usually prompt in her assessments of donations to the museum, her reports were lagging. Her boss had been giving her strange looks for the past week.

Maybe she should tell everybody the whole truth. That might buy her more time.

Please excuse my behavior everyone, not only was my best friend murdered in front of me, I fell in love with a ghost who then went into *the light* leaving me alone forever. I also watched an evil man burn to death then get crushed, and was personally saved by an Archangel from a horrible death. Oh yeah, and there was this priceless religious artifact, probably several, hidden inside statues in a tiny church, so please excuse me if I seem a bit distracted, it's just a lot to take in.

Sure, completely believable, but more likely they'd think her crazy and commit her somewhere.

Surprisingly, she didn't care. That was her problem. Nothing held her interest anymore. Not even her close-knit family. She felt like she was in prison, just marking time until her sentence was up. Yup, that was her, dead woman walking.

Her phone rang, jolting her out of her morbid musings. "Hello, this is Ms. Saville."

"Hey, Laurel. It's Craig. I've got a donor cooling his heels in the lobby."

"Isn't there someone else available?" She asked in desperation, not wanting to leave the safety of her basement cave.

"Ah, that's the thing. He specifically asked for

you."

Of course he did. If she wanted to keep her job, she'd better go meet him. Work was the only thing keeping her sane at the moment. "Fine, I'll be right up."

She tucked the ring back inside her blouse, grabbed her suit jacket, and left her office. The long walk through the narrow corridor led to the elevator. She pressed the button for the lobby, and mulled over what the new donation might be as the doors closed and she was whisked several floors upward.

With a ding, she reached the lobby and went looking for the mysterious donor. *Please God, don't let it be, Meriwether.* The old letch was always trying to hit on her. Granted, he was worth millions, but she couldn't get over the ick factor.

She crossed the floor, stopping by Sue, the T-Rex skeleton and scanned the area. Laurel froze as the hairs on the back of her neck rose, and her stomach turned somersaults. Not knowing why, she slowly turned around.

Her gasp echoed hollowly. She'd finally lost her mind. *He* was here. Simon. He lounged with his elbow on the security's countertop. His silver gaze fixed solely on her.

He was an intense, vivid, hallucination. His long black hair was now cropped short and tight, with a bit of unruly length on top, just enough to leave a tantalizing lock on his forehead. The shorter hair made him look larger, more vibrant. And if she wasn't mistaken he was now dressed in a dark blue Armani suit with a crisp white shirt, unbuttoned and no tie. This illusion of Simon was impossibly more handsome than her memories.

She started trembling from head to foot while her vision tunneled as her blood rushed from her face. Blindly reaching out, her hand locked onto the rail protecting Sue, the T-Rex. Knuckles white, she willed herself not to faint and not to blink. This had to be a delusion. Her brain had finally broken to match her heart.

Simon was dead. He'd earned his peace and was in Heaven. He wasn't in Chicago. She shook her head in denial.

Laurel watched as her imagination had him grin, then walk toward her. Her free hand rose and covered her mouth. As he approached, her heart raced. He paused and gave her an oh-so-familiar frown. She must look like she saw a ghost.

"Simon?" She whispered.

He opened his arms wide in reply.

Not hesitating, she ran and flung herself into his waiting arms. Clinging to him, tears burned her cheeks when his strong arms wrapped around her. She didn't care if this was a psychotic break, she wanted it to last forever.

"*Anigeal*. At last." Simon leaned in, inhaling her scent, then pressed a kiss to her cheek.

She wanted more. Turning her face, she captured his mouth. The months of grief, of separation, of longing poured from her to him. She devoured him, relishing his taste, his heat, her Simon.

He pulled away and chuckled. "Miss me, lass?"

She hauled off to slap him, but he captured her wrist and placed a quick kiss on her pulse.

So many questions raced through her mind, but she didn't care. None of them mattered. He was standing right here, in her arms—all was right.

His silver gray gaze locked on her and he smiled. “I’ve missed you, *anigeal*.”

“Am I dreaming?” Her hand pressed against his chest raised so she could stroke her fingers down his face.

“Nay, lass, you’re not,” he captured her hand and squeezed lightly, then held it.

“How…what…” She stammered, still trying hard to believe.

“After we were parted, I found myself… I’ve never been a religious man. As a lad, religion was something I had to do. In war, it was hard to believe in a God that could allow such carnage, and later, well, I was a wee bit angry about drowning over two hundred times.” A slight smile curled up his mouth. “But now, it’s hard to dispute.”

“You saw Heaven? You were there?”

Simon brushed a strand of hair off her face. “Aye, well, there weren’t any pearly gates or choirs of angels. Just my da, a quiet green wood, and a stream.”

Shocked, Laurel tried to step away from Simon so she could see his face better, but his arms tightened and he pulled her closer, tucking her head beneath his chin. She heard his heartbeat thumping wildly under her ear.

“I don’t know how long I stood there staring, unmoving, but eventually my da strode over and embraced me,” his voice broke and he hesitated before continuing. “We had a chat…he…told me I was forgiven, that he was proud of me.”

“Oh, Simon,” she squeezed him tighter, and felt the onslaught of fresh tears. She knew how much that meant to Simon, to have received his father’s approval after all that had been done and said between them.

"He was given a message to deliver to me. I was to be given a choice." She felt him press a kiss on top her head. "When I learned you lived," his arms tightened around her, giving her a squeeze. "I told Da, Heaven could wait."

Her heart clenched, what had Simon given up? "What about your family?" Her question came out a whisper, but she knew he heard her.

"They're in Heaven, aye? Well protected in paradise and not going anywhere anytime soon. However, more important, *you* weren't there," he swept his thumb across her palm. "If it helps ease any guilt, my da seemed pleased with my choice. He's quite taken with you. As am I."

Her breath caught. She pulled out of his arms and stared at Simon, who was smiling brilliantly, his light-colored eyes sparkling. He chose her? He turned away from Heaven and his family, all for her?

Before her eyes, she watched Simon drop to bended knee. He gathered her hands and clasped them with his. "There wasn't really a choice. My heart and soul belong ever to you. Laurel, *mo anigeal*, will you take me? I'm yours."

Her heart stopped then joy flooded through her. He was hers and there was no question she belonged to him.

"Yes, absolutely yes."

He stood and quickly captured her mouth in a soul-consuming kiss. She flushed with heat and clutched at his shoulders as her legs went weak. Simon was hers, forever.

She wasn't sure how long she clung to him and

kissed him, but the sound of applause filled the air bringing her back to reality. Dear God, she was in the lobby of the museum!

Laurel broke the kiss and felt her face burn. Simon just chuckled. Passersby congratulated them as she led him to a bench away from the middle of the lobby.

She took a deep breath. "There're so many things to ask, so many things I want to know."

"Hush, lass. We've all the time in the world." He picked up her hand and laced his fingers with hers. "Think of the stories we can tell our children."

Children? Somehow the idea made her smile. Marriage to Simon would make her joy at him being alive even more wonderful.

"There are a few things we do need to speak of, so you know everything before we commit ourselves. Once married I'm never letting you go," his gaze was fierce and serious. "Of course, even unwed, you're not escaping me."

Her heart flipped-flopped. If he thought she'd let him do otherwise, he was sorely mistaken.

"First, I know you have your work, which I support," he reassured her. "However, several times a year, we have to return to Scotland. The Orb is still in the MacKay's protection, and will continue with our sons. It's a duty I won't shirk this time, and neither will our offspring."

"Okay. But our daughters will be guardians, too. This is the twenty-first century after all."

Simon laughed and gave her a quick kiss. "Spoken as the true warrior you are. If they are anything like you, it will be well guarded, indeed."

"Um, Simon," she squeezed their linked hands.

"How old were you when you died?"

"Twenty-five."

"Wow, I'm marrying a younger man!" She smiled up at him.

"Or much older, if you count the two hundred odd years of my limbo." Suddenly the teasing glint left Simon's eyes. He hesitated, looking worried for the first time. "I've bought Cleitmuir Manor. It's mine again. I thought we might live there, but…if you can't, I understand…I know—"

"Really? I'd love to live there." She gave him a quick hug. Living in Scotland at Cleitmuir would somehow make her feel closer to Beth. Besides, it was Simon's home and where he was, she'd be at his side. "Home to me, will be wherever you are."

"Ah, *anigeal*, how did I ever get so lucky?"

She chuckled. "Not sure, but you're stuck with me anyway. Hey, how'd you manage to buy Cleitmuir? It had to be expensive. And these clothes?" She fingered the well-made suit. "You hit the jackpot or something?"

"I told you my curse was never about the gold, which was true, however," he said as he pulled her onto his lap. He caressed her face with gentle fingers then his hand swept behind and cupped her head. "I never said there wasn't any Jacobite gold."

Simon swept in and captured her mouth, trapping her gasp.

A word about the author...

First published in Marion Zimmer Bradley's "Sword & Sorceress" anthology, CJ was bitten by the writer's bug and hasn't stopped since. When her pen isn't scribing, you can find her busily cutting and tracking music for film and television. With close to twenty years of music editing experience, her credits range from "Northern Exposure" and "The Muppets Christmas Carol," to "The Kill Point" and "The Middle." She currently resides in sunny southern California with her two cats, great friends, and her horse, Junior.

Thank you for purchasing
this publication of The Wild Rose Press, Inc.

If you enjoyed the story, we would appreciate your
letting others know by leaving a review.

For other wonderful stories,
please visit our on-line bookstore at
www.thewildrosepress.com.

For questions or more information
contact us at
info@thewildrosepress.com.

The Wild Rose Press, Inc.
www.thewildrosepress.com

Stay current with The Wild Rose Press, In

Like us on Facebook

https://www.facebook.com/TheWildRo

And Follow us on Twitter
https://twitter.com/WildRoseP

A word about the author...

First published in Marion Zimmer Bradley's "Sword & Sorceress" anthology, CJ was bitten by the writer's bug and hasn't stopped since. When her pen isn't scribing, you can find her busily cutting and tracking music for film and television. With close to twenty years of music editing experience, her credits range from "Northern Exposure" and "The Muppets Christmas Carol," to "The Kill Point" and "The Middle." She currently resides in sunny southern California with her two cats, great friends, and her horse, Junior.

Thank you for purchasing
this publication of The Wild Rose Press, Inc.

If you enjoyed the story, we would appreciate your
letting others know by leaving a review.

For other wonderful stories,
please visit our on-line bookstore at
www.thewildrosepress.com.

For questions or more information
contact us at
info@thewildrosepress.com.

The Wild Rose Press, Inc.
www.thewildrosepress.com

Stay current with The Wild Rose Press, Inc.

Like us on Facebook

https://www.facebook.com/TheWildRosePress

And Follow us on Twitter
https://twitter.com/WildRosePress